Two Romances

Two Romances

William Young

ISBN: XXXXXXXXX
ISBN 13: XXXXXXXXXXXXX
Library of Congress Control Number: **XXXXX (If applicable)**
LCCN Imprint Name: **City and State (If applicable)**

For my mother, and in memory of my father

JOSEPH AND MARY

A Family Romance

BOOK ONE
Joseph

Chapter I

ON THAT BUSY morning Mom had risen early, as usual, to make the fry bread. The cast-iron skillet sizzled and the smell of fat and sugar filled the kitchen with an Indian aroma. Mom preferred rising before the sun came up. "I've put in half a day's work before you guys even climb out of bed," she liked to point out (justifying her late afternoon nap in the process). By the time I usually tumbled out of bed, around eight, and came downstairs, she had indeed been at work for a few hours, kneading the fry dough in the dark kitchen, her figure illuminated only by a small pool of light above the range, the autolite providing an almost rustic shading. Mom seemed to favor the darkness, having slowly but surely blocked out many of the windows in the house. Some shutters and curtains hadn't been open for years. In other rooms, boxes and stacked-up furnishings prevented the sun from penetrating. Sometimes Mom would just throw a large sheet over a voluminous pile of stuff. And there was no persuading her to change her ways. Only later did I understand Mom's eccentric behavior as something more than mere eccentricity. As something deeper, crazier, more profound, I'd say.

I'd grown used to and even come to like the smell of fry bread, though the smell wasn't anything I remembered from childhood, which had been all pancakes, Cheerios, and scrambled eggs. I'd only recently returned home--an eye injury had forced my return—so I wasn't exactly sure when Mom had taken to making Indian bread; it had something vaguely to do with the fact that our house in Scottsdale bordered the reservation, home of the Pimas, descendants of the Hohokam.

Across two-lane Pima Road lay the vast, empty lands of the Salt River Indian Community. We never saw much of the Indians. At one time a row of rundown houses bordered the road, and the Pimas, a heavy-set, round-faced tribe, would drive their dusty Chevy trucks off the reservation to Safeway for food or to Circle K for a six-pack, three or four kids joking around in the back bed. But recently, they'd retreated to the interior, building better homes, and generally at some distance from the city boundary line. They drove new pickups and rarely came into the city, or perhaps were less noticeable when they did. I couldn't help missing the old days when they weren't so prosperous.

The reservation stretched from just beyond our backyard all the way out to the Superstitions, those jagged peaks to the east of us. On smogless days the mountains appeared quite close, almost superimposed, as though they were just beyond our block fence, as though we lived right below the Grand Tetons or mountains of that scale (I am the first to admit that my injury--I wore a black patch on my right eye--perhaps made this seem more so than it actually was). I had an aesthetician's love for the mountains. Over the years I had painted the landscape in every season and in every sort of light. I especially liked the winter light, and how the stick- dry yellow sage, like fallen buffalo, like a herd of memory, withered in the windless fields. I'd painted the land at all the times of a day, as the color shifted from midnight blue to red to orange and yellow, and back again. I'd even painted the Superstitions at night, the anthropoid silhouettes of the range visible in the darkness. Their fascination for generations of explorers easy enough to understand. One could readily believe some treasure was buried there.

"Morning," I said as I passed through the kitchen, headed as I was for the bathroom off the laundry room.

"Another county heard from," Mom said, still at her labors. Besides feeding her human charges, Mom's early morning duties, as with those of an Irish countrywoman, included feeding the cats and other animals. We had several cats and two ducks. In contrast to the dark interior of the kitchen, Mom wore a colorful, if rather unshapely, house dress. Perhaps the poor indoor illumination encouraged the wearing of bright colors, as it had for the Elizabethans. Mom had a fondness for red and orange: "Southwestern colors," she would explain. A burnt orange scarf, pulled gypsy fashion around her (tinted) black hair, also shone brightly in the kitchen light. She was presently finishing up the dishes.

Mom refused to cook lunch or dinner, just breakfast. Mostly she made fry bread, but sometimes she baked soda bread, with raisins and nuts.

"You get morning eucharist and then you're on your own. No more doing dishes either. I've been working my way through college long enough," she liked to say, her Brooklyn accent ever present beneath the acquired Midwestern and Southwestern flatness. "It's not like you're children anymore," she would say, and indeed we weren't. At twenty-five, Matt was the youngest.

Matthew, Mary, and I all still lived at home with Mom and Dad. Mary at least had a job, and I had money from the injury settlement, but only Joseph, the eldest, had truly managed to launch himself, like that spider in Whitman's poem, out into the big world. Joseph's success had inspired my own attempt at establishing independence: I'd gone to art school in San Francisco. And I had made a life for myself there, going to classes, working--I'd even fallen in love. When we'd first met, Jenny was sixteen, a high school sophomore, sort of in-between girlhood and womanhood, and sort of tomboyish (as Mom had once noted, many of the females I was attracted to had just such yin-yangness, such anima-animus of personality and physical type). We'd met on the Powell Street cable car. Oh I still had hopes of seeing her again!

By the time I came out of the bathroom, Mary had assumed her place at the kitchen table. She was still in her silky underwear: panties and a loose camisole. Her hair, blond, was pulled back in a ponytail. She was reading the morning Gazette and drinking coffee, the smell of coffee mixing with the state-fair smell of fry bread. The front page of the paper detailed White House lawn protests against the visit of the Shah of Iran. Jimmy and Rosalyn Carter were doing the entertaining. Other news included the arrival by freighter, the Huey Fong, of 3,383 Vietnamese refugees in Hong Kong, the British Colony.

I cleared myself a place at the table, moving a few glasses, some magazines, and some overripe bananas in order to set my plate and cup down. The bananas looked like turds. Still the coffee tasted good.

"Sit up straight. Throw your shoulders back," Mom said, as I slouched over my cup. "Well, what do you think of your big bro Joseph returning?" I said, shoulders back, cheerily, to Mary, but of course she didn't respond right away: she was not one to speak until she'd had at least two cups of java and had finished polishing her nails. She also didn't like to be disturbed when she was reading the paper—though she worked from back section to front, from Want Ads to Page One, so I'd concluded that she was pretty much done.

3

The arrival of Joseph was no small deal. He hadn't been home in twelve years, since first taking Holy Orders. But now, for Thanksgiving, he was expected.

"Joseph writes that he wants to see the home movies when he visits," Mom said. "Especially–he's kidding, of course–the first five years with little Joseph."

"Wouldn't it be the first three years with Joseph?" I said, seeing that Mary was three years younger than Joseph, but neither Mary nor Mom responded to this. The gray tin cases that held our movie past were stored away downstairs–in a place without easy access, no doubt–so, for the time being, I was forced to let it be five years. Or was the "five years" part of the joke, Joseph's "kidding."

"I'm looking forward to seeing him," I said, trying whatever I could to get Mary to speak up.

"Of course. We all are," Mom said–speaking (inaccurately) on Mary's behalf.

"He thinks he can waltz back in here after twelve years, like some sort of prodigal son," Mary offered, at last, meanwhile folding the paper in half New York commuter style.

"I'll be right back," I said. Shortly, I stood over Mary with a dictionary in my hand: "By prodigal do you mean 'recklessly extravagant' or 'yielding abundantly'"?

Mary cracked a smile, but then righted herself. "I mean the Bible story. Now leave me some peace, how 'bout it, Peter. I'll be late for my job."

Mary was a "dancer."

But there was a different kind of work that needed doing, in expectation of Joseph's arrival. Housework. The kitchen looked like a combat zone. Mom was running out of room. Even the garage was full up; we had a two-car garage but had never parked even one car inside it. Some boxes brought out from Indiana fifteen years earlier, in 1964, had never been opened (which aroused my curiosity about what sort of clothes I wore when I was thirteen–flannels and corduroys, as I recall).

Mom had kept every picture or scrap of homework any of us had done in school over the years. I'd recently come across a bunch of old exams, on blue-inked mimeograph paper (how unforgettable the smell of the ink!) Victoriana of any shape and size was particularly noticeable among the relics. Hats were legion. Magazines, too, especially *Sunset* and *Arizona Highways*. There were jars full of dried leaves, orange peels, Ball Jar lids, buttons, etc. Mom owned several doll houses, and each was completely equipped, right down to the plumbing--she used hearing aids for toilets. Maps, music scores, tapestries, Chinese fans, chess sets, and various other games (including "Mormonopoly") added what Matt referred to as the "Prospero" touch. Prospero or not, I couldn't figure out why Mom needed to collect all that stuff: it was as if her passion for antiques had become an illness of some sort. Like Matthew's inexplicable drinking.

Mary had turned on the light above the kitchen table to read by, but I insisted upon opening the shutters and letting in natural light. Mom winced; she hated being exposed that way. The window faced the mountains and thus the room was one of the nicest in our split level. The noise of the traffic on Pima Road was one drawback however; the congestion had spurred plans to build a freeway, a freeway that required, should the city fathers have their way, the removal--that is, the destruction--of our house on Cattle Track. Originally, Scottsdale hoped to build Loop 101 on the reservation, but the Indians had decided not to lease any more of their land--the price wasn't right apparently. The community college had been built out there, on a hundred-year lease, but the freeway was still a matter for negotiations, within the tribe and between the tribe and Scottsdale. Meanwhile, we and our neighbors remained in limbo.

November had arrived, and the reservation cotton fields were thickly white, like a sweater stretched out to dry. Our backyard olive trees were filled with fruit. That particular morning the moon was still visible, its fully round shape appearing like a wafer.

Mary held the paper in the most dainty fashion, so as not to smudge her nails.

"Maybe he heard about the freeway," I persisted, now talking to Mom as much as Mary. "Riding in like the calvary to save our scalps."

"Does Joseph have to have a reason to come home?" Mom bitterly interjected.

I assumed (incorrectly, as it turned out) that no one had corresponded with Joseph in the twelve years of his wanderings. Anyway, I felt Mary would probably be forced to point out just how ridiculous my statement about him saving us was, and some sort of verbal intercourse would ensue.

"The freeway will never be built," she said, briefly taking up the argument. "They don't build highways in rich suburbs, Peter. South Phoenix, maybe. Or West Phoenix. Or Guadalupe. Not Scottsdale."

None of the rest of us was convinced of this. Mary was failing to take in to account what Matt called the "street-widening epidemic." Dad, on the other hand, took some solace in the knowledge that the road <u>might</u> be built: we would have to move and thus Mom would be forced to at least get rid of some of what she had collected. Furthermore, Dad liked the idea of freeways: his engineering soul instinctively responded to marvels of technological progress, even if, in this particular case, our own house was under siege.

"Well, Joseph is coming anyway," I said. "Bummer for you, eh, Mary?"

"Don't look for me to greet him at the airport. I wouldn't meet his plane if he were Jesus Christ himself, which he is not, by the way. Or is he, Mom?"

"Well, he's not Elvis," responded Mom. "He didn't buy his mother a Cadillac."

Mary, to her credit I suppose, offered no further word on the subject. She blew on her nails, the usual ghastly shade of red, and retreated upstairs to her room, her boudoir. Her home away from home.

Needless to say, I didn't expect any help from Mary when it came to cleaning up the house for Joseph's visit, nor from Matthew, and my expectations were fulfilled. Since Matt, like myself, was unemployed (I'd lost my cable car engineer-assistant job as a result of the accident), one might think that he could lend a hand with the preparations, but young squire Matt seldom rose before noon, and when he did get up he was usually shaky as a sapling. His drinking had increased during my absence. Earlier that morning, before even Mom had arisen, I'd come downstairs to get a glass of milk and found Matt sitting in screened-in back porch, in his silk smoking jacket, staring out toward the Superstitions (though it was too dark to see much) as though he were a ship at anchor. An eerie smile was stuck on his face, nor did he acknowledge my presence in the room, to the point where it seemed that *he* wasn't, in any real sense, in the room himself, but rather a kind of holograph or film actor. He had stacked up three empty beer bottles, one on top of another end to end, a feat I had never seen before--not even two bottles-- and I concluded that perhaps it was only possible to accomplish this trick with empty Coronas. The tv was broadcasting flickering test patterns; it was apparent that Matt wasn't watching, but I couldn't tell what exactly he was up to, besides drinking.

"Have you ever seen the Superstitions move?" I said, in hope of making contact, brother to brother (a job perhaps more difficult than my attempts earlier in the day with Mary). I was also curious to know if the mountains seemed to him, as they did to me, to be much closer sometimes than others, and not just as a result of the degree of smog.

Matt had heard my query; and he smiled, wryly. "Does Great Birnam wood to high Dunsinane hill come, Peter?"

At night, say past eight or nine o'clock, one was as likely to have Shakespeare answer as Matt. Shakespeare was like another family member, one who appeared after sunset.

Anyhow, the next morning, with Matthew asleep, Mary at her job, Dad at the university, Mom and I were left to wrestle with the house. She wanted to be ready—"prepared"—should Joseph decide to show up sooner than we expected, though Thanksgiving weekend was what he had indicated in his letter. Even when a holiday wasn't in the offing, she spent many days going through her stuff, moving it from one corner of the house to another, never, to my eye, achieving any real progress. It was backbreaking and Sisyphian work. On full-moon nights the house took on the appearance of a grotto.

I'd already moved several pieces of furniture into the backyard (which with its old trailers, rusted contraptions, and broken furniture resembled the Lost Dutchman's Mine), when Mom suggested that I move a few things into the master bathroom, which happened, by the way, to be her bathroom. Dad no longer slept in the master bedroom with Mom. I reminded her that should I do as she asked the six of us would be left with only one bathroom to use, off the kitchen, and that "Mary camps in there as it is" (often leaving rivers of brown stockings on the towel rack afterwards), but Mom, waving her hand, dismissed this concern of mine.

"It's only temporary, Peter," she said, "we can move it all back when Joseph returns to New Orleans. He's only coming for a visit. Besides, I can't think of anyplace else."

"The roof?" I said. We had an Arizona flat-roofed house.

"More work and less repartee," Mom said. "Remember Jesus's robe."

"What?"

"That too was just a cast off."

Still, we were not the type of family to use the same bathroom at the same time--I certainly wouldn't pee while Mary was showering, for instance--so

Mom's sanguine attitude left something to be desired. Indeed, the Wilson need for privacy was often at odds with necessity, not to mention sanity.

Upon my return from San Francisco I'd spent several days clearing out my old room of magazines, odd knickknacks, appliances, and clothes. Also toys and stuffed animals. My room had become, unnervingly, a kind of a graveyard for toys, a kind of memorial to childhood.

"Shall we get rid of these?" I said, holding up two waffle irons. Mom hadn't made waffles in fifteen years or so.

"Those are classics. Look at the design, Peter." I looked: swirling lines, like flames, were etched in silver plating. "I would think an artist such as yourself would realize the value of things. Had to live through the Depression, I guess. FDR never threw out anything either, you know."

The threat of the freeway spurred further packratting. Perhaps Mom subconsciously believed the presence of so much stuff would force the city fathers to decide not to move us, curving the road around our house, even if it meant going out onto Indian land! When one considered how junky some of the Pima properties were, it was not altogether unreasonable to conclude that our property somewhat smudged the line between Scottsdale and the reservation. But again, we'd had virtually no contact with the Pimas over the years, despite living next door, so to speak, and despite my having made many paintings of their land, if one could say it was "theirs"—if one could say anyone owned the land. Or perhaps one could say we all did.

I'd always felt our house and the land it sat on were ours to keep or do with what we wanted, but I was starting to learn otherwise. There was such a thing as eminent domain, there was such a thing as superior force. I'd begun to visualize, in my dreams, not a freeway but a train plowing through our house, something like one of those supersonic trains you read about which run between Tokyo and Osaka. I pictured our family having to move out of the house in the middle of the night, half-dressed, shivering, like some poor refugee family heading off in search of new lands. At other times it was not a train but my Powell Street cable car that would be hurtling toward the house.

Chapter 2

JOSEPH WAS DUE that evening. That morning, just before leaving the house for work, Mary had burst in on me. I was standing in front of the bathroom mirror, shaving. "You don't need to do it every morning," she said. "I"m in hurry. Every time I've come across you lately, Pete, you've got a razor in your hand."

I had decided to start shaving every day, without fail, just as Dad always did—although Dad used an electric ravor, a Remington, which he claimed shaved as close as a blade.

Mom, I felt, was a little too indulgent with us. When we were kids in Indiana, for example, she'd occasionally, on certain cold, dark winter mornings, let me play possum—meaning I'd pretend to not hear her when she came in the bedroom, pretend to be sound asleep, too tired for school. Mary, who shared a room with me until Joseph went off to college, might already be up and dressed or she might also be pretending, we'd be playing double possum as it were (though sometimes you couldn't altogether tell if Mary was asleep because she slept with her eyes half open).

"Petey," Mom would say, "time to get up. You're going to be late. Come on now. You can't miss another day. It won't be dark much longer. It's almost crowfart."

She'd walk out. A few minutes later she'd be back. I could hear Mom breathing above me.

"Oh, let him sleep," she'd say, outloud (she talked to herself even back then). "Let them sleep."

Sometimes I'd miss the entire school day, though other mornings I'd go in in time for P.E. or lunch. Dad blamed Mom, said she was too easy on us.

Over the years I'd gotten into the habit of shaving when I felt like it, but from that morning forward I decided to make the effort daily, even when I was sick, even when I had nothing to do or no one to see (which was more often than not). To rise each morning and shave made me feel more like a man. But–and here's the rub, I suppose–I looked more boyish, like an earlier version of myself. But I shaved everyday anyway. I looked more like the 50's, a more boyish period perhaps but also a more optimistic one, a more self-reliant one. I also, as it happened, looked more 70's, especially since my hair was cut short and around my ears ("Got your ears lowered," Dad would always say when we came home from the barber). In effect by shaving I was erasing the 60's, an era which had been full of wonderful pleasures and conflicts, but a time period also given to indulgence, no question, and one in which I was having a hard time moving on from even though 1979 was just around the corner. I'd graduated high school in 1969 but, for some reason, I hadn't progressed much in the following ten years. My life had a kind of '69 inversion to it.

Following her morning session in the bathroom, Mary would wait on the curb for a ride to work. I'd watch her from the small upstairs bathroom window. How odd it is to have siblings. It seems natural to have a mom and dad. And even though they have individual personalities, you think of them first and foremost as parents. But your siblings insist on their personalities, their individual needs, and certain prerogatives, even the youngest. Of course the oldest gets his own room. It just seems odd that you're living in the same house with these people, and have to share your parents with them. And the older ones–Joseph and Mary, in my case–have a whole history with *your* mom and dad, and with each other, that preceded you.

Around eleven each morning a man would drive up to our house in an expensive car (not always the same man either) and whisk Mary away to the outside world, only to return her (sometimes the same man but not always, and rarely in the same car) back to our house at nine p.m. Mary–twenty-nine, shaped like a Ming dynasty vase–would come in every night dressed in a different outfit than the one she left in, though usually one that at least I recognized as being hers. Then, her hair wet from apparently having showered at her job, she would go up to her room for an hour or so, not reappearing until about eleven when she would sit with Matthew, on the back porch, and watch Nightline. Despite her daily activities Mary claimed to be a virgin.

Throughout the morning Mom and Dad had been hard at work preparing for the return of their first born. Dad's usual duties centered around the pool, the yard, and the cars. Because the interior of the house had declined to a rather wretched state, Dad rarely spent time making repairs inside. He complained even now about not being able to park in the garage. Some nights he would throw a fit and threaten to burn the house down, but by the time he'd return from his nightly dinner at Randy's Grill—since Mom no longer cooked—he was usually calm enough to sit on the davenport downstairs, eat his ice cream, and watch Dallas or Dynasty, or sometimes the Spanish station, even though he didn't know the language. He liked the singing and dancing. Other times he'd retire to the master bathroom and practice violin. But for the most part, the hearth belonged to Mom, the haggard to Dad.

I came upon Dad in the backyard installing Tiki torches. He'd dug several holes in the reddish brown earth that surrounded the pool. Even though he was a violinist, he had large, thick, farmer hands. I've got my father's hands. A bit less stubby perhaps.

Our two ducks, Huey and Luey, watching Dad at his work, toddled around the edge of the water, light whiplashing at the pool bottom like sperm.

"For your brother, Joseph," Dad said, but I knew Joseph's return was something of an excuse because Dad had always wanted Tiki torches.

I wanted to ask Dad about what the deal was between Joseph and Mary. I trusted my father implicitly to tell me all he knew, or at least all he felt it right to share. He wasn't duplicitous. Whenever he talked about the weather, for instance, I knew he was talking about the weather. But maybe, then, maybe Dad wasn't privy to the whole story, or maybe wasn't ready to see it all. There was also this: the more one looked into family relations and events, the more complex it all became. One might never touch bottom. And then what? Did it matter? Life sailed on, didn't it?

Just then, however, he managed to incur Mom's wrath as a result of his bending a window screen while running a power saw cord inside the house.

"You have to break something, don't you, Sherwood?" Mom called out, surveying the damage. "He's not happy unless he's breaking something," she said to me, shaking her head.

"I'm just trying to get some power," Dad called back and revved up the saw.

Mom and Dad were indeed a strange match. Mom was Catholic, baroque, a New Yorker; Dad was Methodist, minimalist, a Midwesterner. She was a rhythm person; he was a method person. She was working class but sophisticated. He was upper middle class but somewhat square. Sometimes I felt my entire life to be but a study in such mixed messages (as a result, I sometimes thought I might go off my nut). Mom was a procrastinator; Dad was a go-getter. She looked to the past (Baroque being a time-soaked style) and he looked to the future. Mom valued individuality; Dad systems. "Your father can't program me," Mom would sometimes say, "that's why he gets so frustrated."

I grew up with a cybernetic father. While Mom encouraged pride and nostalgia, Dad believed in humility and the future, and humility toward the future. The 1939 World's Fair Mom talked about--and of which I'd read up on--actually inaugurated a world more suited to Dad's way of seeing things than to Mom's. Except for the time capsule (containing work by Thomas Mann and Albert Einstein, among others) buried in ritual ceremony by the political fathers of New York, including Mayor LaGuardia, the fair was a celebration of progress--the centerpiece being the General Motors' Futurama, which featured the model of a color-coded future city: bright, rational, functional, completely planned. A place where the past was banished. A place antithetical to nostalgia, and to my mother's instinctive (New York?) contrariness and pessimism. "Prosperity and pessimism don't travel together" was the slogan of Westinghouse during the exhibition.

"Hope it doesn't turn cold," Dad said, as I walked out arms full toward the old Airstream camping trailer, which was now used as a storage. "Just toss that box of stuff in the garbage, Peter. And there's more where that one comes from," he joked.

"Bedlam Manor," I responded.

The trailer was not wholly used up. Several mannequins, most without heads, some without arms or legs, were stacked at various angles—and in various compromising positions—inside. At first glance the mannequin bodies appeared to float in the air as though the interior of the trailer was actually the cabin of a spaceship.

Mom's hoarding was her way of securing her future, even at the price, so it seemed, of her marriage.

I opened the gate to the backyard fence and tossed the carton in the green dumpster. It was a kind of test: Would Mom notice that this stuff (in this case, old calendars) was no longer around? And if at some point she forgot that she had it, did it mean that upon finding it again she could claim that she'd been missing it? And would its value increase for having been gone so long?

When I returned I saw my chance to query Dad about Joseph and Mary's history.

"I thought you knew," he responded, with a puzzled expression, as though everything was perfectly clear and only I was confused. As though, in effect, everyone in the family was boating on a crystal clear lake and only my lack of understanding made the water murky and dark.

"How would I know?" I said. "Mary doesn't tell me anything."

"I think it best you get her version from her. Something happened between Joseph and Mary when they were in high school—some boys, some of Joseph's friends, took advantage of her. I didn't learn of it until later. For a long time Mary and Joseph had somewhat different versions of the incident. And Mary, well...." Dad got a bit choked up. "It was a long time, ago, Peter. Another time and another place. It's bet to let it lie, I think."

Was it? Well, for the time being, I did. Besides, I'd noticed something near the trailer. The ground was still soft from the rains, making Dad's torch installation easier.

"What's that?" I said to him, pausing as I headed back inside. He was holding up a piece of pottery. He held it above his head, turning the piece to the light. It appeared to be Indian pottery. A design, in yellow, was painted on the reddish-brown glaze. Although the paint was faded and the shard was covered with dirt, a portion of a human figure, perhaps the torso of a woman, was etched in relief below the design.

Dad didn't respond right away. He had Zenlike concentration when engaged in some activity; he was an absent-minded professor as a result of this ability.

"It looks Indian," I said.

"You think so? I doubt it. Probably from Deseret or Pic & Save. Probably your mother bought it."

"It could be Pima. Who knows, it could be Hohokam."

"More likely Chinese I've been digging straight down."

Once in a while my father came out with a good one. (When Matt graduated high school and someone asked what his graduation present was, Dad said: "New shoes.")

"Well, I don't think it's Chinese," I said.

"But I'm half way to the Middle Kingdom already. The holes are so deep not even a dust devil could blow these torches from their standards."

I could see Dad wasn't too impressed by the pottery; as for myself, I was wondering what else the rains might have excavated and I was determined to take a closer look at some point later in the day.

"Well, don't throw it away," I persisted, but Dad had already moved on to other concerns.

Chapter 3

AT CLOSE TO ten that evening Joseph arrived at Sky Harbor. He looked taller than I recalled him as being. He'd always cut a very striking figure, especially when wearing his robes and collariam, which was the last garb I'd seen him wear that day, some twelve years earlier, when he became a priest. It wasn't until he removed his coat that we saw that he was dressed in everyday attire, a beige Shaker sweater and tailored slacks, although a cap--a Milan bonnet (as I learned later from Matthew, who praised the "splendid virility" of Joseph's clothes)--provided a dandyish touch. Joseph had a suitcase in each hand. He was quick to hug each of us.

"I can't believe I'm really here," he said, which I took to mean "among the family" rather than "in Arizona," although Joseph, visiting at Christmas during his junior year at Notre Dame, had also only once before been to the Grand Canyon State.

We headed for the baggage area.

"Where's Mary?" Joseph said, certainly a question that he'd wanted to ask immediately but had held back.

"At work," I said. "She'll be home later."

"Tired from being on her feet all day," Matt said.

"She always loved to dance," Joseph said. "She had happy feet." Joseph apparently knew all about Mary's occupation.

Before we left the airport, he stopped at the bathroom. It was a little awkward waiting for him, awkward in ways it wouldn't have been for any other member of the family. The years of separation changed things.

The two suitcases gave one the idea that he had come for a lengthy visit. This impression was reinforced by our trip to baggage express, where we picked up another suitcase, a leather briefcase, a duffle bag, golf clubs, and a tennis racket. Inevitably, such an array of grips and equipment put me in mind of Mom's collecting passions. Joseph looked a great deal like Mom: both had pale-white Irish skin, full lips, and jet-black hair (Mom, who thought long hair unbecoming on older women, had nevertheless let the worldly luxury of her long hair hang loose that evening). Joseph hoisted one suitcase and the duffle bag. Dad and I each grabbed a suitcase. Matthew slung the golf clubs over his shoulder. Mom carried the tennis racket. Soon we were piled into the "Nimitz" headed for home. It was a beautiful fall evening, the lights of the city, this city I rarely ventured into, glimmered in the soft darkness like points on a solid-state circuit. Joseph ran his window all the way down in order to enjoy the air. He removed his hat and let the wind flow through the twenties-style finger waves of his (still) dark hair. "It's a grand evening," he said. He was riding shotgun. "Lovely."

Inevitably perhaps the conversation turned to a discussion of the Pima Freeway, Mom bringing it up.

"They'll need a crane to move me," she said, referring in this case, I believe, to her personal self rather than her belongings.

"I would hate to see the old homestead dismantled," Joseph said, despite, as I've said, his having only once before been to the Scottsdale house. "You know, in Atlantic City, they had to build this big steel casino around a little house because the guy wouldn't move. Now his house is a gift shop."

Already in his evening mode, Matt was quick to offer observations of his own, or rather observations culled from his reading.

"No, thought Oedipa, sad," he said from his seat next to me in the back, "as if their home cemetery in some way still did exist, in a land where you could somehow walk, and not need the East San Narciso Freeway "

Joseph spoke into the rearview mirror: "I remember what a fine memory you had as a child."

"And bones still could rest in peace, nourishing ghosts of dandelions, no one to plow, them up. As if the dead really do persist, even in a bottle of wine," Matt continued, apparently completing the original quote.

Then, we were home.

The main rooms of the house looked quite nice, even elegant—"undrugged," one might say—for Joseph's homecoming, especially if one didn't notice certain corners where Mom had thrown a sheet. We were in the livingroom. Dad immediately set to making a fire because it was a rather cool November evening. The wad of newspapers quickly caught and flames licked up the sides of the logs. It seemed but a fortnight had passed since Joseph was last part of the family.

"Sit here," Mom said to him, pointing to a red, high-backed Victorian chair.

Matt, who sat near the open sliding door, lit up. We talked in part about the freeway. At Dad's direction, about the weather; and in part of Joseph's life in New Orleans. However, this latter subject received rather sketchy and inconclusive testimony from Joseph. "I've been with the same small parish church several years now," he said, almost mechanically. "Of course New Orleans is a wonderful place, especially the food. I've traveled a great deal over the years, when I could get away from church work. Turkey, Morocco." Not much else of substance was revealed, though he did add, less mechanically, "I so wish you all could have come visit sometime." Yet why we couldn't have had was not explained.

So a little montage of Joseph's wandering years played before our eyes, a lot of the meaty scenes edited out. It struck me as we sat there how odd it was to discuss Joseph's life, or anyone's life for that matter, and never make any reference to relationships, to never mention a lover or a fiancee, and of course to never mention the possibility that the person under question might be planning on becoming a parent some day. Joseph, a priest, lived without these things. But, to various lesser degrees, Mary, Matthew, and I also were doing without. Perhaps it was at that moment I first truly feared for the future of us Wilsons, a fear that even superseded fears aroused by the projected Pima Freeway. Wilsons without future Wilsons seemed a terrible nullity, a denial of life, a perversity. Joseph's long absence seemed to speak to some entropic nature within our family. Nor was there any mention of why Joseph had decided to return home now, at thirty-two years of age.

Which is not to say I wasn't glad to have Joseph home. I'd missed him. I regretted the absence of a big brother, my big brother; I longed to recall in his presence scenes of our Hoosier childhood—cutting through someone's backyard to get to where we needed to go, for instance. Scenes like that, simple, unforgettable. But now he was home. Indeed everything was going quite well that evening, until about nine o'clock—Dad had just gone into the kitchen to fix the spumoni—when Mary, the likes of which I had never seen before, arrived home.

She glowered at Joseph, biting her lip as she did, her eyes narrowing into the shape of little fishes.

"So you're back," she said, and then ran up the stairs to her room and slammed shut her door, as though, so it seemed to me, she had suddenly become a little girl again, and in true Wilson fashion clung to that notion that she could keep out the world by simply closing herself off in her room.

Meanwhile a silence fell upon those of us left in the parlor, a silence that greatly amplified the crackling of the mesquite logs in the fireplace.

We waited, though what we were waiting for was not altogether clear. For my part, I hoped Joseph might say something helpful, something that would ease the situation even if there wasn't anything to be said sufficient to clear up or remedy the situation, whatever the situation was, which was also not entirely clear, at least to me. But apparently Joseph didn't have anything very helpful and/or revealing to offer.

"I recall that vacation I spent here," he said suddenly, changing the subject. "Remember how we woke Christmas morning and found all those sheep from the reservation in our frontyard. It was surreal, wasn't it--those white sheep blanketing the yard. At first, I didn't know if that was a usual occurrence for you guys, having a bunch of bleating sheep in your yard."

"Only on Christmas," Dad said.

We laughed.

But Joseph abruptly stood, nearly hitting the ceiling with his head as he did. Saying, yawning: "I must be to bed now. I'm really quite tired from my trip, though happy to be home. The house looks lovely, Mom. I hope Mary feels better tomorrow. I...oh well, tomorrow's another day, isn't it?" The phrase about tomorrow was one of Dad's favorite commonplaces.

Joseph retreated—recalling, for me, the way in high school he would withdraw to his room right after dinner and stay there most of the evening. He was studious; I would walk by his half- opened door and see him doing his homework, the neck of the black desk lamp bent over the paper, casting its small pool of light. In fact, once he entered high school I saw little of him; in all but actuality, he had already left home. But I came to understand, later, that Joseph escaped to his room not only to study but also to avoid the family, perhaps especially Mom and Dad, who were often at odds.

He appeared to be waiting for us to say goodnight.

"Perhaps we all *should* get to bed," Mom said. "A busy day we'll have tomorrow." Eschewing her no cooking rule once more, Mom would be up before the crack of dawn to fix the turkey.

"Nebraska and Oklahoma at noon," Matt offered, a reference to the annual Big 8 Thanksgiving Day football game.

My father said: "The weather is supposed to be warm this weekend. Just like the Indian summer we used to have in Indiana. What do you say we go boating Friday?"

But there was no response to Dad's inquiry. And before long everyone, except Matthew, retired for the night.

To my surprise, the scene in the parlor was not the worst spectacle I witnessed that evening; it was but a prelude to what I saw later, as wind and rain sometime prefigure a hail storm.

I awakened once more from a bad dream—something to do with Jenny and the day of my eye accident--and was reading in bed, Van Gogh's letters to Theo, when the thought crossed my mind that I might never have another chance to see my whole family together again, I mean to see them quiet and peaceful, all in one house, for I had a vision of Joseph suddenly concluding it would be best for him to fly straight back to New Orleans, or of Mary going out at eleven the next morning and never returning, or of the freeway itself abruptly displacing our home, as capitalism has displaced feudalism. But more to the point, I began to wonder in a general way if ever there was, or ever had been, a single time in the history of our household when, like most families come nightfall, each person was asleep, no one was awake, no one was prowling: Mary was home from her dissipations and, alone, in bed; Dad had got up from the couch, where he liked to nod off in front of the television; Matt, the primary obstacle to the realization of this quiet hour, had gone off to his stuporous slumber; Mom, the ever vigilant, had not yet started frying; and Joseph, whose sleep patterns were, for me, a matter of speculation, had not risen for matins or some such early morning ritual you would expect a priest to perform.

Why, I wondered, was there always at least one of us awake, keeping the watch, as though our house, our little ark, were in jeopardy of sailing off into dangerous waters?

And so, at four a.m., I rose from my own bed to find out the answer to my query, discounting, as was necessary, the fact that should I indeed find all asleep I, myself, was nevertheless awake. I began with Dad. He was a pretty masterful sleeper; no doubt he had acquired this talent out of necessity, since he was largely responsible for the fiscal solvency of the family. Or perhaps the ability to shut things out is endemic to university professors. Dad was sleeping quite soundly, wearing only his white jockey shorts, stretched out face down on the pillow, snoring, exhausted. The guest room, a small room off the pantry, served as Dad's sleeping quarters, as well as his study. Many times he left his computer going, its blue screen the color of airport runway lights.

I couldn't help but pause in front of Dad's bed before moving on; my gratitude to him, for all the years he worked to support his family, was one of the inexpressibles. In fact, as I silently and stealthily wended my way about the house, only a backyard moon shining through windows for light, I felt strongly that everything was going to be all right, that all was exactly as it was supposed to be, and this simple but singular feeling of peacefulness vanquished--at least for a moment--all my frustrations and fears, including even the fear that I had apparently lost Jenny and the verdant years we might have spent together.

I looked in the refrigerator for something to eat before moving on, but settled on just a glass of milk.

Having discovered that Dad was asleep, and also that Mom was not in the kitchen and thus, presumably, was also in bed—since she locked her door at night, I couldn't actually check on her—and discovering that Matthew was safely and securely asleep in his downstairs, window- blackened bedroom, I climbed back up the stairs confident that Joseph, tired from his trip, would also be slumbering and that even Mary, despite being upset, would also be in dreamland. Mary rarely missed her eight hours (she was always fagged out when she got home from work). One of the most reassuring things in my life was to see my sister home alone in bed, hidden beneath her blue comforter, the only visible part of her being the top of her head, her eyes covered by black patches she wore to block out the light, having borrowed the patches from me.

Mary slept with the light on, a small, Tiffany lamp which she also used for reading. She was, like the rest of us Wilsons, an avid reader, her own taste running toward Southern Gothic.

I couldn't bring myself right then to open Mary's door. I suppose I wanted to hold on as long as possible to the hope that everybody could be sleeping peacefully at once. A kind of nativity scene was what I had in mind, but more like the day *after* Jesus was born, the whole thing settled, everyone gathered and at ease (also tired from the journey and from tending a crying baby).

In the end I decided it might be best to look in on Joseph. Surely his return had been a physical and emotional drain on him. Surely he was, as we say, sound asleep.

So it was indeed a great shock–how confidently I had opened his door!--to find not only that Joseph wasn't sleeping but that, instead, he knelt before his bed weeping, and in a manner so abject and heartrending I cannot bring myself to fully describe it. His body, however, I can describe, for the visual detail before me was forged into my mind as though by a soldering iron. His long naked body was turned toward the window. Scars and deep scratches ran across his back, causing a resemblance to a map of the Tigris and the Euphrates (something I remembered studying repeatedly during my grade school years).

Joseph's iconographic bearing at that moment–his prostrate form, the way the light from the moon shone on his skin–was almost too much for me. I considered closing the door again, leaving him to his orisons. I never had been able to envision my elder brother in merely human terms; the years of his absence had furthered the mystery Joseph had become for me someone extraordinary, and, to a degree, alien.

He hadn't heard me come in. At last, sensing my presence, he turned around and spoke. "I have been defrocked, Peter. Suspended from the Order. I am homeless now."

At first I thought he was making some kind of joke, some reference to his present naked state, but I soon realized that wasn't the case.

"Defrocked?" I said, once and then twice, more repeating the word to myself than actually addressing him. At that moment I even felt powerless to ask the simple and most relevant question, "Why?" I felt numbed by the news that my brother was no longer a priest.

I also was helpless to comfort him. Though I wanted to embrace him, I felt incapable of doing so--partly, I admit, because of the unsettling appearance of his body. He was not only scarred but I saw now, now that he was out of his clothes, Joseph had become, except for his beautiful face, older. Prematurely old. His chest was sunken. His hands liver-spotted. His legs and arms, however, were still muscular.

It was terrible, of course, to share such an intimate moment with a member of my own family. It was more than terrible, it was indecent, like the time I had to visit Matthew at the detox center. And yet, I had a feeling it was necessary, indecent or not. Somehow we Wilsons, as a family, needed to unearth the past. There appeared to be no other way.

"I'm sorry to hear of your troubles, Joseph," I managed to say at last. And, despite the somewhat cold way I had phrased it, I was sorry. Deeply sorry. The church had been Joseph's life.

But this moment alone with my older brother was soon interrupted.

"You've no need to feel sorry for him," I heard someone say from behind me. It was Mary. For a moment there, I'd thought it was our mother—I'd never noticed how alike Mary and Mom sounded--but it was Mary, standing there oddly triumphant, the black patches resting on the top of her head like Mickey Mouse ears.

"And why not?" I said to Mary, turning toward her, feeling that it was about time the cards were out on the table, that, despite my family's reticence when it came to personal matters, it was time to be a bit more forthright, a bit more open. Surely Joseph, who had already confessed to some degree, would appreciate the same sort of candidness on Mary's part. I knew I would. I was tired of being so much in the dark. Conspiratorial interpretations lent themselves to my ears.

Joseph used the momentary exchange between Mary and me to slip into his bathrobe. Mary was focused on other things however.

"Well, our father forgives," she said, distractedly, somewhat cryptically--while waving her hand, her beautiful petite white right hand, in a dismissive manner. She, herself, was dressed in nothing more than a nightie, a slip of a thing. "Forgive, Ex post facto," Mary said.

"Meaning?" I said, turning first to Mary and then to Joseph, and then back and forth between them. I didn't appreciate Mary's wordmongering. And forgive *what* was the question.

"Meaning your older brother will have to forgive himself," Mary said. "He and Leslie Feelers."

Joseph appeared to almost wince at the mention of this name, Leslie Feelers. I remembered him, vaguely. Joseph also appeared to be waiting for me to say something, waiting for my reaction, but I didn't have one that I could easily articulate.

Meanwhile Mary backtracked to her bedroom, shutting the door, shutting us out. I stood in the hallway.

"Come in, Peter," Joseph said, shutting his own bedroom door behind us.

"No need to explain unless you want to," I said and sat down on the edge of the bed. "We are just happy to have you home."

Joseph looked at me searchingly. "Which?" he said.

"Which?" I said, repeating the word, unable to decipher his meaning.

"Mary's actions or my defrocking?"

"Uh..." I said, faltering--realizing that Mary's actions and Joseph's defrocking were separate issues, but that in my mind I had linked them.

Joseph again waited for me to continue, to draw him out on the subject, or subjects. Then, he didn't wait.

"Mom wrote me that for a while, after your return from San Francisco, you got letters from a little high school student you knew there."

I was astonished to hear that Joseph knew about Jenny: astonished to learn, as I would shortly, that Mom wrote to Joseph, and, furthermore, that she told him about some of the more intimate details of my life, and had apparently been doing so for twelve years. But I couldn't see what my friendship with Jenny had to do with Joseph's defrocking or his relationship with Mary.

"Mom would write to you?"

"Of course, didn't you know? I've kept abreast of things these twelve years."

"I never saw any letters from you?"

"Well, I didn't write back. But Mom knew I got _her_ letters."

"Pretty weird arrangement, I would say. Makes me wonder about this family. Not that I'm being critical."

"But as to your high school friend?" Joseph persisted.

He was turned to the window, looking out at the moonlit and now underlit sky. Soon it would be sunrise.

I recalled how my room at the Y in San Francisco, where Jenny first came to visit me, caught the morning light off the bay. My window at the Y also looked

out–prophetically, so it seemed to me upon returning to Arizona–on the unfinished Embarcadero Freeway, on the concrete pillars of the last section of that
elevated monstrosity, the final sweep disappearing, in almost mystical fashion,
into the misty air of the surrounding water.

"Yes," I said at last, "what about her?"

"Well, Peter, sua passion' predominante e la giovin principiante–that's from
Don Giovanni, who also liked young girls. I've had my temptations as well. I too
have been prone to weakness."

Weakness? I thought to myself. Was Jenny my weakness? Joseph obviously
wasn't aware of Jenny's interest in art, not that even that mattered. I loved Jenny,
that was the long and short of it. Furthermore, Joseph bringing up Jenny seemed
a wholly inadequate response to matters of both his disappearance and his sudden return to the fold twelve years later.

However, his statement did have the effect of shifting the focus of the interrogation back on him.

"What's your weakness?" I said.

"Not exactly sexual," he said, which implied that my Jenny thing was about
sex, "but..."

"Yes?" I said.

"Wildness," Joseph said. "Wildness?"

"Yes." He suddenly peered out the window. "In what way?"

"Every way. That's why I had to become a priest."

"Because you were too wild?"

"Yes."

"Is there something I'm missing in what you're telling me? Something more
specific you should tell me?" I said, pressing Joseph about as far as I was felt
comfortable doing.

"No."

"Which?"

"No, I can't be more specific, right now. Later, maybe, once I get to know
you better again."

I didn't much like the sound of that, as though I was going to have to pass
some test, some trial, before becoming privy to what I considered to be basic

knowledge, knowledge fundamental to my understanding of myself and my family on an even cursory basis.

"Is that you two boys?" Mom suddenly called in from behind the door. For a second I'd thought it was Mary.

"Do you think Mary will be all right?" I said, quietly.

"Mary will be hard to bring round," Joseph said, whispering now. "She's stubborn. And she's hurt. But in the long run she too will be converted. I think the family will be all right now. We've got that damn freeway to fight, don't we?"

I found it difficult to disagree. The freeway suddenly seemed like a dream, or like a two- dimensional cartoon some fool city planner hoped to breathe life into.

"We were just talking, Mom," I said, opening the door.

"Doesn't anybody sleep around here," she said. "Even in the middle of the night, like Grand Central Station."

"Or Atlantic City," Joseph said.

"Oh, how I miss the ocean," Mom said, heading downstairs.

Joseph was still staring out the window, out toward the Superstitions. The sun was sneaking up the backside of the mountains.

I thought once more of Jenny. I imagined myself painting her again, catching her in a lambent light, and I thought about how nice it be to watch her grow into a woman.

I looked back, and up, at Joseph. I concurred—we indeed had something to rally around. Everything would be all right, I told myself, as long as we were together. Surely Joseph has some regrets, I was thinking; surely coming home wasn't his first choice. He was an impressive figure when he was in the world. As Matthew once said of Joseph: "It was not his wont to be the hindmost man." Yet, it was also true that we needed him at home right then.

"When did Mom start collecting all this stuff?" he said.

"I can't remember. It seems like it has always been with us."

"I've always collected myself of course," Joseph said, intimately. "Old tinted postcards...various things. I've got a storage full in New Orleans. But, well, they say wagon trains had to dump things along the way. Stoves, bedsteads—anything to lighten the load."

"I don't know exactly when it started to get bad," I said, though Joseph's question started me to thinking: Had Mom revved up her collecting when he left?

"Quite a while, it's been," I said. I saw Joseph wasn't sure how long I meant. "Some years. It's been some years," I said. "Too many."

Just to top it off, I discovered Matt downstairs, on the patio. "Are the Superstitions moving?" I joked.

"Did you know Mom's stuff is like a physical manifestation of my own disease," Matt responded. He liked non-responsive dialogue. As a child he engaged in what they now call "parallel play." "Every time I'm home, which as you know is pretty damn often, I see manifestations of my drinking piled up around the house. You know what I mean?"

I was a little too tired to discuss it, right then, however.

But I set to thinking about it later when I went off to bed. For indeed while a drinker can, at least for a time, conceal his illness--hiding gin bottles in dresser drawers, for instance--and whereas a sex fiend can park his car in the back lot of the adult shop he too frequently visits, Mom's problem could not be easily hidden. A sheet thrown over boxes was the best she could do. Perhaps Matt was right, the family was in this together. Perhaps Mary's "dancing," for instance, was a symbolic interpretation of Matt's alcoholism. And perhaps his shakes were a kind of manifestation of her exhibitionist tendencies. Maybe Joseph's disappearance was in some way a playing out in visible form of an unspecified, invisible illness of one family member, or the family as a whole. And what did it mean his coming home?

Chapter 4

DESPITE OUR PROBLEMS, or troubles, we had a pleasant Thanksgiving, one that recalled those spent in our Hoosier homeland, and perhaps even reminiscent (sans Native Americans) of the original Thanksgiving. The dining room table was set with cut glass goblets as well as the usual blue willow dishes, glazed with Chinese scenes, such as a man and woman crossing a little arched stone bridge-- the scene delicately portraying the relationships of man and social life as well as man and nature. We sat in the straight-backed chairs Mom had recently bought at Deseret, chairs that made the family appear as a subject worthy of the artist Grant Wood, best known, of course, for his "American Gothic." Indeed known, if at all, almost entirely for that one painting.

Dad, at the head of the table, said grace, Joseph having begged off despite Dad's importuning.

"Thank you, Father, for this beautiful day, for this Thanksgiving dinner, for the opportunity to have the whole family together, now that our eldest, Joseph, has returned to spend some time with us. In your name. Amen."

"Amen," we all said–Matthew, however, adding a gospel and faintly humorous intonation to the phrase. Matt was also keen to show us that he preferred praying brass-knuckle fashion. "Open the doors and there are all the people," he said, wiggling his fingers.

"I suppose Matt should make the toast," Dad said, a reference to Matt's literary ability, I guess.

Matt took this charge seriously. He stood and filled each wine glass to the brim. Then, rather than look at us, he turned to look out the window into the middle distance, out toward the reservation, out beyond the wide spreading olive tree of our backyard past Pima Road to where, near the confluence of the Salt and Verde rivers, stood the McDowells and the Superstitions.

"Confusion to our enemies," he said, and sat back down.

And thus we spent our Thanksgiving, my favorite holiday, the true American holiday, the best holiday--just food and family and conversation and celebration of our arrival in America.

And soon we were into a routine, Joseph just one of the family again. He spent his time reading, and gardening, relandscaping the front patio as it were--planting low-water shade trees and rose bushes. For starters, the rose branches were cut back. And then over the next couple of months they began to grow and bloom, the leaves turning from green to rose--and I realized (me, a painter, how humiliating!) that it's the leaves, beet red almost, almost purple, rose, not the flowers, red, white, or yellow, that we know as rose. Even more I was struck, as I looked out the window one day at the bare branches, live green or almost rose, several to a bush, stripped but just then refashioning themselves--by the thorns, I was struck, and their beauty, translucent, sharp, along the patio in December.

But the less said about Christmastime the better. Mary didn't even show Christmas morning; we opened presents without her. In fact, Mary, sulking, was rarely at home. Many nights she no longer came in at all. Although she would try to get back some evenings to watch Nightline with Matt, she would often go right back out again. Matt most definitely missed having her around, though I too felt the lack. No doubt Joseph felt some guilt, since his return had obviously provoked Mary's increasing absence. Indeed, her behavior was apparently the primary reason for Joseph's return, soon after Christmas, to New Orleans, though his professed reason was to clear up some of his affairs. He was gone for two months. Two months wasn't much after twelve years, but still it felt odd to have him absent once again.

Joseph returned Easter week. In the interim Matthew, responding to Joseph's urging, had taken up golf. So it followed naturally that the four of us, the men of the family, took in a round.

"You all spend too much time inside. Housebound," Joseph said as we drove to the course. "Dad and I will take on you and Peter, eh Matt?"

"Lead on," Matt said, feeling a bit cocky.

Papago was a municipal desert course, long and rolling, and near impossible to score well on unless you kept it in the fairway. The rough was rocks, dirt, and small desert bushes, like tumbleweed, sage, and sweet smelling creoscte. But it was a popular layout, difficult to get on during the winter when the snow birds were in town, and especially on such a fine warm day as that particular Palm Sunday. The blue sheet of morning stretched out before us like a whale skin, the green links themselves like the isles of a foreign clime or some ancient world. The desire to be elsewhere was often satisfied by a simple round of golf.

The exotic feel of Papago was enhanced by the presence, or near presence, of the Phoenix Zoo, which happened to border the course. The animals were enjoying their late morning feed just about the time we teed off. Standing at the first tee, we could hear them rooting about in their cages. Even the usually sleepy lions and tigers were awake, their roar echoing across the landscape, across the buttes and mesas of the park. The first tee box was close to the tiger enclosure. The tigers, neon orange, black, and white in the sun, paced back and forth on a path they'd worn just the other side of the fence. Strangely, they ignored us until we were ready to hit.

But we still had to wait. Joseph was a big hitter and he didn't want to take a chance of sending a ball bounding into the group ahead, four women golfers, who, though good for women, nevertheless couldn't punch the ball much more than a hundred yards at a time--though strangely this didn't appear to detract from their enjoyment of the game.

On the course that day Joseph made light of the woman-playing-golf issue. "Once in a while one of the nuns would want to join our New Orleans foursome," he said, leaning forward on his driver, watching the group in front of us. He was wearing a blue windbreaker. "But if God had intended women to play golf he would have made triple bogey a good score."

"Or designed nun's habits with knickers," I said, shamefully joining in, and wondering how Joseph could so blithely talk about his church experiences. Perhaps the pain of his defrocking (for exactly what I still didn't know) had begun to subside.

"Nuns in knickers, you say," Matt reiterated, laughing through his teeth. "I knew there was a reason I got out of bed this morning."

29

"Besides the danger of forgetting what morning looks like," Dad said. Normally Dad was pretty quiet, but he was always thinking.

"Every man and woman should be forced out of bed soon after the sun has risen: particularly the nervous ones," Joseph said. Adding--"And forced into physical activity. If not, they will soon be nervously diseased"--before returning to the previous topic: "In New Orleans, you know, the men try to keep women off the golf courses."

"Oh, are nuns women?" I said.

"Not Sister Mary Louisa," Joseph said, recalling the Mother Superior of our church back in Indiana.

"Well, we are not men," Matt said, apparently borrowing a phrase from a song. Then, it was time for golf.

Matthew hit first. He dropped his cigarette to the grass and, with a nice easy swing, sent a solid straight drive some two hundred and twenty yards over the fairway trap into a perfect approach position for his second shot. Matt was a natural golfer. Somehow when he stood over the ball his shakes disappeared, his concentration became immaculate, his address fundamentally sound. His swing was smooth and fluid, like a pendulum. It was almost as if he'd missed his true vocation--though what his actual vocation was no one exactly knew, unless poetry counted. "This one's for Bonnie Prince Charlie," Matt would say when addressing the ball, or "This one's for the Boy Pretender," for Matt claimed, but only when we were golfing, that we were really more Scottish than Irish. (Furthermore, according to him, "We're more Dutch than Irish" when boating with Dad. Mom's claims to Canarsie Indian blood had yet to assume an esti-mable place in Matt's cosmography of the family heritage. However the Welsh side--have I mentioned the Welsh side?--was often in play, too, Matt insisted, but he couldn't say just how.)

As a golfer, Matt's downfall was Tiffany, the beer girl. She was a fine lass, blond as Mary, young--endowed with both beauty and a certain pleasing sense of herself. Matt had a thing for her. Yet she could have been the worst old hag, one of Macbeth's witches, and he would still have been her best customer. Joseph's golf therapy--he believed golf better therapy than religion--was dealt a more than glancing blow by the presence of the beer girl. But Joseph claimed that golf had practically saved his life and could do the same for Matthew.

And so it had come to pass that, at noon each day, Matt would head out the door in his tartan shorts and white golf shoes. He drove to the course in his golf shoes, his usual rara-avis behavior in many ways still intact. But he was happier. He was shooting in the low 80's, and also considering graduate school. As for the beer girl, she knew not to approach him before the 13th hole, unless he was having a particularly miserable round.

"Faulkner played every afternoon," he had informed me back in February, after he'd been playing regularly for a while. "Willie Faulkner didn't start drinking until after the round. Malcolm Lowry was a champion schoolboy golfer. Remember when the Consul says, 'I should have become a sort of Donne of the fairways at least?'"

Literary precedent was important.

"Well, never a drink before five o'clock and never to bed completely sober," I responded. Matt was like those early Scots golfers, Willie Anderson and the like, rural lads who took to golf and the pub in equal measure.

But Mary took a harder line.

"Half measures avail us nothing," she had said to him one time, quoting the AA bible.

I considered her assessment rather harsh. She seemed to miss the noticeable differences in Matthew's physiognomy as a result of his strenuous (for him) golf regimen. It occurred to me that Mary might resent the change in Matthew. Joseph's return had caused a visible shift in the family structure. Matt no longer seemed so dependent on Mary. He was spending time with his girlfriend, Lacey; he was writing poems again; and, along with contemplating grad school, he was considering getting a job.

"I often thought I might go crazy, I might break my vows, but golf was there to get me away from things," I'd once heard Joseph say to Matt in the hope, now fulfilled, that he would take up the game—though I must say upon hearing Joseph the first question I put to myself was: Well, eldest brother, I thought you did break your vows?

"As a priest, I had plenty of time to practice," Joseph said as, again, we waited for the women ahead to clear the green. His religious order was called the Congregation of the Sacred Heart. The four stages of Christ's life on earth-- Childhood, Hidden Life, Teaching, Crucifixion-- served as a model for the life of the priests. Their vows were Poverty, Chastity, Obedience. "I especially liked beating lawyers and doctors," Joseph was saying. "I'd wear my collar, you see, and make a friendly wager on a round. Yes, it's a grand game. They could hardly say no, especially lawyers. So competitive. 'Father, it's a bet,' they'd say, smiling. Many secretly want a chance to get back at us Holinesses. 'Please, hit away," I'd say. 'Your honor.' Then I'd take them to the cleaners. I loved betting—too much, I'm afraid."

"Too much?" I said, hoping Joseph was, in his oblique way, trying once again to tell me something about his recent troubles. Matt and Dad were not within earshot.

"I was a gambler," he said—though he also looked at me harshly, as if to say: Now, will that satisfy you? I could see Joseph would continue to resist my attempts to probe too deeply, and I suppose I could hardly blame him.

Meanwhile Dad was in the next fairway. Dad's strategy on the course was predicated upon his possessing a wicked slice, and yet sometimes he still didn't compensate enough. His swing was all arms, almost no wrist action whatsoever. A real outside-in swing, the kind God mocks at every turn. Dad always "played" for his slice, often aiming far out into the desert or even out of bounds. On the third hole his alignment meant that his ball, if hit as planned, would travel high above the gorilla cage before returning to the fairway. But often, no matter how much he played for his slice, he'd wind up far right of the hole. Once in a while he was actually two fairways to the right of us, as though he were playing with another foursome or playing a different nine. "Dad's playing an entirely different game," Matt observed. Sometimes during the round Dad was but a speck in the distance, a small buoy drifting upon a vast green sea.

I was sharing a cart with Matt, riding being something I'd only gotten used to that winter: as a kid, I'd walked the course, even in the 100+ Phoenix heat. Back then I was something of a fighter, a daredevil—urged on by friends one time, I climbed over the fence at the fifth hole, into the yak cage, and started throwing stray golf balls over to my buddies, tossing them, as it were, as rapidly as I could because the yak were herding together and beginning to inch toward me. I picked up a few more balls and then scrabbled over the fence at the last minute, just when it appeared the shaggy-haired beasts were ready to charge, though I didn't really know if yak (recent of Tibetan highlands) would charge. Somewhere along the way I'd lost a lot of that boyhood brashness, and acquired, in its stead and to my general dismay, a strange passivity—the passivity and indolence of the artist, I suppose, though I found little consolation in ascribing my absence from active life to artistic inclinations. I mean, art is great but it can't touch boyhood.

We were on the seventh hole, alongside the buffalo habitat, when Joseph and Matthew briefly got into an argument. Apparently Joseph had made some slighting remark about Mary.

"Mary is one the great women of the belle epoque," I heard Matt say, from his spot in the front bunker. "There's nothing wrong with dancing." This last was perhaps a bit disingenuous, since some dancers wear clothes. But Matt had become increasingly annoyed with Joseph's desire to improve our lives—with his sort of all-knowing attitude. Although it should also be said that in Matt's case real improvement was apparent. He still drank but he also golfed.

The sand trap was so deep only Matt's head and shoulders were visible from where I stood. He kept raising his head to check the flag position. The pin was but a few feet in front of him, sloping away; it was a near impossible shot to get close. Matt's head bobbed up and down like a marionette as he surveyed the problem. Ready, he blasted out over the green right into the buffalos. Perhaps he was still mad at Joseph.

"Picked that one clean," he said.

The buffalo, still wearing their shaggy, Vandyke brown winter coats, were not amused. One big mother stood at the fence snorting.

"Play it from there. That's the rules," Dad joked.

"Stroke and distance and reparations to the American Indians," Joseph said. Matt smiled. Their tiff had apparently blown over.

In fact, the rest of the round Joseph rode with Matt, switching bags with me. Joseph wanted to show Matt some of the finer points of the game.

I enjoyed riding with Dad for a while, though his game took us over all the course. When I complained at the tenth that I couldn't find the yardage marker and had no idea what club I should use, he asked if I'd ever seen a parallax yardage estimator on the market. I said I hadn't.

"Probably someone has already invented it," he said. "But you know a parallax focus on the pin would tell you the distance. Maybe I should get to work on that."

"You should. I'm pretty sure I've never heard of any such thing. If I can't find the yardage marker, I try to estimate the length of my drive and subtract that from the total yardage of the hole."

"That's dead reckoning. Ships use that. But a parallax camera would work better." I could tell Dad was thinking about this invention over the next few holes.

The unforgettable nature of that Palm Sunday round was a result of what we came upon at the 13th. An older man—a snow bird perhaps—had expired right on the green. His form was stretched out prone near the pin. A bright yellow vinyl golf jacket had been placed over his upper half out of respect. His golfing partners stood on the apron of the green like statues in a park. Beyond covering him up, they apparently had yet to decide what they should do about him. I don't mean they were deciding whether or not they should play on and finish their round, but somehow the event, the death of their playing partner, had left them helpless, catatonic.

"What shall we do?" one of them said to Joseph, Matt, and me as we approached the green. Only Dad, far to the right of us, in an arroyo, had yet to hit up. Joseph's shot had rolled to within three feet of the man. A sure birdie putt.

"Dead?" I said.

I knew the man was dead, but there was something so incongruous, and yet so fitting, about dying on a golf course that I needed some verbal confirmation.

Another of the playing partners, a skinny fellow who looked positively terror stricken, spoke up: "Yes, he's gone. Could you play around us?"

"Play around you?" Joseph said.

"Yes. I mean, we don't want to hold you up."

I looked at Joseph, wondering what he would say. I mean the fellow's suggestion was not so ridiculous. The man was dead; we didn't know him; it might be hours before the cops arrived.

"We could put him in our golf cart," I said, looking now both at Joseph and the skinny man. His foursome--now threesome--were using pull carts. "We could take him into the clubhouse and wait there for the authorities."

Joseph too seemed to be at a bit of a loss. He seemed to hesitate, to not be his usual assured self.

"Is the man a Catholic?" he asked, and suddenly I saw his dilemma. Should Joseph, now defrocked, administer last rites? Or should he call in another priest? Once, at catechism, when Mary dropped a wafer Father Boyle had given her and went to pick it up—old Boyle had left the room--the nun insisted Mary not touch the body of Christ herself, nor could the nun touch it. Instead they must fetch the priest.

But perhaps the man isn't Catholic, I was thinking, and so his soul was not Joseph's responsibility. Joseph, no doubt, was hoping the same. And yet, instinctively perhaps, he knelt down by the man (while I marked Joseph's ball) and then asked once again: "Y'all, is the man Catholic?"

"Don't know," answered the skinny man. He still stood at some distance, frozen on the apron of that long, oval-shaped, undulated green (a very difficult green to putt--lots of "bends," as Dad would say). "I never asked him." He walked nearer to Joseph. "He was just my golfing buddy. I'll ask Mike. Hey, Mike, was O'Leary a Catholic? Any idea?"

Matt, huddled with Tiffany on the fringe of the green, let out a howl at that one. It was like we were near the hyena cage. "Is the Pope..." Matt began, but mid-sentence restrained himself.

However I could see, for all the inherent humor in the situation, that Matt was sick at heart at what had happened to the man, as well as what had happened to the normal pleasures of reaching the 13th. He turned away, apparently unable to look on any longer. I watched his shoulders sag as he stuffed his putter back in the bag. Tiffany handed him another Tecate, in the red and orange can.

Joseph concluded that the dead O'Leary was quite probably a member of the Church. Without asking anyone's approval (Did O'Leary belong more to his playing partners than to the Church?), Joseph uncovered the dead man's head and in a soft voice performed last rites--gave the man a proper if late and not altogether official send off. "In nomine Patrais, et Filii, et Spiritus Santi," etc. The murmured Latin, much of which I no longer understood, but which Joseph's religious order still employed, evidently was also some solace to O'Leary's playing partners. They no longer looked like stone.

"Why don't one of you fellows ride in with Tiffany and get some help," Joseph said. "We'll direct golfers around the hole."

The design of the course made it easy to go from the 12th green to the 14th tee. We would see to it that no one played the 13th and that play, otherwise, continued uninterrupted. Though no doubt some of the golfers would surely feel uneasy about playing just seventeen holes.

"Must Tiffany go?" Matt said.

But Joseph wasn't listening. He was leading. I caught of glimpse of what he must have been like prior to his return to us.

In the meantime Matt was able to procure another beer as well as a consolatory hug from Tiffany before she left, but he remained upset.

"Come back after this is all over," he called to her as she pulled away. For her part, Tiffany seemed happy to be leaving the vigil part to us.

Dad arrived at the green.

"Couldn't find my shot. I think I'll just ride along the rest of the round. I'm out of balls."

"I've got some," I said.

Then, he noticed the dead man, whose upper body and head were again hidden beneath the yellow slicker.

"Who's this?" Dad said.

We waited for the cops to come. It took a half hour. We answered the requisite questions and then closed out on thirteen (Joseph insisted on tapping in for his birdie despite our having conceded him the putt). By the time we teed off on fourteen the russet and purple flush of Phoenix twilight, clouds overhead like glowing pipes, filled the sky. We played the rest of our round in near dark. But we finished respectably, Joseph especially strong in the closing holes.

Matt, it's true, did not do so well. He'd had time for a couple of extra beers at the 13th, and he seemed flustered by Tiffany's failure to return after rendering escort service. His normally smooth take away became jerky and fast; on one follow-through he nearly toppled over. Indeed, Matt's overall recovery from alcoholism was dealt a setback that day. He avoided the golf course for the rest of Easter week, superstitious of what could befall him there.

"If it hadn't been the 13th," I heard him say, as he sat on the back porch, drinking. The tv was on. In the twilight, part of the garden behind the house was reflected in the backroom windows. The porch seemed to me right then, as it had at other times, to be situated more on Pima lands than in Scottsdale. I often got a sense that Matt was living on the reservation and only visiting us now and then.

I had a rough night myself following upon O'Leary's death, waking at one point from a dream in which the pin on the 13th green was a candle atop a birthday cake, and then a fuse to a bomb. In short, I began to imagine the worst again, for Matt and the rest of our family. I began to see Matthew's case as hopeless. I began to think it was time–high time, I suppose–for us all to go our separate ways. Though why I considered this such a terrible fate I don't know. After all, at a certain point it was only natural.

Mary, for her part, continued to throw cold water on Joseph's golf therapy theories.

"Can you imagine, a priest," she said to me the next day in the kitchen–she rarely spoke directly to or of Joseph–"or rather ex-priest, who believes golf can save your life. Maybe an ex- priest."

"Just Matthew's life. He didn't say it was universal salvation. Nor even a <u>cure</u> for Matt. Should Matthew spend the rest of his life watching Nightline, Mary? You know, he even talked of getting a job as a golf course groundskeeper. He said he felt good when he was playing; it was like walking in nature, he said, but competitive. He also likes talking to the animals."

"He likes the beer girl."

"Well, yes, that's true. But he was doing rather well until that damn death-- O'Leary's--put a crimp in things. Not that golf is everything. But it was a start. People are capable of changing, I think."

"There's always one in every family who can't cope," Mary said, echoing Mom's judgement of Matt. "Matt is our one. You know that as well as I do, Peter. He's <u>too</u> sensitive. It's a flaw."

"No, I don't know that Matt is our 'one.' If it comes to that, everyone in this family is our 'one,'" I said--also thinking, suddenly, that splitting up the family didn't sound so terrible after all. Sometimes all I wanted to do was clear out, head for the open territory, like Holden Caulfield. No, Huck Finn.

"We have to protect him," Mary said.

"Enable him, you mean. Didn't AA teach you anything?" I said. Mary, like Matt—and Joseph?--had done an AA stint. I wanted to use it against her. I was angry now. Livid. I suddenly saw the Mary-Matt alliance as an unholy one, as a big sister-little brother arrangement which unmanned Matt.

Mary looked at me. The AA thing had taken her back a little. But she was stubborn, a "dry drunk."

"What AA taught me is that the first thing is giving up drinking. And the second thing is giving up drinking. And the third is giving up drinking."

Well, this took me back a little. I mean, I saw her point. Matthew was a bit stuck in the pleasure stage and needed to enter the success stage (incorporating pleasure). He needed a substitute for drinking. A replacement. A new passion of some sort. Golf was part of the therapy, but it wasn't the be-all.

But unlike Mary, I felt any sort of attempt was better than complete acquiescence. Taking some sort of action was better than doing nothing. Acedia was the great crippler. Joseph, for example, felt better when helping Matt straighten out. Joseph needed a project of some sort, something in addition to gardening; he had a fair amount of Dad's go-getterness—something Matt and I, and perhaps Mary as well, could have used a little more of.

"I'll get Matt back on the course," Joseph said, at breakfast the same day, Mary having already vanished to her room. I could see a change had come over Joseph. "Maybe it was no accident that we were there at the snow bird's death, if he was a snow bird. It made me realize that, sooner or later, I'll have to go back to the Church. It's the only life I know."

But at this, this pronouncement, one that had nothing to do with Matt, I was stunned. I couldn't believe what Joseph was saying. For one thing, I assumed his defrocking was permanent. But I now realized that perhaps it was only, as he had said, a "suspension." Maybe he could go back. Maybe he would. Maybe his return to the ancestral home was only a layover, a way station. Maybe his essential life was elsewhere. Maybe mine was too, now that I was twenty-eight! I mean, I had almost come to just such a conclusion, hadn't I? (Although Robert Louis Stevenson didn't live home for good until he was twenty-nine.)

BOOK TWO
Mary

Chapter I

ONE COOL, MIDDLE of the month day in February I decided to follow Mary to her job. I felt it was pretty ridiculous not to know more about what she did for a living. There were other things I wanted to straighten out as well. West Phoenix was a rather amorphous working class area, which I usually avoided but now found myself in, tailing Mary. Apache clouds hung overhead and cast shadows across the city. Brown pueblo style apartments, that looked like free standing prisons, scarred the West Side landscape. Dry sagebrush dotted the surrounding hillsides.

At one point I feared I'd lost track of the car Mary was riding in--her chauffeur was a tall, black gentleman, with a goatee—but for once the construction work that never stopped in the city (anymore than workers ever stopped painting the Golden Gate Bridge) was beneficial, for it contributed to my being able to keep up with her. Both our vehicles, the bright yellow Cadillac Mary was riding in and the family Nimitz, were forced to wait at the corner of Indian School and Grand Avenue while behemoth-like caterpillars crossed the intersection. I dared not follow Mary too closely into her parking lot, but I did get there in time to see her give the guy driving a peck on the cheek. "Her boyfriend," was my first thought; he had given her a ride more than once. But he wasn't the only fellow who came for her, so I was forced to conclude he was one of her boyfriends, or perhaps just a friend. At any rate, he drove off, smiling.

I parked beneath the girders of the huge, red sign, which read: "The Great Tundra Bush Company. Open at noon. Closed at two a.m. $5 admission—FREE ADMISSION when you buy lunch or dinner." Below this, in neon, an open-mouthed grizzly bear was pictured, accompanied by the words: "We Grin and Bare It For You." Mary obviously worked the early shift.

There were only a few cars in the asphalt lot: two Plymouth Dusters, a Mustang Mach I, a Chevy truck, and a big old Buick Electra, complete with Landau top, three holes along the running board, and console bucket seats. On the back of the Buick a bumper sticker read: "My Child is an Honor Student at Sweetwater Elementary School." Slowly, a few more girls as well as a few more customers pulled in. One young woman, with long blond hair, arrived in a pickup along with what appeared to be her husband and child. She kissed both her old man and her little boy and then hopped out of the cab, hurrying into the club, a small white suitcase in hand.

It was then that a tremendous wave of melancholy and tenderness washed over me. To think that my sister—my only sister—worked as a stripper! Of course I had always assumed as much, but now it was more difficult to avoid confronting the question of why Mary had chosen such a path through life. Why this and not—for example—college?

I was able to convince myself that I might find the answer by going inside the establishment of her employ.

Once inside the door, I took the mimeographed lunch menu handed to me by the bouncer, a man befitting the title, and then I sat myself down, in a red felt booth toward the back. None of the girls had started dancing, though music, rock music clearly suitable for stripping, was blaring from several speakers. A huge brown stuffed grizzly stood in a glass case in one corner of the bar; heads of high-racked antelope, a bison, a moose, coyotes, and even a snub-nosed wild boar hung from the wood-paneled sideboards. All in all, I found the western baroque decor pleasing, cheerful.

The waitress, a dancer now a little past her prime, came to take my order, her belly and breasts shiny as apples in the rosy light. Long horizontal mirrors—Alaskan lakes, no doubt—reflected the swirling red and blue lights of the stage as well as, as I was soon to learn, the bodies of the girls on stage and "table side." ("Get yourself a dance up-close and personal," our DJ was fond of saying, I soon learned. Had I not been there for the expressed purpose of checking on Mary, I might have given it a try. All my life-drawing classes notwithstanding.)

At least one question remained: Did the girls—did Mary—dance topless or totally nude? At last a couple of the girls came out of the dressing room—Mary not among them—and sat smoking in a corner together, rather Toulouse-Lautrec fashion. My damaged eyesight perhaps contributed to the flat, poster-like quality of the scene. Both young women were blond. Little wisps of smoke rose from their cigarettes as in the 60's magazine advertisements of my childhood. The girls were so young I couldn't help but reflect back on Jenny--in a positive manner, that is. I reflected on how, coming over to see me afternoons, changed out of her Catholic School uniform into her washed-out blue jeans, and then slipping out of those, she sat so very gracefully, so very...animal-like, moving only very occasionally to push her long, shoe- black hair away from her breasts and her forehead. Although I'll admit, too, to now being slightly more uncomfortable about my memories of Jenny—I mean, she was quite young, as Joseph had so pointedly intimated.

The waitress came to take my order. She stood directly below a wagon wheel light fixture, which cast an attractive glow on her.

"Sir?"

"The round steak, and a Budweiser," I said.

She returned directly with the Bud and mentioned that the steak would be up soon. "Medium rare," I said, though perhaps it was already too late for that.

The waitress bent forward and poured the contents of the Bud Long Neck into a tall glass. I handed her a dollar.

They didn't seem to be in any hurry to get the show started, which anyway I was not too sure I wanted to see, being that it involved my sister and all, and seeing that she might not take kindly to my spying on her. "Why are you doing this, Peter?" I queried myself in words I thought I was likely to hear from Mary, should I get caught.

The Bush appeared to be waiting for a larger crowd. I counted eight guys, including myself. One man up front had come in right off the street. Head down, he was asleep and breathing heavily, as though hooked up to a respirator. Three young fellows, laughing and carrying on, sat up front in seats that ringed the stage and put them in position to see everything, which they were quite intent on doing.

DJ "Bob" cranked up some Heavy Metal–Z.Z. Top, I think it was--and we were on our way. "Welcome to the Great Tundra Bush Company," he said, "your home away from home. This is your party, guys, so undo that tie and have some fun, and be generous with these girls, who are working on tips and tips alone."

Instinctively, I once more took a dollar from my wallet.

The first dancer turned out to be the young woman I'd seen in the truck with the guy and the little boy. Her name was "Cheyenne." She was, I soon discovered, covered with tattoos, though from my seat toward the back I couldn't make out the individual designs. She had a large tattoo between her breasts, one on her left shoulder, and one high up on her rear-end. Cheyenne was a pretty good-looking woman, but even from my vantage point I could see that she was not a good dancer. Still, she'd mastered a trick which kept the men interested--rotating her breasts. She moved them in circles, counterclockwise and in opposite directions from each other, a feat I, for one, had never seen live. The silver tassels on her nipples flashed like fishing lures. Cheyenne danced only one song, and then, naked as a jaybird–yes, totally nude!–bent over and picked up her clothes, the dollars she'd collected held in her fist. She climbed down from the stage, ready for table side work. Almost immediately, she was hired, by the only fellow in there who wore a white shirt, and a tie. As "Bob" had suggested, he had unloosened the latter.

It was then that Mary came out from behind the curtain.

"All the way from Hollywood, California, for one song only–so treat her right, these girls are working for your tips and your tips alone–let's hear it for Angel."

I still held the dollar in my hand.

My sister, Mary, alias "Angel," came skipping on to the stage, with an elan and speed reminiscent of her cheerleading days. Her hair was pulled back ballerina-style. No one who'd ever seen her slothfulness at breakfast could easily imagine the energy and grace she now exhibited. Her outfit, however, was not unlike her usual skimpy morning attire.

Mary was well served by the ballet lessons our folks had paid for over the years. She was perhaps at the far edge of her career, like an aging basketball star who's lost a step, but she successfully managed all the moves, such as the splits (which she'd performed at Coronado High), the pole wrap, the backbend, etc. I watched Mary, now topless, bend backwards in front of one young guy and tongue a creased dollar bill from his fingertips into her mouth. Then, standing, shaking her rear-end, turning around, she brought her breasts right up close to his face, as he, "generous," slipped another single between those very breasts she held tightly together between her arms.

Fortunately, she still wore a g-string. Maybe she only danced topless, I was thinking, seeing that she was only supposed to be out there, or up there, for one song? But it was long song—by Van Morrison—a song I'd long been familiar with. I knew I had time to slip away before being forced to see more than I'd bargained for, so to speak.

And that's just what I did. I left ten dollars on the table and headed out the door. Blinding sunbeams from outdoors flooded the womblike interior of the Bush--I believed I'd escaped without Mary recognizing me; though, between the brightness of the scene and problems I had with my vision, I couldn't be sure. And if truth be told, just as the door was closing, I turned to look at Sis. She had nothing on but high heels, I'm afraid. In that momentary ray of light, she was indeed the "Angel" of her stage persona, her bush on fire (Mary a true blonde as it turned out).

I was relieved to once more be breathing the open air, to be in a sense myself again. And I wasn't sure I'd learned much that I didn't already know, about Mary and life, though seeing things first hand did make a difference.

And while I'm admitting things, I might as well admit I was intrigued: it crossed my mind to perhaps check out one or two more Grand Avenue dancing establishments before heading home. But at the same time I can hardly tell you what it feels like to see your own sister turn herself inside out and upside down for a bunch of no-count men. At any rate, I was saved from any further no-count adventures of my own by Mary herself: she stood at my car window gesturing at me.

"Mary, or is it Angel?" I thought it best to take the offensive.

"Mary, to you, buster. So would you like to explain yourself? How could you do this to me, Peter?"

"Buster," I said, but Mary wasn't laughing. A little bead of sweat graced her upper lip.

I didn't have a ready answer to her question, and besides I was rather non-plused to be having such a conversation at all with my sister, standing there as she was in the parking lot half- dressed.

"All the way from Hollywood, California?" I said, which once again failed to elicit an amused look from her.

"Eight o'clock. You meet me here at eight o'clock."

"Sounds workable," I said. After all, it had been a long time since I'd spent some quality time with my sister. It was almost as if, like Joseph, she'd not been home, in any real sense, for years. Or so it seemed to me sometimes.

I spent a few hours at the art museum, looking at sketches of Frank Lloyd Wright buildings, most of which were never built. Wright was one of my culture heroes. After a while I moved on to the Oriental collection, which reminded me that it was a book on Tantra that first gave Jenny the notion that she would like to pose for me.

The rules at the San Francisco YMCA governing visitors were strict, almost Draconian, so Jenny, a minor, could only visit me by climbing the crooked, girded steps of the fire escape and entering through my window. After a while she didn't even knock, but usually I'd hear her coming up the stairs. Sometimes I'd hear her say "good-afternoon" to the birds out on the landing. Why, I sometimes wondered, did she come to me at all? And why, I wondered also, though less often, did I let her? Perhaps, in part, it was the way she came, as though from the trees, on high, filled with the afternoon air, immaculate as our transgressions of the house rules.

The Mexico collection was my last tour. Rivera, Siquieros, and of course, Frida Kahlo--a very big cultural hero in my book, a wonderful painter of family life, and still life, and of herself, of everything that mattered most in life. All before a most beautiful ethereal background. I would come downtown more often, I told myself; I'd visit Frida on a regular basis, I said to myself, as I sat there on a wooden bench before one of her paintings.

When I returned for Mary I was a half an hour late. It was dark out, and raining. Really raining. A cold February rain. A Biblical rain. It doesn't rain in Phoenix but that it pours. The sewerless streets flood, the washes become rivers, trees and telephone lines come down-- inescapably reminding one of the Old Testament.

Mary was waiting for me under the eaves of the Bush entrance. Having just showered, her hair was wet, but wet or not the wind was blowing it wildly across her face. She'd put on jeans and a t-shirt.

Quickly she hopped into the car. "God," she said, a reference to the rain. "I'm half soaked. Where have you been?"

"Shall we wait it out?" We had a long trek ahead of us across town should the rain not let up.

"Let's get some coffee," Mary said, her anger towards me lessened somewhat so it seemed.

We drove down Grand to the Coffee Cafe, famous throughout the Valley for the huge cup which slowly turns on the roof of the restaurant. We had to hopscotch parking curbs in order to escape drenching our shoes on the way in. Mary was especially put out by the rain, fearing for her makeup: she knew many of the waitresses and regulars and didn't want to be embarrassed.

"Is the chocolate cream pie good, Mary?" I said, once we were seated, in an uncomfortable and worn booth.

"Order what you like, Peter."

Mary's tone made me reconsider my earlier analysis. Meanwhile the rain pelted the windows, like gravel spit from car wheels.

I wanted to work my way around to discussing Mary's job, since I had the feeling Mary, pissed off, wasn't going to bring it up on her own, though I also couldn't recall any recent occasion when my sister had allowed me to enter the sanctum sanctorum of her thoughts and life. Now, I at least knew why Mary may have been disinclined to tell me about her work.

Mary asked June, our waitress, for a refill on coffee. June was an attractive women, if, like her colleagues, a bit too West Side in appearance: her makeup was overdone and her hair too big.

"Well, what is it you hoped to learn by spying on me? Any questions I can answer for you, little brother?" Mary said.

"I'd like to know how that girl Cheyenne gets her breasts to spin like pinwheels, for starters?"

"Her arms. While you're ogling her tits, she's moving her arms. Next time watch the arms. The pecs."

"I doubt there will be a next time."

"You might be surprised. A lot of men get addicted, besotted. There's always another girl, a different girl, coming on stage. It's hard to get bored. At least until maybe you've seen the rotation. ...But that's all you want to ask?"

"Well, what gives in your case, Mary? I mean, how long you been...dancing?"

"Since high school. Since the day Mom and Dad said they couldn't afford to send me to Loyola Marymount—they sent Joseph to Notre Dame all right, didn't they?"

Mary blotted a few drops of rain from her forehead. Her green eye shadow ran, like the tailings of fireworks, along her temples and cheek bones.

"Don't say it," Mary continued. "I could have gone to ASU like you and Matthew, I know."

"Twelve years, twelve years...stripping?" I persisted.

"Yep, the Lost Years, I guess. Everyone in the family knows. I thought you did too."

"Dad knows?"

"Well, Dad is sort of oblivious. But yes, I think even Dad."

"Mom?"

"You're trying to tell me you didn't have a clue?"

"I thought maybe topless," I said, wondering why it took me so many years to investigate for myself. I suppose I'd always felt it didn't make any difference, topless or nude, though now, now that I'd seen Mary perform in the buff, I wasn't so sure about that.

"Topless gets boring," Mary was saying. "The money is better at the Bush."

"Joseph knows?"

"As far as I'm concerned, Joseph is not part of the family. I just hope he stays in New Orleans."

"What got you started anyway?" I said, leaving the Joseph reference alone. "Ballet?"

"Is this an interview? But yes, to support my dance. And then, after you do something for a while, and are making some bucks—in some ways I even like the job—it's not easy to walk away from it." Mary paused. "Joseph is partly responsible, if you really want to know."

Did I want to know? I wasn't sure.

"Joseph?" I said, tentatively.

"Joseph, your brother. Father Joseph of New Orleans. The ex-priest."

"I know *which* Joseph, Mary."

"Jesus, Mary, and Joseph!" Mary laughed. It was an old family joke--and it helped mollify Mary's displeasure with me.

"Explain," I said. "You're better off in the dark."

"I'm not."

"In this case you are. Anyway, it wasn't directly his fault. Since joining AA, I've learned to take responsibility for my actions."

"You belong to AA?"

"Didn't you know?"

"No," I said, wondering why I should be expected to. Why didn't people—my family especially—just tell me things, straight out. I knew Mary didn't drink. And I'd seen some AA literature around the house, but I'd assumed it belonged to Matthew. And since one "A" in "AA" stands for anonymous, I didn't feel it was my prerogative to ask about such things, even if a member of my own family was involved. I'd felt the same about Mary's dancing. I'd assumed she used her body to make money, but...well, how to explain the reticence that victimized our family? Though I was beginning to think I was perhaps the most victimized of all.

"I celebrated my fifth A.A. birthday last month."

And still dancing, I thought to myself.

"We'd better give Mom a call," I said, changing the subject, thinking I'd wait till later to talk about Joseph. "She'll worry when you're not home by nine. Especially with this rain."

"You call her, Peter."

"All right. But she'll wonder why you're with me."

"Tell her you're my brother."

"And that makes you my sister?"

As it turned out, we didn't make it home at all that night: the roads were flooded, the freeways crowded. Dark clouds banked the sky like headlands, promising more rain.

The Grand Avenue Motel 6 was but two blocks from the Coffee Cup. It was Mary's idea to stay over, further evidence that her anger had subsided.

"I have to be at work at noon. It might be fun to sleep somewhere else for a change—but just like when we were kids, eh, sharing a room. Though I'll miss watching Nightline with Matt. It's the best time of the day for him, I think. But one more night won't matter. When you call Mom, speak to Matt for me, will you?"

I'd never watched Nightline with Mary, nor done much of anything else with her. But I felt pretty sure this one time—though recently the times were mounting—wouldn't much bother Matt.

He answered the phone. It was a first, to my memory, for Matt to answer a call, even if it were for him. He insisted that people write him letters.

"What's happening?" I said, breezily. "Who's this?"

"Your bro. I'm over on the West Side with Mary. Is it raining there?"

"Cats and dogs. Pigs and chickens."

"We're going to come home in the morning. We got a motel. Tell Mom, will you?"

There was a pretty long pause then.

"Ten Our Fathers and three Hail Marys," Matt said at last, turning the phone booth I was standing in into a makeshift confessional, as he also abruptly hung up on me. Upset, I guess.

I walked back toward the room. The motel looked strangely beautiful in the pale neon light of the rain. Daddy-long-leg spiders floated upside down beneath the eaves of the building. Clouds had blocked out the stars; weeping willows threshed back and forth, the leafy branches blowing up like skirts.

Once we were inside, Mary spent fifteen minutes meditating, while I listened to the weather report. The storm was expected to continue through the night.

"I didn't know you did yoga?"

Mary showed me her lotus. The white bottoms of her feet were shiny with calluses. "Every night in my room after work," she said. "Gets me out of my body."

"To where?" I said, but Mary, chanting some mantra, didn't appear to hear me.

In the *Art of Tantra*, Jenny and I had read the chapters on 'mantra' and 'yantra' together. In those pictures she could see that the body was an eternal delight and some cultures were right up front about that. They worshipped the body: the world was made beautiful through desire. "Looks difficult," she'd said, laughing, surveying the painting of the sexual posture Cakra Asana, a rather tortuous position, which is supposed to affect the pattern of energies in the spinal column. But it was a lovely painting, a miniature, with a bright, India-red border. The woman in the picture looked a little like Jenny--perhaps it was this also that fueled her desire to pose. Jenny's skin was a attractive color, a lightish brown, like oak, or oak mixed with ash; her father was Filipino, her mother Caucasian.

Mary, at that moment in the motel, was also a study worth painting. I could see her reflection in the bathroom mirror, her face grown ghostly with cream.

"You know, they say Vaseline works just as well as that expensive stuff," I said.

"That doesn't take into account a belief in magic potions. The fountain of youth can't be bought too cheaply if one's to trust in its powers. Indeed one's whole soul is the cost."

Mary finally came to bed. All that was available that night was a single room, with one double bed.

"I want to ask you something, Sis?" I said.

"What now?"

"Well, two things."

"You're on thin ground already."

"Did you ever do anything at the Bush besides dance?"

"Curious George, aren't you? Well, if you must know, I was the janitor."

"You know what I mean."

"The impertinence. Okay, nosy. It was standard practice for the girls to meet guys away from the club. Guys were always making offers--offers it was difficult to refuse. You know, come outside with me for five minutes for two hundred dollars."

"Sounds like what some professional ballplayers make. Two hundred a pitch, one thousand a basket."

"Well, I refused. Except once. There was one guy who came in I liked. He was a businessman, in the 'bottled water industry,' he said, which made me laugh. 'Just a matter of time before bottled water becomes a staple,' he said, which I found hard to believe. Anyway, he was sweet. And fab looking. An Adonis."

"So?"

"I had an affair with him. He bought me presents, but I didn't take money."

"I thought you were a virgin."

"I am. Except for him."

"I think that violates the definition," I said, joking, but surprised that Mary had lied to me.

Yet the knowledge that Mary had, perhaps, slept with only this one guy allayed some of my worse imaginings with regard to Mary and Joseph, which I never for a second believed but was glad anyway to have confirmed as not true, unless of course Mary was still lying. Still, I felt relieved, like when water in your ear at last seeps out, unmuffling the world.

"All my life," Mary said, "I've been searching for one other human being before whom I can stand completely naked, so to speak, stripped of all pretense or defense, and trust that person not to hurt me, because that other person has stripped himself naked, too. I thought I'd found that person in my bottled water man, but I hadn't. He turned out to be not much different than the other men who came to the club."

After that statement I felt the wind go out of my sails in terms of further challenging Mary regarding her virginity claims.

Yet I gave it a try. "What happened in high school between you and Joseph?"

Mary hesitated. She crossed her legs again, yoga fashion, though no longer doing yoga. "Get the story from Joseph, if you must. His version should be amusing. As for myself, I am trying to forget it, all these years later. In fact, until that son-of-a-bitch came home, I'd pretty much put it behind me."

"If he is a son-of-a-bitch, what does that make me, or Mom?"

"You artists take everything personally. Or literally."

"I doubt he'll tell me, should he ever return," I continued.

"I'll let him know that he either tells you or I will. Just mention 'hash' to him."

"Hash?" I was picturing the hash Mom sometimes made for dinner when we were kids.

"Marijuana."

"Oh. Seems rather roundabout, me going to Joseph. I'm not going to write him a letter. I think at this point I deserve more than a hint."

"Okay, I'll tell you this much--it was his friends. A boy named Leslie. Leslie Feelers. They were all on drugs. Leslie was Joseph's best buddy. That's all I'm going to say. So leave it, me alone, Peter. I've had a rough day already, which you made rougher. I'm going to sleep."

"But..." I said, as Mary turned over on her side, away from me. I was alone with my thoughts.

I looked at Mary. Her soft form—she wore panties and a tee shirt—was not so different from the girl with whom I shared a room, who at fourteen, after Joseph's departure for Notre Dame, finally got a room of her own. (Though it was also soon after that our family, minus Joseph, left Indiana for Arizona and moved into a five-bedroom house, our present home on Cattle Track, and thus each of us acquired, including the absent Joseph, a room of one's own. How quickly the subsequent years had passed.)

Chapter 2

INCREDIBLY, BUT AS promised, Mary drifted speedily off to sleep. No doubt eight hours of dancing was wearing, and, despite her claims otherwise, somewhat dispiriting. However her nodding off that way left much unresolved, including here-to-fore virginity claims. So I was left to probe not her but my own imagination with regard to the subject.

I couldn't rightly be expected to sleep myself under such circumstances, could I? Out of desperation, I turned to the provided Gideons. Fortuitously, my eyes happened to fall on a passage which I considered highly relevant to the day's events. Jesus says–I've forgotten exactly where–"If spirit came into being because of the body, it is a wonder of wonders. Indeed, I am amazed at how this great wealth has made its home in this poverty." Of course I didn't altogether agree with Jesus on this point–how could I after my experiences with Jenny--but what Mary had told me, even the little she had told me, about the Leslie Feelers incident raised some doubts in my mind about bodily desires, I'll say that. Yet all the while I was thinking, also as a result of my remembrances of Jenny, that I might go down to the Coffee Cup and see if June, the waitress, was still there. I'd gotten the feeling earlier in the evening that she wouldn't mind if I stopped back by to talk to her--though I couldn't be sure I read her signals correctly. Still...

But naturally I decided it wouldn't be right to leave Mary there in the room alone. Indeed, how I could have even considered such a thing I don't know, except–not to excuse myself–the withdrawal from physical affection that I'd experienced since returning home was, at times, physically painful, for after all isn't that we need, affection. Mom had recently mentioned in passing that she too was suffering from a lack of "affection." Maybe it was all pretty simple, when one stopped to think about it. A simple lack of affection, including physical affection. It didn't take an Einstein to figure this out I suppose, but sometimes when you look at the excesses people are prone to—not *good* excesses, not William Blake's "the path of wisdom is excess" (one of my favorite painters, Blake)—but neurotic excesses, drinking, nymphomania, etc., it's all just a lack of being together maybe, a lack of affection maybe, including physical affection. But, unfortunately, there was nothing to be done about that, nothing acceptable, on that particular night.

So at last I turned out the lamp. A few minutes later the thunder and lightning began. Our room lit like the body of a firefly. Mary's body lit up as well, translucently and rather eerily, I felt. But through it all Mary didn't stir. She seemed quite peacefully asleep, as though drugged or something, even though her eyes, it's true, were, as in childhood, half way open, or, to put it differently, only half way closed. I thought again about how we'd shared a room as kids, and I felt at that moment in the motel a particular tenderness for Mary. I felt love for her, naturally. Although on the other hand I wasn't sure I'd ever got, or could ever get, quite enough affection from her in return. Though I was determined to see about that.

The rain was gone as quickly as it had come. A few patches of the motel parking lot, I noticed, were mirrored in water but by afternoon those too would be dry. I was waiting for Mary to give up the bathroom. Not until noon, check-out time, were we finally ready to head out.

I drove Mary back to the Bush.

"I'll have to wear the same getup as yesterday," she said. "The regulars will notice."

"Not when you take it off."

"More of the same," she laughed.

I kissed her on the cheek and sped off.

It was a thirty minute drive across town. Our house stood at the end of a cul de sac. Having driven all of the way across the city, through the West Side suburbs, the downtown neighborhoods, downtown itself, and then following a similar process heading east, having driven, as it were, through all the avenues and streets, through miles of trees, buildings, and cars—Scottsdale Cadillacs waltzing through the boulevards like old bandleaders—I arrived at our house with a new sense of it being situated at a far edge of modern civilization: beyond Pima Road lay seemingly unending stretches of Indian farmland. A kind of dream landscape of paleolithic dimensions—satellite dishes notwithstanding—beckoned the weary city traveler.

"Is Mary okay?" Mom asked.

She was sitting on the front patio—I was surprised to see her in the outdoors. But there she was, nicely dressed in shirt, pants, and vest, and sun hat, reading the morning "Republic," the roses a beautiful backdrop.

"Mary's fine. Back at work. Quite a storm, wasn't it?" I said.

"It freshened things."

The mountains, for example, were suddenly "right there." With the air clearer, the sunshine itself seemed especially bright. I stood under the porch overhang, the sun butting my head when I leaned forward--although when I leaned back the sun appeared to be but a nimbus, a spider's web.

"So are you satisfied?" Mom said, peering at me over the "Valley and State" section.

We exchanged glances. I understood her meaning. "Not completely."

"Why's that?"

"Well, I know that Mary dances, and where...and how! But still not really why, except for the money."

"Exercise, too," Mom said, though it sounded a bit catty to me. Mom and Mary were not that close. Of course there was love there, and even mutual respect, but a certain distance, too. A certain difference. Of course I had no idea what was behind it—well, Joseph, maybe. "Anyway, Peter," Mom continued, "Mary has a mind of her own, always has. I just hope that someday she'll find someone to look after her. Everybody needs that."

"Maybe we Wilsons are not made for wedlock."

"She needn't marry necessarily. It's okay to live someone. Marriage isn't all it's cracked up to be. Your father wanted me to learn typing and be a secretary, you know, but I was too good for that. I love your father. But answering to someone isn't easy sometimes. Mary has her own life, even if it's a bit of a bedraggled of one."

"It's the men who do the answering, no?" I said. "In marriage at least."

But Mom let that comment go unanswered. "I'm glad you two had a chance to talk," she said.

She then turned back to read, moving on to the Front Page, in which she quickly became absorbed. The back of the front section carried a story about Vietnamese refugees taken ashore in Hong Kong, the British Colony, after having spent twenty-nine days abroad a crowded freighter.

"It goes both ways," Mom said, looking up. "I sacrificed for your father's career."

Chapter 3

My opportunity to query Joseph arrived later the next day. Joseph had arisen with single-minded purpose: get Mom to face her collecting addiction.

"Let's get rid of some of the trash. Just some of the broken things," he said, pleading, between mouthfuls of scone. "I'm feeling claustrophobic. And you know Dad won't put up with this much longer, Mom."

"It's like living in a refugee camp," Mary said, standing at the stove. "Like we just got off the boat."

I was surprised to hear Mary support one of Joseph's causes. Perhaps she had something up her sleeve, something that would take her away from us. Joseph also appeared to be operating under some sort of time-line. I feared this would be our last Easter together, that the Easter Bunny would never again come to the Wilson house on Cattle Track.

"Instead of a hair appointment every Friday, like the other faculty wives, I found something more interesting to do," Mom said in response to Joseph and Mary. Adding: "And what about you, Peter, do you care to offer a criticism or two?"

Before I could answer, Mom had left the room, crying. Joseph poured himself some coffee and also walked out.

Mary said: "A real charmer, isn't he?"

"Well, the refugee comment didn't help."

So Mary, too, withdrew, leaving me there alone at the circular kitchen table to think about Mom and Dad.

Mom's insecurities–her childhood years fatherless and poverty-stricken, her mother's alcoholism, her fears that Dad would leave her for some younger woman, some Babette Catkins–were taking their toll on all of us. She collected stuff as a hedge against the future, as though she could sell off her items one by one during the coming lean years, her social security years. "I'm not going to be one of those little old ladies that survives on cat food," she'd said more than once. "You can't count on your children to take care of you." In the case of us Wilson siblings, this was perhaps doubly true. But Mom's hoarding was creating a greater sense of insecurity than security; she was pushing out the humans, us, her tribe, in favor of things. She now lacked even a concept of "trash." Over the years her idea of collectible things became more and more inclusive. Bric-a-brac, porcelain figurines, musical toys, brochures, plastic bags. No need to rehearse it further: Mom was of the Egyptian you-can-take-it-with-you school of thought. "My career," she would joke, moving a box of stuff from one room to the next. Occasionally I was allowed to drive a Nimitz-full of junk out to the Tri-City dump on the reservation (that the Indians ran a landfill for white people's trash was just short of surreal), but I could have motored out there weekly with an overflowing station wagon and not made a significant dent in the aggregate. Which is not to say there weren't treasures mixed in with the rest; Mom knew a great deal about antiques and had a fine eye for beauty. Whatever artistic talents we possessed probably derived mostly from her (although a love of nature and mathematical design came from Dad).

Joseph brought the collecting issue to a head. That evening, behind Mom's back, he organized a yard sale. Mom was scheduled to spend Saturday at a doll show in Prescott, so Joseph saw an opening, figuring she'd never suspect us of organizing a yard sale Easter weekend. On Good Friday we gathered out by the pool to discuss the matter.

At first Matthew had refused to have anything to do with the plan. "She'll never forgive us."

"It's for her own good, and the good of the family," Joseph argued.

"I don't like people who talk about doing the world some good." ("Will no one rid me of this turbulent priest?" he added, as an aside). But in the long run Matt relented. "Nothing of value," he insisted. "We sell nothing worth anything."

"We won't make much money that way," Dad said.

"Nothing Mom considers valuable," Matt said, discriminating. It got pretty abstract.

Mary didn't say anything, nor did I. We were both more inclined to let events control us. Or at least I was.

"Do I sense an intervention coming on?" Mom said, suddenly discovering our little gathering--Mary's willingness to discuss something with Joseph probably caused Mom to surmise that something was afoot. "I thought old women were just set out to die on the reservation when their time came."

Mom's appearance meant that the meeting was disbanded, which left only Mom, Joseph, and Dad by the pool, although Dad had gone in for a swim. Huey and Luey, their feathers like Indian headdresses, followed him back and forth as he did his lengths, the light beneath the diving board flooding the water like the beam of an oncoming train (reminding me, also, of my coming out to the pool one night and finding a little mouse swimming frantically across it, his tiny legs churning, his plight as hopeless as a man gone overboard in Lake Michigan).

No doubt Dad couldn't hear what Mom and Joseph were discussing, and I only heard their comments by accident, as I'd come outside to tell Joseph he was wanted on the phone.

"Anyway, you can't go on blaming yourself, Joseph," I heard Mom say, from my spot behind the oleanders. "It's time we put that particular incident behind us. It was sixteen years ago, for God's sake. You know your father doesn't have any animosity toward you. Mary will have to forget, too. Forgive and forget, it's the only way. Maybe you could have stopped it, but there's nothing to be gained by berating yourself endlessly."

"I don't."

"I can see better than you. I can see it in your face sometimes. The waxy, masklike look, the Flanagan look. After losing the business, Grandpa Flanagan was never the same, you know. He blamed himself. I think we inherited his melancholy."

"Instead of his money," Joseph joked.

Meanwhile I'd begun to feel uneasy about eavesdropping. It was one thing to pursue certain questions in the open and quite another to act stealthily. Even at the risk of missing my chance at the true story, I felt it was unseemly to stand in the shadows that way. Unseemly, and melodramatic.

But I emerged into the open too late: already I was privy to the thrust of the conversation and more quickly followed.

"I do blame myself, still," Joseph said. "I could have stopped it. I still see Mary at the mercy of those hoods, whom I thought were my friends. Especially Leslie Feelers. His betrayal hurt almost as much as seeing Mary there, imploring me to do something."

At that point Joseph apparently sensed my presence; he looked up to find me standing, indeed looming, overhead. He was perhaps unaware that I'd heard so much, though his face looked, just as Mom had indicated, masked by woe, by the Flanagan *petite mal* as it were.

"The phone's for you, Joseph," I said, trying to appear nonchalant.

"I wonder who it could be," Joseph responded, more to himself than to me. "I didn't think anyone knew I was here."

When I came back inside, I could make out enough of what Joseph was saying to recognize that he was speaking to someone in Louisiana. The longer he talked, the thicker his Southern accent became. Once he even used the word "sugar." "That's right, sugar," he said.

"Joseph fathered six children in New Orleans," Matt said, passing ghostlike through the room.

I didn't want to disturb Joseph so I went back upstairs. I noticed that one of Dolly's kittens had climbed inside of Mom's doll house. It was curled up among the little tables and chairs of the livingroom. Amazingly, nothing had been knocked over.

Something–the doll house maybe, the shade of Matt as he walked about the house, my "spying" activities–put me in mind of our favorite childhood board game, Clue. Slowly the clues added up and then you made your guess: Colonel Mustard killed Miss Scarlet in the billiard room with the candlestick, or, Mrs. Peacock killed Professor Plum in the conservatory with the wrench. Father Joseph chastised Sister Mary in the cenacle with the stole, etc!

When I came back downstairs Joseph was off the phone. He was sitting, partly slumped over, on the sofa, a stiff old green thing with Spanish carvings on the legs. All the life he'd shown while talking long distance now appeared drained out of him.

"I was looking at your high school annual a while back," I said to him, not altogether innocently.

"Where is it?"

I brought it in from the book depository.

"Dare I?" he said, peeking inside the cover. "It's been so long. Remember the good old days in Indiana, Petey?"

"Yeah. But how come you went to Crockett?" I said.

Suddenly Joseph's face grew cloudy, as though he had just emerged from under water. He gathered his breath. He sat up straight, looking at me in a curious manner, either puzzled or appalled by my insistence–which indeed make me wonder about it myself. Did I somehow feel jealous of this special even if terrible thing that had happened between Joseph and Mary?

"Of course you needn't answer," I said.

"Dad and I had an argument," Joseph began. "Or really several arguments. He didn't like that my hair was long. You know, his Navy background. His basic conservatism. Republicanism. It all blew up one day when I used a cassette tape that had Grandpa Wilson's voice on it."

"That was a problem?"

"Well, rather than write letters, Dad and Grandpa had started exchanging tapes through the mail. I needed a cassette for English class. Somewhere along the line that year my English teacher, Mrs. Guess, decided that she wanted to record her responses to our compositions on tape. We were to take it to the library and listen to her comments, in the privacy of a booth. We were the Advanced English Class. She seemed to see something experimental in this process."

"And?" I said. I was sitting across from Joseph in Dad's desk chair. The story he was telling was not the one I'd expected.

"I'd failed to bring in a blank tape to school," Joseph continued. "And Mrs. Guess was angry. She gave me an ultimatum–a 'tomorrow morning' ultimatum–or I would fail the course. I remembered seeing a cassette in Dad's dresser drawer. I often borrowed his socks, especially when I was late for school and didn't have time to sort through the mound of socks on the dryer. I was standing in Mom and Dad's dimly lit bedroom--they slept together then, as you know--and I was looking at the tape when Dad came in. 'I have to have it,' I said, even though Dad had just informed me that it was the last recording he had of Grandpa; in fact, the only one. 'She says I'll fail English if I don't bring one in today,' I said, and Dad, almost disbelieving I think, you know, exhausted, said: 'I don't think you should use it, Joseph,' which I took to be, of course, not a definite 'no.' I needed it. I was going to fail Advanced Junior English. I barely hesitated, I think.

I was in the habit of taking what I needed when I needed it. It wasn't until I went into the booth for the first time to hear my teacher's comments on my paper—and glowing comments they were—that I realized what I had done. Something that I have regretted ever since. Something that could never be made right again. Though, at times, even now, I find myself shifting part of the blame: Dad has been a good and generous father, but I wish he would have stood up to me that day. For once."

I nodded, acknowledging Joseph's story more than agreeing with his idea about blame. "So after that you went to Crockett?"

"Yes."

"And decided to become a priest as expiation for the sin of the tape?" I said, half joking. "No, though it played a part. At the military academy I found God. Or, to put it differently, I decided while I was at Crockett that I wanted to be a soldier for God. And join other soldiers for God, other priests, in making this world a better place for mankind. But that was a long time ago, Peter. Many moons."

Joseph rose from his spot on the sofa. It appeared that he didn't really want to say more about Crockett. He hadn't even looked at the yearbook. But I had one last question, the most important of questions. Underneath all the Gnostic layers of Joseph's psyche, lay some sort of ultimate truth, I was pretty sure.

"What did he or they do to Mary?" I said.

Understandably, Joseph was shaken by this inquiry. He sat back down on the davenport. His face seemed to darken, now, like the sun or moon just before an eclipse. "They—he— deflowered her."

"Leslie Feelers?"

"Mary told you?"

"Not much."

Joseph look at me, quizzically.

"If you want to hear the rest of the story," he said, following a rather awkward pause, "you'll have to come for a ride with me. I don't want to talk about this around the house. Mom knows, but I don't think Dad..."

"He doesn't. Not everything. Nor does Matt."

"I'll get my coat," Joseph said.

Of course I agreed to go with him, even though it was almost my bedtime and, most likely, I'd be short-shrifted of my usual eight hours sleep.

By the time we set off in the car, it had started to rain. I left the window down, letting the drops spatter my face. It must have been the rainiest spring on record. We headed north along Pima Road, just driving I assumed, though Joseph appeared to have a destination in mind.

"The others held her down," he said, as we drove past Taleisin, toward Verde River and the lake. "But Leslie Feelers did it."

"You didn't hold her down, too?"

"No, damnit."

Joseph seemed genuinely outraged that I would suggest such a thing and for a few moments just stared straight ahead, his eyes fixed on the road. We were in the McDowell foothills, the mountain silhouettes stretching horizontally around the valley like giant figures of sleeping cowboys or cavalryman.

"Well, what did you do?" I said, pressing for details.

"Nothing. That's the problem, you see, I didn't stop them. Though I wasn't quite sure what they were doing."

"How's that possible?"

"We were all high, tripping. On hash. Kif. And it was nighttime, down by the river. Leslie, Aaron, Ted, and I--Mary and Lisa."

"Your groupies."

"I'm not excusing myself; I'll never be able to do that. I'll go to my grave grieving over what happened to Mary—and our family—that day. Things were never the same again. I've never been able to forgive Leslie, either. Nor Aaron and Ted, my so-called blood brothers."

"Blood brothers?"

"Yes. We'd sworn allegiance. Kid stuff. But even though I am a priest, I can't absolve them." Joseph phrased it all with his usual formality. He ran his hand through his wavy hair. "Even now."

"Were they tripping?"

"Yes. We all were. The summer light was at last gone from the sky and it was dark out, except for a little moonlight and a few stars. The Wabash was hardly distinguishable from the woods and the muddy banks. But at the same time, once we dropped acid, everything was strangely distinct, tactile, the whole scene infused with black light. The water looked like it was on fire, to me; as though it had caught on fire, like the Cuyahoga. I've played the scene over in my mind a thousand times."

"Well, what happened next?" I said. Joseph looked to be in a near-trance.

"Leslie was the first in the water. He left his clothes on the bank and swam out. The river was still pretty chilly, but the night was humid, fetid, Leslie's body flashing like a firefly as he moved in and out of the moonlight. Then Aaron and Ted were in the water. 'Come on, girls,' they called. I could see Mary and Lisa were considering it. Mary liked Leslie, you know. She was infatuated with him. 'If you do, I will,' Lisa said. 'Not with my brother, here,' Mary said. I remember. But then Lisa sort of freaked. Maybe it was the drugs. She split. And it was like they took out their frustrations on Mary once Lisa had left; Lisa was a tease."

"What did Mary do?"

"She walked down to the shore. And then took off her t-shirt, though she had a bra underneath. The guys were whistling. It was all so slow, understand. Every second lasted hours. I think Mary felt almost like she had to go in after had Lisa fled. I watched Mary pull off her top, take off her bra, slip down her cutoffs, and then even her panties, which wasn't really necessary. The next thing I remember she was in the water, up to her neck."

"Did you go in?" I said, wondering why Mary had more or less stripped for the boys.

"No, I didn't."

"Why not?"

"I don't know. It was like the river was far, far away. Way across a football field or something. God forgive me, Peter. It was like I was in another dimension. The Twilight Zone."

Joseph was almost praying now, his face smokey, unnatural. "They did it in the water?"

"On the bank. In the mud. Mary was crying. Though at first she was laughing. I thought they were horsing around. They were chasing after her as she tried to put her clothes back on—it made me uncomfortable, but it didn't seem too serious. Then Leslie was on top of her. I don't know what Mary was thinking, but I heard her say, 'Get off, Leslie.' And then, 'Joseph, Joseph.' She was crying."

"But how could they do it to your sister? With you standing right there?"

"I don't know. But look what I did–or didn't do. People do terrible things. It sounds cliched, but it's true, isn't it. Leslie was naked on top of Mary, and I couldn't move. I mean, finally I did run to her, but it was too late. He'd already...I think it wasn't until I was standing there that Leslie and the others really understood what they'd just done. I could see the fear in Leslie's eyes. I pushed him down–I was a lot bigger. I slugged him in the face. But when I went over to see to Mary, he scrambled off with Aaron and Ted. Ted left his shirt. It was evidence, should it have come to criminal charges. But it didn't. I don't know how Leslie explained his swollen cheek to his parents."

Before I could say more–and, after hearing Joseph describe the assault, I wasn't sure I could bring myself to say anything–Joseph pulled the car to a stop in a gravel lot, some hundred yards or so from the Verde River. It might have been the Wabash. Except right in front of us, shining in the dark, stood a big aluminum-sided warehouse. On top of the warehouse was strung a sign, in red, white, and blue bulbs. "BINGO," it said. "BINGO."

"B.I.N.G.O., and Bingo was his name," I murmured to myself, absurdly.

Chapter 4

I'D SEEN THE sign from the road while traveling past there over the years, but I'd never gone in. On the Fort McDowell reservation casino-style gambling was legal. The cars in the parking lot, wet from the rain, glimmered in the moonlight and neon.

"It's been two years since I bet on anything," Joseph said. Apparently he was determined to say little or nothing more about the rape.

"Were you defrocked for gambling?"

"That was one thing, but not the worst."

The rain had stopped, and the night air was soft and fragrant with the smell of eucalyptus—reminding me of California, and thus of Jenny.

"I told you, Peter," continued Joseph—killing the engine, his face meanwhile underlit by the glow from the dashboard—"I've done everything. I became a priest to get away from temptations, but it just drove things underground in my case. I suppose you don't know that I once had a drinking problem? It only got worse when I became a priest. I used to carry a breviary flask in my prayer book. But finally I joined AA and quit drinking altogether."

"You were in AA?" I said, flabbergasted.

"Well, I don't go to meetings anymore. But I used to."

Joseph started out of the car, but I had one more question, at the very least. "How did you keep knowledge of the rape from Dad?"

"He knew something happened, and I finally confessed to Mom, and to Father Michael at Central Catholic, but I've never told anyone else the story ever--including Dad. But I feel better for having confessed to you, Peter. I do, somehow."

"Why weren't those kids prosecuted?"

"The publicity. It was a small town, and a different era. Mary would have had a tough time living there, as would have the rest of us. Besides, we were taking drugs and that was bound to come out. The fact that we were into drugs would have probably been the big news. 'Reefer Madness.' Anyway, Mary didn't want the story public."

And so there it all was, at last, out in the open: already I sensed how I too would now replay this new-to-me chapter from our Indiana days over and over. Perhaps I should say almost all out in the open: I still didn't know what Joseph had done after Leslie and the others had fled.

But already Joseph was out of the car and walking up ahead of me. I noticed again how really tall he was, how quickly his long strides moved off. But he stopped outside the bingo building, His blue windbreaker shone brightly, neonlike itself, as he stood waiting--waiting for me to finish my interrogation, I guess.

"Did you go home with Mary?"

"I wrapped my shirt around her. She was cold. And almost in shock, I think. And still high, I suppose. She wouldn't look at me. In fact, I can't remember Mary ever looking at me straight on since that day. She won't meet my gaze even yet. 'After great pain, a formal feeling comes.'"

"What?"

"Emily Dickinson—my favorite poet."

"Matthew's is Wallace Stevens, I think. So you got Mary home?"

"Yes, and into bed."

"What did Mom do?"

"She took care of Mary. She also forgave me, though she thought it best I go away. Crockett, then Notre Dame, as you know. The one time I came home from college for a visit I didn't feel comfortable. Mary was angry at Mom for sticking by me, but what else could she do?"

"I can't believe Dad didn't pursue the story. He must have known something serious happened. Mary was his only daughter."

Joseph gave me a rather strange look, as though I was being obtuse. "At that time Dad was involved with Babette Catkins."

Once I'd accidentally come across Dad and Miss Catkins. Dad often worked on Saturday and I would occasionally stop by or bring him his sack lunch. Not that I liked the engineering building much. The place was a maze of cubicles, like in an industrial plant. In order to get to Dad's office I also had to pass through a large gray room full of metal machines, the machines inert, heavy, shiny objects— ominous objects, to me—but from there you could look into Dad's cubicle. And there I saw Dad, tie undone, Babette sitting on his desk. With the exception of the slide rule handing from Dad's belt, the scene was like a picture out of Playboy (50's style)-- incongruous with everything I'd known of my father up to then. I left without giving him his lunch. I'd always believed Dad didn't see me that day.

"She's one reason you all moved to Arizona," Joseph was saying. "Babette Catkins compromised his position as far responding to my—or rather Leslie's— sexual untowardness."

Joseph phrasing it that way, Freudian slipping and all, made me ponder to what extent Leslie stood in for Joseph.

"Yes, I suppose," I said, in reference to Dad, thinking perhaps I should tell Joseph about finding Dad that day at his office, but I decided otherwise: What purpose would be served by my tattle telling? Indeed, I was beginning to won- der what purpose whatsoever was served by my dredging our collective past the way I'd been doing, consciously and subconsciously, since my return from San Francisco, and especially, since Joseph's unexpected and now unnerving reinte- gration into the family chronicles. "Let's go in," I said.

The bingo hall was a colorful, tacky bazaar. The green and red gaming ta- bles, garish lighting, and oddly dressed Indian operators and dealers all contrib- uted to the fleshy, unseemly ambience. I was reminded of Mary's Bush. It was as if, walking across an arid landscape, we'd suddenly came across a watering hole, a fluorescent oasis, a place where desert dwellers could find relief from sun and wind. The place was packed, mostly with Anglos, and most of them elderly, which accounted for all the Cadillacs in the parking lot.

I think Joseph felt a sense of freedom there—a respite from family, from re- ligion, even from country--though of course this freedom was tempered by the fact that he appeared to be addicted to gambling. I didn't know if he had ever attended Gam-Anon meetings, nor just how serious his problem was, but I could see by the light in his eyes that he was itching to get at the tables. Perhaps gambling, like confession, offered something more like relief than freedom. At any rate, Joseph stood before a blackjack table, waiting, eyes circling in their sockets, like those around him, for the silver ball to land on a number. He was about as happy as I'd seen him since his return.

However his, or our, sense of liberty, that feeling that we were released from the usual societal restraints, was brought to an abrupt end, for Mary, our very own sister, was standing at one of the bingo tables, in a strapless, eel green dress, next to a short, slightly rotund man. This man was of Arab descent, I surmised. Apparently, Joseph had yet to notice Mary, nor she us; but when Joseph did espy her, he wanted to leave–immediately. He thought we might be able to escape unnoticed. Perhaps he thought Mary would assume that we had followed her there–this worried me as well–or perhaps he didn't want Mary to know that he, himself, frequented such places, but at any rate, he was anxious to depart, even more impatient than he'd been to get there. His countenance clouded again, his physiognomy tensed, his voice grew anxious.

"Quick, Peter, please, let's go."

But should we? I mean, why shouldn't we speak to Mary? Even though Joseph had told me the story of the rape, were things really any different now? Wouldn't it be worse if she saw us sneaking away? It was ridiculous not to speak to your own sister. A sister you deeply loved, to boot. It was rude.

Mary spotted us as she was walking over to get a refill on her drink--her soda. There was no alcohol allowed on the reservation, in any case.

"Come meet my friend," she said, to me, including Joseph only by inference, though a few moments later she would introduce him first. As we made our way past around the tables and through the rows of slots I briefly caught sight of something new--a small blue tattoo on Mary's left breast. I couldn't make out the design however; rather just the color--marine blue-- and the emblematic shape. "This is my brother Joseph and my brother Peter, Ihab. This is Ihab Abelnaby," Mary said.

An Arab, I concluded definitively (Mom's blood lines preoccupation buried deep in my own psyche).

"Oh, I've heard so much about you," I said, which considering the recent publicity about him and the Bush Company was perhaps not the best choice of wording. "From Mary," I added.

"All good things, I hope."

"Indubitably."

He laughed. We all laughed.

"Both from Phoenix, are you?" He had a broad, bright smile, like a Miss America contestant.

"Joseph's from New Orleans," Mary said. "Oh, a beautiful city."

"Yes, it surely is," Joseph said.

And the conversation got more stilted—for one thing we were not free to ask Mary what she was doing there and why she was with Mr. Abelnaby. He was her employer, yes, but something more than that as well it appeared.

"We thought we'd play some blackjack, some winning blackjack," Joseph said, successfully extricating us from at least the immediate situation. "Will you excuse us?"

But just before drifting back toward the bingo tables, Mary whispered a shocking, and damning, piece of information in my ear. Perhaps she suspected that I had talked to Joseph about the long-concealed sexual assault, or maybe she had some premonition that the time was ripe, or overripe, for clearing the air. Whatever her reasoning, I wasn't at all prepared for her revelation.

"Joseph was in love with Leslie Feelers," she said.

I found this statement startling, to say the least. I tried to look directly into Mary's eyes, to stare her down, to make sure she would stick by her incredible claim. She didn't flinch. Nor say anything more. She walked off, blithely, leaving me to ponder, without benefit of her explication, the word "Love" (which I pictured in compact Caledonia script, a Linotype face that borders on Scotch Modern). The word flashed before my mind like a talisman. "Love," she said. Did Joseph love Leslie Feelers like a brother, is that what she meant? Or more? Did Mary, that night along the river, indeed stand in for Joseph!

Joseph was on a streak and wanted to play out his luck. While he placed his wagers (an activity of little interest to me), I occasionally looked over at Mary, watching her with Ihab but also hoping she would come over and, out of Joseph's earshot of course, tell me what she'd meant in reference to him and Leslie. However, Mary didn't deign to meet my gaze. In fact, she appeared to be quite taken with Ihab. She'd looped her arm in his—his other free to pull the one- arm bandits.

But later when she did at last look over I approached her. Ihab, like Joseph, was now at the tables. "Want to go outside for a minute?" I said, and Mary nodded.

We stood beneath an overhang, looking out on the landscape. The "Bingo" lights flashed against the widely scattered trees. Mary lit a cigarette.

"Love?" I said. Mary stared at me blankly. "You said Joseph loved Leslie Feelers."

"Yes. Did you finally get his version?"

"He didn't mention love. But he did say you 'liked' Leslie."

"That's rich."

"Did you?"

"Joseph thought I did."

"Did Leslie?"

"How would I know?

"Did you strip for him–him in particular?"

Mary dropped her cigarette. "What are you saying?"

I didn't answer immediately; I looked down, the cancer stick glowing at my feet. I felt that perhaps I'd overstepped my bounds. We were family but that wasn't license for anything, I suppose. Still, I continued.

"Joseph implied that you led them on."

"I was fourteen," Mary said.

I could see she didn't want to say much more.

"Were you aware of his gambling?" I said, gesturing with my head to the bingo hall.

"We played strip poker as kids," Mary dead panned. She wasn't beyond a sense of humor about the whole thing, the whole family thing.

Her linking sex and gambling reminded me of something I'd once read: if you give a rat a beer, he'll want a cup of coffee, and then want a beer, and then coffee, etc.–one addiction feeds another. Addictions overlap like branches of a sycamore.

"I shouldn't ignore my date," Mary said. As she started to walk off, I held her arm. She shook loose. Mary wouldn't talk more; we went back inside, me still thinking, among other things, of Ihab being her "date."

By the time Joseph and I called it a night, Mary had long since left with Ihab. On the drive home, Joseph said (he'd won big): "What was it that Mary whispered to you back there?"

I hesitated, again. Did I want to go into it further right then? What would further discourse yield?

It was past midnight; I was tired. Tomorrow was another day, I was thinking. And not just another day–Good Friday, a time for mourning. For forgiveness. For starting over. For Easter celebrations (I was approaching the full flower of my manhood: Who could say what lay ahead?)

"Nothing important," I said, sure that Joseph knew otherwise.

"Nothing?"

"You really want to know?"

"Yes."

"She said you were in love with Leslie Feelers."

And so there it was, it was out in the open, too--out of the closet, I was thinking–though I still didn't really know what to make of what Mary had told me. Was Joseph gay?

Perhaps Joseph would even deny he was in love with Leslie Feelers. Maybe even three times before the cock crowed.

"I loved him," he said, his voice flat now, metallic. "I was taken with him for a time, in adolescence."

"Taken with him," what sort of euphemistic gibberish was this? Should I-- could I--ask Joseph about his sexual orientation? No way. I had my limits.

"You liked Leslie enough to sacrifice your own sister?" I said.

"I didn't think he'd go that far. It broke my heart when he did. I thought we were friends, for life. After that, I never spoke to him. I don't know what became of him. It's like he only exists in dream time or something. He's always a boy, slim, handsome, circumscribed by a certain place and time. I've never gone back to any Central Catholic reunion. And never will. He'll always be a boy to me."

I let things stand like that, at least for the time being, thinking, for one thing, about my own reunion, but more importantly, thinking about the apparent coincidence of meeting Mary at the bingo hall. Surely it was but a chance thing. I thought it couldn't be anything else. I'd always believed coincidences were looked for, that people are struck by the way certain events tally, but that they are in reality creating the connections themselves, in their minds. One word colors another, one event colors another, until–wouldn't that philosopher,

Wittginstein, assent?—one event seems to deja vu another. I was convinced I was right, the I Ching notwithstanding. But the strange and striking paralleling of persons and events made me wonder. I began to believe in the possibility of the marvelous. Even the Easter story could not be wholly discounted.

Joseph and I got out of the car and ran hurriedly through the downpour into the house. "When you all moved West," he said, "I felt my connection to the past weaken. I was ready to remake myself somewhere I'd never been before. Somewhere where I could be myself. The Church."

Chapter 5

RANDY'S GRILL WAS a wedge of light on the corner of the Camelback Shopping Plaza. Safeway, a travel agency, Bob's Liquor, and Randy's (the pharmacy went out of business). Randy was from Nebraska; the restaurant offered Midwest fare. You could get a good hamburger or meat loaf, and especially good corn bread. They had delicious blueberry pancakes. It was the only place in the valley where, according to Dad, you could order right off the menu a "Tin Roof"—ice cream with nuts on top. But the vegetables, from California, weren't up to Midwest standards. The coffee was terrible. Randy had tried, at one point, to offer a gourmet coffee but his regular customers wouldn't hear of it.

Randy was a born-again Christian. Right next to the toothpicks little two-inch books about God were free for the taking. *The King Is Coming* (and All Shall See Him)—books like that. One of my favorites had on its cover a guy shooting a gun below words that read, "How To Get On Target." The shooting metaphor was carried throughout. "According to the Bible everyone, including you, has 'missed the mark' of living a perfect, sinless life." Inside all of the booklets were printed a selection of verses from the Bible: "For the Lord himself shall descend from heaven with a shout, with the voice of the archangel..." etc. Most of the passages were from Acts, Romans, and Corinthians; all were revelatory and dramatic. In the flat, open spaces of the Midwest it is possible to imagine strange appearances; one feels as if almost anything could happen there.

"More Postom, Mr. Wilson," the waitress said, ready to pour.

When she bent over, Dad, Joseph, Matt, and I got an eyeful of her pasty but nice breasts. "No thank you, Louise," Dad said. "You know my sons, Peter and Matthew. This is Joseph, the oldest."

Joseph tipped his glengarry hat.

"Nice to see you," Louise said. "Nice to meet you," Joseph said.

We ordered dinner. Then, as soon as Louise left, Dad made a big announcement.

"I think I should tell you boys. I said to your Mom last night that I want to sell our house to the city officials. The freeway's coming through whether we like or not. The city will give us a good price for it, and I'm ready to move. I want a fresh start. I think it's about the last chance your mother and I have. I want to pull into a new driveway. I've told her I want to move up north, to Prescott. Too blasted hot here anyway. I'm tired of these Russian winters we have each summer. They have a symphony orchestra in Prescott. And a doll club for your mother..."

"You don't need to justify it, Dad," Joseph interrupted. "I think it's best that you do move."

I looked at Joseph. I couldn't believe what he was saying; I felt betrayed. Didn't he want to save the house, our home, from the freeway? Didn't he want to maintain the family homestead? Of course he could, perhaps, return to New Orleans, but what about the rest of us?

"What does Mom say?" Joseph asked.

"Oh, you know your mother. She's negative about everything at first. Unless she makes things difficult she feels taken advantage of. Programmed. But I really think she's ready. It would best for all of us, I think. We're all a bit stuck in neutral right now."

"Well, I'm planning to get married," Matt suddenly said.

I looked at him just as I had looked at Joseph. Were they all putting me on, I wondered? "To Lacey?" I said.

"Yes."

"I thought you'd backed off from that scenario?"

"You've forgotten, Pierre, we're descended from the mercurial Marquis of Montrose. Besides, a writer needs a muse, doesn't he. We're running short of muses these latter-day saints days."

"Fuses, maybe," I rejoindered. "Ruses," said Joseph.

"Well, Matt, that's exciting news," Dad said (inadvertently continuing the rhyming), "as long as you know what you're doing."

He reached over and vigorously shook Matt's hand.

"When are you moving, Dad?" Joseph said. Obviously he didn't put so much stock in the marriage announcement, even though, as I've indicated, Matt had cut down on his drinking some and was more clearheaded. He even looked more like marriagable material.

"As soon as we can find a house in Prescott." Mom and Dad in Prescott, I couldn't believe it.

But I should have. Or at least parts of it. Work had begun on the freeway. They'd started by constructing overpasses—a huge, beige-colored bridge had risen near our backyard, partially blocking our view of the Superstitions. As yet, one could take solace in the fact that the overpasses led nowhere, in two directions; but someday they would—to more freeway. And Dad, maybe Mom, Joseph, and Matt, should he indeed be considering marriage, were apparently already planning their escape. That left me and Mary.

"I hope all of you, including you and Lacey, Matt, will come and visit your poor sister and me sometimes," I joked.

Suddenly, I had this vision—Mary and I living alone together in the big split level. She upstairs, me downstairs; she up above the world, me below. She dreaming of her bottled water man and me of Jenny. The two of us, sister and brother, sitting down at breakfast not speaking to each other. And then later, as if we'd regressed or gone back in time, sharing the same room, furnished with the two little wagon wheel single beds, the very same ones we'd had in Indiana.

And yet, it was also different from Indiana, or rather like Indiana but colored now by what I'd learned of the Leslie Feelers episode. Now all the innocence was gone out of my Hoosier childhood, tainted it was, the way the Babette Catkins incident also tainted it a bit. But that was different again. The Leslie Feelers thing was retrospective coloring. I mean, now I no longer knew which version of my youth was true and real, the original version or the retrospective one—I was descending Duchamp's staircase; or I was protopostmodern. In short, I wasn't too sure who the "I" in I was. I'd always assumed, wrongly perhaps, that we are a product of our environment. But which environment, which family? Such, at any event, were the drift of my thoughts.

I returned from Randy's filled with imaginings and anxieties--sitting alone in the backyard for a while, in order to get *away* from my family, seemed the best immediate solution, even if, as was ever the case, I was once more residing on Wilson land. Still, there was always the reassurance of the fields and mountains. If it weren't for the reservation, Scottsdale would have long ago built right up to the mountains, and then right on the mountains. No open spaces would remain—instead just houses and more houses, as if they were capable of reproducing themselves.

The storm of the previous night was hanging around, though was diminished. The back windows of the porch shone blue black, like oil. The setting sun underlit the dark clouds; the backyard palo verdes were shiny as wet suits. I could see my breath as I looked out over the fence at the reservation, car lights flashing across the black harvested fields and across my own upper body.

It was then, standing there near the pool, that I heard a whimper—a low, long cry, almost religious sounding actually, as one might expect to hear from a Tibetan mystic or some such personage. The sound came in intervals between the Pima Road traffic noise. At first it was a little hard to identify the source and direction of the cry, but then I realized it came from the other side of our block fence. I opened the gate and looked out, but, at first, saw nothing. But soon came another short, little cry—there in a ditch on the reservation side of the road, she lay. A dog. She'd been hit by a car, I was soon to discover. She lay on her side, in profile, her chest inflating and deflating like a bellows, her cry now sounding to me like squealing tires. Once the way was clear I jogged across to her—the asphalt shiny as wet hair, and slick. The sky had turned cobalt black, strangely luminescent.

I knelt down near the dog. She looked up but didn't move. I wasn't sure if I should try to move her, fearing that I might injure her further. In the end, we brought the dog home in the Nimitz, wrapping her up in a blanket, and lifting. Dad, Mom, Joseph, Matt and I. Fortunately, Maud, as we called her, was only slightly hurt. She was wet and shivering, but the vet, who came over an hour later, believed she'd suffered no internal injuries, which indeed turned out to be the case. Our cat-loving family was suddenly a dog-loving one as well. Maud was a year old, mostly Husky, part Brittany Springer (when she recovered she could leap straight up onto the hood of a car). She was burnished gold and white spotted. Her yellow eyes were bright, penetrating, warm; her tail curled up like a plume. She had big, soft paws. When muddied, they printed hieroglyphics on the kitchen floor.

When Mary came in later that evening, an hour later than her usual nine p.m. arrival, she was of course surprised to see we had acquired a dog. "Acquired" I say because Maud didn't have a tag; we had no obvious way of contacting her master.

"She probably belongs to a reservation family," Mary said, "I think you should try to find its owner."

We all agreed that was fair enough. The Pimas were a close-knit group and would likely know whose dog it was if it were one of theirs. On the other hand, we were chauvinistic enough to wonder if the Indians always took good care of their dogs—we had no hard evidence of this of course, but still, no one wanted to give Maud up and so we convinced ourselves it was best to keep her. And who were the Pimas anyway? Americans or a nation within a nation. Of course they were the original or native Americans. But how odd it was to enter their lands, how like entering a foreign country. We kept Maud. Nationalism is the parameter of love, I'm afraid.

"You know," Matt said—all of us but Joseph were gathered in the living room—"one of my friends' family, back when I was in the fifth grade, moved out to a house on the reservation because it was the only place they could afford. His father had lost his job, I think. They moved into ones of those shacks you used to see near Pima Road." Matt sipped his beer, his first of the evening. "Man, it was depressing to visit them out there. No grass or even desert landscaping in the yard."

"Just desert itself," I said.

"Exactly. Terrible," Matt said, and we laughed.

Following Matt's example, we were soon telling a round of stories, most of them humorous, about our dealings with our Pima neighbors, including a recounting of the time Dad got fined for riding a home-made motorbike out along the Salt River canal.

Once Mom and Dad, like Joseph earlier, had retired for the night, Mary joined in the story fest.

"At one of the first Alcoholics Anonymous meetings I went to the topic for discussion wound up being the loss of a pet. One older lady started talking about having lost her dog, Fluffy, after some fifteen years together. She was a woman in her fifties, white haired, with an old, smooth face, like a sawed off tree limb."

"That's good. That's very good," Matt interjected.

"She said she didn't want to go on living after losing Fluffy. She didn't want to live and took to drinking to excess. And thus she came into AA. 'If my dear Fluffy hadn't passed away I might never have come into the fellowship,' she said. She was weeping, a trace of her Jersey accent audible in the sound of her crying.

"Well, new to AA as I was, I was aghast. I also assumed the others in the circle were embarrassed for this woman; it wasn't unusual for someone to cry, but over losing a pet? I couldn't relate."

"Don't you remember how it felt to lose Cleveland when we were kids?" I said, remembering the only other dog we'd ever had.

"She's getting to that," Matt said. "'E in anticipo.'" Apparently Matt already knew the story.

"Well, dead pets weren't a regular 'Share,'" Mary continued. "Usually the topic was something like 'My Last Drunk' or 'Why One Is Not Enough.'"

"You can plainly see why I am not a member," Matt said, raising his beer in a kind of toast. Within the hour he would not be good company.

"'My Fluffy saved my life,' the woman said, gesturing upward—lacquered wooden beams ran along the high ceiling of that Presbyterian Church. The place looked more like a lodge than a sanctuary. 'I know she is in doggie heaven and that God realizes Fluffy rescued me.' Well, imagine my dismay when the fellow sitting next to me, a middle-aged Southerner, picked up right where the woman had left off. This man had also lost a dog. A swamp hound. A good hunting dog, he said. A pet he'd had since he was a boy and kept through two divorces. He'd brought the dog with him to Phoenix, only to lose him soon after arriving. He too started crying. The man himself looked like a hound."

"A booze hound," said Matt.

"Others in the fellowship were soon recalling their own experiences in losing a pet: a dog, a cat, a turtle, a goldfish. One woman spoke about her dead llama, Susan. She told the whole story. She told how she let Susan sleep in the house, but how, one night, the llama got into poisons under the sink."

At that juncture Mary paused, leaned back in the recliner, and borrowed a cigarette from Matthew. I liked the v-shaped feminine way she brought the fag to her lips, if for no other reason than its contrast to Matthew's (equally interesting) clawlike method.

"Talking alcohol 'to death' is part of the therapy, you know," Mary said. "But when it came time for me to speak, I was at a loss. I was forced to tell the story of how Mom and Dad got rid of Cleveland, even though he was Joseph's dog and I'd never felt the way Joseph had about him–I was younger for one thing–but there I was describing how Joseph felt, seeing things from his point of view, something I don't care to do usually. 'My parents gave away my dog without even telling me beforehand,' I said, a touch of outrage in my voice, nearly convincing myself, if only for a moment, that I'd felt as badly as he had. In actuality, as Mom tells it, I used to push the dog away with my hand when it came up to me."

Our Cleveland was a Schnauzer, solid black, with thick, matted fur. He was lively, a yipper, an energetic but not, to my mind, a fashionable dog–a dog bred, in Germany, to kill rats, grabbing the rat by the neck and shaking violently. Joseph would throw him a rolled up sock and watch him tear into it, his teeth flicking back and forth faster than a sprinkler head. Mom and Dad took him to a kennel just prior to the family's annual summer vacation to Florida, saying they'd pick up the dog upon their return, but they never did, never intended to.

"Well, my audience was all ears," continued Mary. "Newcomers are afforded special attention in AA, and anything related to family problems is of particular interest to some members. 'There were complaints from neighbors about our dog getting into their yard and ruining their garden and such,' I said to them–for fairness sake giving Mom and Dad's side of the story.

"But I told the group, 'I can't say I've ever quite pardoned my parents for doing this to me.' Of course I couldn't put my whole heart into what I was saying"--Mary took a drag on her cigarette--"but the group provided the emotion I lacked. They seemed genuinely moved by my story. 'We learn to forgive in AA,' said the older woman, Fluffy's former master."

"That's a good story," I said to Mary, encouraging her, in my own perhaps unsubtle way, to continue, with more AA stories or other ones–Mary's life outside of the house was of constant interest to me. But even as I had said "a good story," Mary and Matt were in the process of retreating to the porch, for it was time for Nightline. Maud followed after them, stiffly, but eagerly (the back room an area she soon made her home, producing there an odor acrid and rich, dog and dog food mixed in with the vapors of Matt's cigarettes). I had little choice myself but bed, though certainly Mary and Matt would have not prevented me from joining them. In fact, Mary had said, her green eyes looking at me kindly, "Come on, Petey, it's time for Ted Koppel," as though I was a part of the nightly ritual and always had been. But the truth was that, at some point in the past—I'm not quite sure when exactly—Matthew had replaced me in Mary's affections, as I had once replaced Joseph, I guess.

And the truth was, also, I was ready for bed, exhausted from golf death, dog injury, and family, though perhaps not exactly in that order, but the cumulative effect was the same irregardless. I was thinking about Dad's moving plans, about Matt's erstwhile marriage plans—I was thinking time was piling up on us, so to speak, and, having just read, at Joseph's urging, Franz Kafka's *The Castle*, I was not unaware of the difficulty, at times, of actually ever getting inside something. Yet I was determined to try and do something about that—just what Kafka appears to imply we shouldn't do.

Chapter 6

MARY WAS ON stage when the Bush was raided. It was her last dance as a stripper, ever. But she was resigned to it.

"Twelve years is long enough," she explained. We were at the lake together. "Some of the girls are disgusted I had the balls to dance as long as I have. Graceless, that's the way they thought of it—some sort of blind spot on my part, to their way of thinking. One girl, Wendy, even implied that I was a spy for the management. I don't look *that* old, do I, sweet Peter?"

"Of course you don't. You're just coming into full bloom. No doubt it was one of the younger ones who suggested you stop dancing?" I said, leaving the spy comment alone for the time being.

"Those young girls just want quick cash. Their biggest dream is a boob job, so they can make more money. 'I'm getting my boobs on Tuesday,' I overheard one say the other day. They don't dance very well. They don't really take care of the men. The ones with kids are more humane, and work harder, but some of these young ones are loyal only to the dollar."

"Young turks and turkettes," I said.

At that moment Mary was posing for me (her idea), her usual daily pattern of being picked up at eleven and dropped back off at nine forever relegated to the dust bin of her history, and the history of the Wilsons. My sister had no real plans to retire before the Bush raid, but once retirement was forced upon her (or almost, since she could have worked at a topless club), she decided it was time to move on.

"Were you a snitch?"

"I was strictly a stripper," Mary said, offended, glaring at me.

"Don't move. Stay still, won't you, please?"

"That's just what the men at the Bush would say when they wanted a good look. Though rarely, 'please.'"

"If you say things like that, I'll be too embarrassed to continue."

"You mean, 'please'?"

"You know what I mean."

Anything sexual is awkward within a family, I felt, family life being too intimate to begin with. Mary's skimpy bikini barely covered her. I could see the brown ring of her nipples plain and simple.

It looked bad for the Bush proprietors, who also owned the only other totally nude club in the Valley, as well as the original Great Tundra Bush Company in Anchorage. Allegations in the paper--front page allegations--said the Bush owners were part of a Middle Eastern crime family—yes, the Abelnabys—who used strip joints as a front for prostitution, drug dealing, and money laundering (for me, that last term always provoked amusing, colorful images).

"I was totally naked when the cops burst in," Mary said, moving once more, determined, I suspected, to complicate the process I was following even though she had first suggested I do her.

"Okay, let's take a break," I said, resignedly.

My painting was not going too well anyway. It was a picture of a woman taking off her clothes on a beach, but abstract, motion achieved through arabesque. A fallen saguaro completed the picture—I'd once witnessed a saguaro's death, its eight tons crashing through the brush like a dinosaur.

We rested on the sand: Mary sitting, with her knees up; me stretched out, my legs speckled with white paint.

"Hand me a beer," Mary said.

"A beer?"

"You brought them to drink, n'est pas?"

"For me to drink," I said. I'd taken to having a beer or two. And an occasional stogie.

"Five years is long enough to go without a brew, little brother."

"Nah, you don't need it, Mary."

"But I want it."

"You can't always get what you want," I sang. "But if you try sometime..."

"Now," she said.

I was a little disheartened by Sis's decision to drink again, but I handed her a can. A Dutch beer, "Peter's Brand," which I always bought.

"Tastes like death," Mary said, just sipping. "The thing about getting sober is that you get glimpses of your early self, your pre-drinking self. Your youth. Though to be reminded of that is not altogether pleasant either. But beer taste good, doesn't it. It's refreshing."

"Continue the raid story, you old lush," I said.

"Well, the cops wouldn't even let me get dressed. It was humiliating. They wouldn't let me move. 'Nobody move,' they said, just like in the movies. One officer was female. I appealed to her. 'No way, sister,' she said. 'Nobody's looking at you.'"

Since I'd visited Mary at the Bush, I could picture the scene: the smokey red and blue lights; the pool tables; the girls, guys, and cops frozen in place, reflected in the long mirrors, gangster-like.

"I already miss it," Mary said. "I think I even miss the lecherous men. They knew what they wanted at least. Most of them were simple as hell."

I wasn't sure I wanted to hear about that, but I did have it in mind to ask Mary a few other things.

"Truth or dare," I abruptly said to her, hoping to make a game of my probings.

Mary stood up and stretched and looked down at me, wondering, so it seemed, where my questions were headed. Her rear-end, I noticed, had left a clamshell imprint in the sand. "You first," she said.

"Me?" I'd sort of forgotten that truth or dare was a two-way street. And for perhaps the first time in my life, it occurred to me that Mary, and the rest of my family, were maybe as curious about my secret life—my time in San Francisco—as I was about their life away from home. I had spent so much time and energy trying to figure out the dynamics of our family, and to what extent the past impinged on the present, that I had not taken enough time to think about my own path in life and my family's perceptions of the path *I* was following. Perhaps I needed to step back, the way a Chinese ping-pong player steps back from table in order to see better and gain more reaction time, not that one could ever get enough reaction time in ping-pong.

"After a couple months I moved into the Sunset District, near Golden Gate Park," I said to Mary, but not so much to satisfy her as to reminisce. "Right at the fog line. The blanket of summer fog seemed to stop right at my flat. Sometimes my bay window in back was fogged in and my front window was clear and sunny. The backyard, which was very small, was often ten or fifteen degrees cooler than the front stoop. The City was like that: one spot cool, one warm; one foggy, one bright as Berkeley. You had to dress in layers."

"I don't think you understand the nature of 'Truth or Dare,'" Mary said, in response to this pleasant reminiscence. "Revealing the different temperatures between frontyard and backyard doesn't qualify."

"Well, I asked you first, as I recall."

Mary looked at me. "Hand me another beer," she said.

I gave her a cold one. I didn't like to see Mary drink, to ruin all that good sobriety, but I did think--God forgive me--Mary would be more loquacious if she were tipsy.

"Truth or dare," I said, again.

"You're so childish sometimes, Peter."

But I wouldn't be dissuaded. "Joseph," I said.

Mary walked to the shore and put her feet in the water. I followed her. We sat down, the surf running up to our feet and then receding. Alternately, our feet appeared to be ours and then, as the water submerged them once more, someone else's. The lake was freezing cold.

"What's the dare?" said Mary.

"You jump in the lake," I said. "Here goes, then..."

"And get your hair wet," I added.

Mary again sat down on the sand. She'd recently cut her hair pageboy short, but she still didn't want to get it, or her makeup, wet.

"What was with this blood brotherhood Joseph and Leslie had?"

"When we were kids in Indiana, Joseph was always organizing some club or another. A Zorro Club, a Tecumseh Club, a Rock and Roll Club. The other kids, the boys that is, went along with him. He was persuasive. And also big for his age. You know we had Happy Hollow just beyond pear tree ridge, and it was natural for us to play in the woods and, well, regress to some more primitive tribal state. A Lord of the Flies sort of thing, remember?"

"Yes."

"Well, I began to worry about Joseph when he told me about the Naked Club. The boys-- they were ten, twelve years old–would go into the woods and just take off their clothes. I asked Joseph: 'You just take off your clothes, that's all?' 'Yes,' he said, 'and we howl.' Sounded pretty stupid to me."

"I would think a club like that you would understand."

"The point is, dear Peter," Mary said, annoyed, "Joseph always needed some sort of club to belong to."

"Some sort of ritual," I said, thinking how wonderful it was to belong to a club, how much nicer than a "society" or "group"–although I could only remember one such affiliation from my Happy Hollow days, the Saint Francis of Assisi Nature Club Steve Lyman thought up but which only lasted a week.

"I suppose you're right," Mary said, "about ritual. Of course no girls were allowed, no matter the club. One time they got Liz Dockery to go with them and take off her clothes--they wanted to watch her pee–but she still wasn't allowed to join."

I was picturing Liz, who was a couple years older than me and a friend of Mary's, squatting for the boys in the woods, her bottom white as a bird egg against the damp brown leaves and the trees. (When Steve Lyman and I were ten, or thereabouts, we pinned Liz down and demanded she show us top or bottom, which was an easy decision for her–she was flat as an arrowhead, and as smooth, though stacked in later years). And I was also thinking about that time in another woods I'd inadvertently surprised Mary; we'd driven up to a ranch near Prescott to see a branding and I came across her with her pants down. In order to get out of the wind–the windmill for the well was spinning and clanking–I'd retreated to the van only to find Mary kneeling there behind the back bumper, holding on to it for support, peeing. "Sorry, Sis," I said, ducking quickly inside, though guessing even then that I was more embarrassed than she. "Next time I'll have to try the scrub oaks," Mary said, "but I'm afraid of snakes. You boys have it..."-- not needing to finish that sentence, as I recall.

At the lake, I was again enjoying being out in the wilds with Mary.

"I remember being confused about how many holes a girl had," I said, perhaps exceeding the boundaries of "Truth or Dare."

"Ten."

I counted. "Ten?"

"Well, eight then," Mary said, and laughed, and then continued without further prodding. "In high school, at Central Catholic, it was the Wambats. Another club Joseph formed."

Mary was really talking now—maybe about things she'd never revealed before, though I couldn't be sure about that. Maybe she had told those stories to Mom and Dad and Matt, and maybe to friends, and maybe, in bars back when she drank, to strangers. But she was talking now, to me, and I was happy. Thrilled.

"Here, have another beer," I said.

"Let's sit out of the sun."

We found a shady spot under a blue palo verde; I think there is no tree more beautiful. And the flies weren't so fond of the shade. Flies weren't a usual feature of Arizona, but we'd had an especially rainy spring. The lake was high, like a bathtub ready to slosh over the sides.

"What does Wambats mean?" I asked. "Aren't they an Australian animal?"

"It had something to do with Sir Walter Scott, I think. *Ivanhoe*."

I'd never read Scott so I didn't know the reference. There were some gaps in my education.

"For a while Joseph was enamored of Scott. Later it was D.H. Lawrence, but first it was Scott. Joseph liked all that medieval stuff."

"A real antiquary. Like Mom."

"He's Mom's child, isn't he?"

"Mostly," I said. "Who's kid are you?"

Mary reached in the cooler for another Peter's Brand.

"I was never Daddy's little girl, if that's what you mean. Dad loved me, and there was a time when I was something of a substitute for the lack of affection he got from Mom, but..."

Mary trailed off, unwilling to say exactly whose child she was. Perhaps it was more difficult to associate her personality with one parent or the other because she didn't look much like either one, nor like the rest of us. Besides her dissimilar coloring—if Matt, Joseph, and I were the land, Mary was the sea—Mary also had a somewhat more angular face, and a little bump at the bridge of her nose. She looked less Irish, or Celtic, than we boys.

The sun was directly above us at that point. It was getting hot. I watched the spidery shadows play across Mary's face and body. It would have been a fine time for an impressionistic painting of her.

"You're Dad's kid, aren't you?" she said.

"I guess. But I've always been the least loved, don't you think?"

"You feel that way?"

"Sometimes."

"You may be right, I'm afraid. You're so reserved, Peter, so...reticent, shy. Most shy people feel deep inside that no one is worthy of their company!"

"Let's go for a swim," I said, squirming a bit at being put under the microscope, and a bit put out at Mary equating reticence and arrogance.

When we were in the water—and it *was* cold—Mary decided it would be funny to take off her top. She waved the halter of her yellow bikini in the air above her head. Her hair she managed to keep dry.

"Very amusing," I said, "you can put it back on now. One would think it would bother *you* to sit here topless in front of God, nature, and the water patrol."

There weren't many boats on the choppy, mineral green lake, but the water patrol seemed ubiquitous.

Mary appeared to have a compulsive need to take her clothes off. Her breasts were whiter than the rest of her. They stood out above the water like a fishing dock.

"Tell me about the Wambats," I said.

Mary slipped back into her bikini top, putting it around her body and hooking it in front of her, and than swiveling it around and pulling it up over her breasts. That was nearly as impressive as when, returning from work, she would reach under her blouse and unsnap her bra, and then, slipping one strap from her right shoulder, would suddenly pull her bra, like a scarf, from out of her left sleeve.

Before continuing her story, she pushed her blond bangs away from her face.

"Joseph would let me come to the club meetings, but he wouldn't let me join. No girls. He also let my friend Lisa come too, but she couldn't join either."

"Yes, he mentioned Lisa. Why did you two want to even go?"

"Why must you know? Can't you see these are painful memories for me?"

"Just tell me why you wanted to hang out with the Wambats."

"I thought Joseph was some kind of god, I guess. I suppose I was half in love with him. He was good at everything, you know. A top student. Top gymnast. A good golfer. A fine musician. Just very talented. No one suspected how weird he was. This tribal thing. At first it was kind of thrilling. I think one of the attractions, for me, was that I couldn't join. You know they were men–all of seventeen, mind you–and Lisa and I were just young girls. Just fourteen. I liked that. But I paid a price."

"Which was exactly?" I said, pretending to know less than I did–a unique situation. But Mary wouldn't answer me. "So you don't know what Wambat meant?" I said, taking still another tact.

"In *Ivanhoe*, Wamba is a jester of some sort. You should of seen the clothes Joseph and his friends wore. They were harlequins. Pre-hippies, yippies. They even wore brass rings around their necks, dog collars; though Joseph kept his school self and his Wambat self separate. To school he wore button-downed shirts and preppy slacks. Always color coordinated, important in a college town. Most of the time he looked normal. Mom and Dad didn't even know about the club."

"Where did it meet?"

"Down by the river."

"The Wabash?"

"Yeah. On the banks of the Wabash," Mary said.

"You and Lisa were Wambat groupies."

"I guess."

"So?"

"That's it," Mary said.

"That's all? Come on."

"What *exactly* did Joseph tell you?"

"Not everything. Well, almost everything. But I want your perspective."

"I don't want to talk about it anymore, Peter. There's no law says your family has a right to know everything about you."

"But somebody's got to be the family annalist," I argued, thinking that after all I might be Mom's child more than I realized. "Somebody's got to know the history. Though apparently I'm the only one who <u>doesn't</u> know–or didn't. I want to get your version."

Mary's face was suddenly an oxymoron, both florid and ashen. Her eyes were fixed on the distant cliff sides and the cloudless sky.

"Why do you need my version?" she said, still not looking at me.

"To put the two together."

"Why do you need to do that?"

"Don't know," I said. "Curiosity. And I can't help feeling that in someway I'm implicated in all this. That the whole family is. It's part of our common history—our common destiny."

Also, submerged as we were in the water, I felt as though whatever she told me would be acceptable, even blessed. In the water we were different creatures, Wambats maybe, unbeholden to the taboos of shore Life. And I felt, too, that it would probably do Mary some good to tell me the rest, though I realized I was no father confessor, just her brother.

"Truth," I said, again, though it wasn't really my turn.

"Fuck you, Peter," Mary responded, and swam to shore.

I followed, toweling off when I got to where she was under the tree. Mary was crying, streaking her Covergirl makeup with lizard tracks. And I badly wanted to say something to Mary, to reassure her, or hold her, or something, but couldn't bring myself to do it. She was too angry. Even too angry to continue the game. Though she was beautiful when she was angry.

Not that that was the end of it for one day. Just like when we were kids, Mary and I had changed in the car out of our suits into dry clothes. She in the front seat and me in the back. And we remained that way the rest of the trip home, in different compartments, Mary driving, neither of us talking. But the truth revealed at the lake was a drop in the bucket that was the small ocean that was the Wilsons. For Mary boldly came to my room late that evening—near midnight it was. In fact, she shook me awake from my dream. But as it was kind of a nightmare, I didn't mind so much, though I pretended to. I'd been dreaming about Jenny again, modeling, about how, though thin—like a refugee girl—she had enough curves to make use of whatever light and shadow was available. Her shoulder blades were like cut off wings, shifting plates of the Continental Divide even. Her breasts were smallish, plums. But her...well, clitoris was prominent—a running brook, an envelope slot, a Horner harmonica. In my dream as once in real life she was stretched out on her side, turned toward me, along the inside shelf of the bay window. She was virtually hairless, like most Orientals. The sun was burning off the fog, creating a lovely light, a light I recalled and now dreamed, when—and this too happened in San Francisco—her father appeared.

"It's your turn," Mary said, even before I was fully awake. Mary, of course, was wearing her usual silk skivvies. She sat down in my reading chair. "Jenny," she said, not wasting time.

"What about her?" I responded, meanwhile struck by Mary's timing.

"Did you shack up with her?"

"No."

"Did you 'do her'?"

"Her picture?"

"You know what I mean. Fuck her."

"No, I didn't."

"The truth."

"She wanted to, I think. But it was a professional relationship in addition to being a friendship."

"So you're a virgin, Peter."

"I'm not proud of it. Or happy about it. It's like a tragic flaw." (I thought Mary would enjoy this reference. She'd been a thespian in high school.) "At least I meet the definition of what a virgin is fair and square."

"I've never heard of a guy saying 'no.' You're so odd."

"It's a family thing," I said. I sat up in bed. "It's funny, I was dreaming about Jenny when you walked in."

"I want to hear about your eye injury," Mary said. "The truth. No one in the family ever believed the story you fed us about being mugged."

"On the day in question, the day of my injury, Jenny's father had followed her to my apartment. When I was at the YMCA Jenny could just walk to my room, but once I moved to the Sunset she needed to take a bus. She didn't come so often, but when she did she stayed longer. We looked at books. We talked about the world. Some afternoons I served ginseng tea. Maybe only San Francisco could have produced a girl like Jenny: a girl both sophisticated and dreamy—a sixties throwback of sorts."

"Oh, free love," Mary said.

"It was more innocent than you might think, as I've already told you. Sometimes we'd go to the park. You could walk for hours in Golden Gate Park, making new discoveries all the time. A steep grade would lead up to a lake; a hillock would appear, covered with wild flowers, blue lupine and California poppy; a path would end at the ocean itself. Near the Presidio, down a steep, sandy path, Jenny and I once came across a nude beach. But we didn't take our clothes off for there was something a little too adult, and gay, about the scene.

"Mostly, we worked. I paid her seven dollars an hour. Not much, but I couldn't afford more and she was happy for the money. Seven dollars an hour wasn't bad for a high school girl. Beat working at McDonald's or some corner grocery store. Modeling is hard work, as you now know, but Jenny felt an artist needed a good model. She was good."

And as I said that Jenny appeared before my eyes again, naked, beautiful, a phantom. "Jenny's father nicked my eye with a knife," I continued, "it was an accident."

I could see Mary was surprised by my revelation.

"How could that be an accident?"

"Jenny came between her father and me, and so her father, pushing her away, scraped the knife--used for cutting cane in the Philippines, I think--across my cornea. I don't think at any point he intended to hurt me. He just wanted to scare me, which he'd already succeeded in doing."

"That's everything?"

"That's not enough? I believe in being forthright whenever possible, whenever you can be so without hurting someone else."

"I see," Mary said, smiling. "How did all this affect Jenny?"

"Well, she felt somewhat responsible for my injury, though it wasn't her fault. But I never saw her after that. Her father paid the medical bill. I think he's actually a decent guy."

"Sounds like it."

"Raised with perhaps different social mores," I said, laughing.

Mary laughed, too. But then grew serious, wrinkling her eyebrows, her eyes once again like little fishes, like tadpoles.

"I want you to do something for me, Peter," she said.

"What is it?" I said, reluctantly. I gazed at the clock. It was past midnight.

"I'm leaving," Mary said.

"What? First Dad and Mom, and then Matt and Joseph, and now you?"

"I've got to."

"Why?"

"For one thing, I've lost my job. For another, it would be too weird with Mom and Dad gone. And then there's Joseph."

"But he's leaving. Returning to the priesthood."

"So he says."

"Where will you go?"

"Alaska. Anchorage."

"Oh no, not the Abelnabys. I thought you were through with dancing."

"A non-dancing job. Supervisor. I've never had a non-dancing job, you know. But I'll still be around the life I know, just like Joseph and his church, I guess. Anyway, maybe something extraordinary will happen to me in Alaska. I'm ready for an adventure."

Remembering my Frisco days, I couldn't help thinking: you may be back before you know it.

"What about the freeway?" I said.

"The freeway will be moved out onto Indian land. Wait and see. Scottsdale will bribe them."

"So what is it you want me to do for you?"

"Two things. Don't tell Matt I've started drinking again for one."

"Well, Sis, such things aren't easy to hide."

Mary looked at me very seriously: "I'm leaving this weekend, he'll never know."

"This weekend, Jesus."

"And Mary and Joseph, ha."

"When exactly?" I said, staring at Mary's beautiful face, floating in the reading lamp light like an angel's.

"Sunday night, after Easter. I won't drink at home, not even during Easter dinner. Matt will remain in the dark. It's not like he's a bloodhound. I've fallen off the wagon, but I'm going to get back on and ride it out of town. Matt doesn't need to know I've fallen."

"At least you're getting out before the blast furnace starts up," I said, a reference to our summers.

"The second thing is this," Mary said, "I'd like you to do a nude of me."

A nude? I flashed on Mary squatting behind the van, and dancing at the Bush, and of the occasional glimpse of her coming out of the shower.

"Very funny," I said.

"You're a very good artist, Peter—not a genius like Matt..."

"And the least loved," I added.

"Oh, Gomez, don't be upset. There's room in the family for one and half geniuses."

"What?"

"From the Addams family. Morticia to Gomez. Don't you love how Matt can quote things out of nowhere?"

"Sometimes."

"Well, I'd love it if you'd paint me, Peter. I want something that sort of memorializes my youth. What I really want is a picture of me dancing. Not stripping, just dancing. I know it's sentimental, but, will you?"

"Is this a dare?" I said, my mind flashing back again, this time to sharing a room with Mary when we were young. Her sleeping with her eyes half open frightened me.

Mary said it wasn't a dare. "A double dare?" I said.

"No."

"I think I prefer truth. But I'll do it, I guess. Don't expect miracles though."

"We can arrange a time and place."

"One last thing," I said.

"What?" Mary said, sighing.

"Are you really a virgin, except for the bottled water man?" I said.

"No," she said.

Chapter 7

SATURDAY MORNING THE sky was silver gray, like the lining of an old coat. The mountains were different shades of charcoal. Mom and her girlfriends had left for Prescott early in the morning, Mom failing to even make fry bread before her departure. I was still thinking about the other night, at the casino. The tattoo on Mary's breast–also visible at the lake of course–as well as the sight of her hanging on a man's arm, again invoked memories of that trip I'd taken with her to a ranch back when Mary was sixteen and I was fourteen, that trip north when I had surprised her behind the van. For some reason, not altogether clear to me, I felt it was an important day. Mary's friend, Rick, who'd joined us, was already in college. I got the feeling Mary had invited me to go along so it wouldn't look so bad her going off with a college guy. I was sure, or almost sure, she had slept with him. Was he one more blemish on her virginity claims?

At any rate, at home that day, at our suburban ranch, all of us, Matthew included, rose at sunrise to set up tables on the front patio. Most of the olives had fallen off the tree, darkening the white, Spanish tile with purple juice. People squashed olives as they walked around handling our stuff. Of particular interest was our bathtub Madonna (which however wasn't for sale). Mom had stood an old bathtub on end--it must have weighed two hundred pounds–and then buried the nozzle end underneath the ground half way, leaving the curved, aboveground extremity for use as a little shrine to the Virgin Mary. It looked like something you might see hiking the Tyrol.

Matthew's baseball card collection was a featured item of the sale. When it came to this collection, Matthew was Mom's kid–he had three hundred cards. In keeping with his nothing of value stance, Matt was only selling off cards of negligible worth.

One exception was a rare, mint '56 Ernie Banks, "Mr. Cub," encased in glass; however it was priced at a prohibitive $2,000. Matt wouldn't take less.

"I need the money for wedding rings. Lacey wants a wedding band as a symbol of my capturing her."

Perhaps, as Matt alluded, it was the Shrovetide season, and Matt's engagement--if indeed he did marry—would be a catalyst to several Wilson marriages. Mary might find her soulmate in Alaska, perhaps even an Eskimo; I might propose to Jenny at her graduation ceremonies; and Joseph, well, was he still a priest, or might he too get hitched? Who knew? However, it was a melancholy thought, at least in some ways, to imagine the family disbanding into little nuclear units. It would absolutely signal the end of my childhood, for instance. And it would signal, unambiguously perhaps, that we Wilsons were pretty much like everyone else, at the mercy of pairing off, though of course we siblings wouldn't exist had Dad and Mom not done just that, become a couple.

Dad informed us that he was keen on selling off the Airstream travel trailer. It was the only other big ticket item. Hawking the trailer seemed a particular risky move to make in Mom's absence, but he was adamant.

Unfortunately (or so it seemed initially), Mom's guilt over being away from home on Good Friday or perhaps her general instincts brought her back early from Prescott. She arrived around eight a.m. Saturday, just as the sale was hitting full swing. And upon returning, she nearly leaped from The Nimitz at what she saw before her laid out on the front lawn—having returned just in time, as it were, to accost a young man who happened to be carrying a "prize" high chair out to his car (a chair all four of us siblings had once used).

"Where did you get that?" Mom yelled, to the startled young family man.

"What do you mean?" he said. "I just bought it. This is a yard sale."

"But that's my chair. My baby chair. You'd take someone's baby chair?"

"Well, lady, someone just sold it to me."

"For how much?"

"Five dollars."

"Five dollars?" Mom said, disbelieving. She looked the four of us, the four men of the family—especially at Joseph who sat before a cash box: "Five dollars?" Mom mouthed, silently.

"Yes, five dollars," the young fellow said. He seemed a decent enough guy.

"That's a steal. I'll give you seven for it. Seven dollars."

"I don't want seven," he responded. "I need it for my kid. I want the chair. For my baby."

"Eight, then. That's a fair offer. There's no robber blood among my ancestors. No Kittredge swindlers."

I was wondering if her father was exempted somehow.

"Is this an auction or a yard sale?" he said, incredulous, but also, I think, starting to enjoy himself a little. He was smiling now, like a kid himself.

"Nine," Mom countered.

"Ten?" he said.

"How old's your baby?"

"Three years old tomorrow, Mam."

"Boy or girl?"

"Boy. Tim Jr."

"I have three myself, you know. Three miserable boys who are pulling a fast one on me. They have all their Grandmother Wilson's shitty, sneaky traits." He laughed. At last Mom said, frustrated yet now involved: "Take the chair and enjoy it, Tim. But don't ever sell it. Keep it as something to remember your children by. Understand? Something to be passed down."

Mom had a soft spot for boys (something Mary resented). As for the young fellow, he was only too happy to agree to Mom's provisos as long as he was allowed to leave. He stuck our baby chair in the back of his minitruck and drove away, quickly, yet smiling still. No doubt he had a story to tell, and remember, and pass down.

And a bad scene had been averted. However it wasn't long before my mother was removing several articles from the sale as well as marking up the price of others—indeed many items had a low price crossed out and a higher price written in below it in large numerals, a system which provoked Matt to tell about a poem he'd once read called "Sad Hour."

"Unlike Happy Hour, during Sad Hour drinks were twelve-fifty a shot. Popcorn was five dollars. And the jukebox is unplugged. But funny thing, in the poem everyone likes Sad Hour better than Happy Hour."

After a while Mom did start to enjoy herself; once the first step had been taken (in her absence), she started to barter. Many offers, of course, were far too low, insultingly so. "It's a collectible," she'd say, or "I've got a home for that. I don't need to sell it."

Dad had the bad fortune of making a run for hamburgers at McDonald's just prior to arrival of a serious buyer for the trailer. Mom took over, walking the short, mustached prospect to the backyard where the Airstream, our Hindenburg, was parked, somewhat hidden behind two yellow palo verdes, which were in blossom. I followed Mom, leaving Joseph and Matt to man the till.

"How much you want for it?" the man asked.

"It's written on it," Mom said.

"It's not really worth much, you know."

"Says who, you?" He laughed at that. "You're from New York, aren't you?"

"Yeah. The Bronx," he said.

"Well, so am I. Queens. (Brooklyn really.) I know what you'll do. You'll turn around and sell it to some snowbird for twice the price. I've been around the block, you know."

"What do you care what I do with it?" he countered.

"I grew up among all kinds of people in New York--Jews, Italians, Poles...," Mom continued, but her fellow New Yorker, who was probably of Jewish or Italian origin, was no longer bartering. One got the feeling he never intended to make a serious offer. But he was, like Mom, enjoying the conversation.

Pretty soon the two of them were reminiscing about New York, about Battery Park, and Harlem during the good ol' days, and of course Coney Island.

When he left, Mom said to me: "New Yorkers are real people, Pete. You've got to watch them, but generally they are real, they like other people."

By the time we returned to the frontyard it was packed with people. And fortunately, another buyer, a winter visitor from Minnesota, a tall, Scandinavian type, arrived directly, accepted the asking price for the tailor and paid in cash. Eighteen hundred dollars. "It's a deal," Mom quickly said, though the figure was fair enough. The gleaming silver Airstream was aerodynamic as a missile and, for purposes of the sale, had been emptied out and cleaned. Mom seemed happy to have sold it, which meant extra money, but more importantly, provided proof to her claim that, if she set her mind to it, she could "sell anything." (She rarely set her mind to it).

And so, the yard sale was counted a success—but what was to be revealed as a result of the yard sale was truly amazing. However we were not to know this until late in the day, as the sale wound to a close—the sight of the picked over, scattered, and overpriced unbought items only mildly dampening our feeling of accomplishment. Indeed, as we sat there on the patio, I felt strangely peaceful. The sky was smooth. The sinuous arms of the olive tree rising high above the roof of the house cast pantomime shadows on the walls. And intermittently, a small lip- shaped leaf, the color of papaya, would drift down. Some of the leaves had perfect little semi- circles sheered off by cutter bees.

Dad, informed that the camping vehicle had sold, asked Mom how much she got for it.

"The asking price. You would have sold it for a soo," she said, opening her Happy Meal (she saved the toys). "I'm a super salesman."

"Exactly how much?"

"$1800.

"That's good."

"You forget my side of the family are business people. They'd be rich today if they hadn't squandered away their inheritance. Their vaudeville house was the most popular spot on the Boardwalk. Not to mention the value of the land itself. Always get 'a piece of the prop,' my grandfather would say. All the celebrities of the day performed at his place."

Mom told us again the story of how relatives on her mother's side had once owned one third of Coney Island.

"Everyone knew the Flanagans," she said. "Did you know Cousin Jeannie was married, for a short time, to Johnny Ray?"

We did know this. We knew most of the stories. Singer Johnny Ray, the "Prince of Wails," revolutionized popular music in the early 1950's by combining rhythm and blues, country and gospel, punctuating the mix with real-sounding sobs. Screaming teenage girls couldn't get enough of Johnny Ray, whom, for a time, I'd tried to emulate.

While we all sat in the front yard, Maud was furiously digging at the spot where the trailer had been. Dad, who'd walked around to the back just to enjoy the sight of the trailer's absence, was the first to see that buried at the barren spot where Maud scratched was a circular structure of some sort—a wall of mortar, perhaps early adobe. Returning to the front where Mom, Joseph, Matt and I sat distributing the proceeds (Mary having gone inside), Dad announced, his face uncharacteristically florid, even flushed, that he believed there was something interesting in the backyard, something we should all come to take a look at, that Matthew should get Mary and bring her as well, that—Dad seemed positively flustered—we perhaps had been, all those years, including many years before the threat of the freeway, sitting on something extraordinary. It appeared we had some sort of Lost Dutchman's mine right in our backyard; in effect, the Superstitions had come to us.

"Ruins," he said, though at first Dad's Midwest accent caused me to think he'd said "Runes."

"Songs?" I asked.

"No, he says we're ruined," offered Matt.

Dad didn't know if Matt was joking, but it was no time for that--"Ruins. Indian ruins, I think. Peter was probably right about that old piece of pottery being valuable."

Said Matt: "Makes me think of Freud's metaphor for the unconscious. The unconscious is like an ancient buried city..."

"Quite," Joseph said. "Fetch Mary will you, Matt?"

Mary was detained, but the rest of us, the five of us, could only gape open-mouthed at what we saw before us, even though, at that point, we couldn't see much. I suppose it was our imaginations that set us to gaping. The Minnesota man, returning with his hitch and pulling the Airstream from its moorings, uncovered—though he was never to know it—ruins. Yes, honest-to- goodness Indians ruins, it appeared. Hohokam ruins, we surmised. The heavy rains of that spring had apparently washed away some of the topsoil that covered up the remnants of a past and as yet unrecovered culture. Right there in our backyard!

Immediately I began to imagine the presence of extraordinary artifacts (al-though it also occurred to me that someone else—the city fathers? the Pimas?--might feel our new collectibles were not our property to dispose of as we wished, not that we would have done anything inappropriate or irreverent—after all, we were Wilsons). I was familiar with Pima and pre-Pima arts; many times I'd gone to the Heard Indian Museum, in central Phoenix. Indeed my own art, in its use of color and mosaics was, not surprisingly, influenced by Native American arts and crafts. I'd always especially liked the fired clay figurines of Hohokam origin.

Just as importantly, I realized that—even as I was still trying to comprehend the possible magnitude of our discovery, or recovery—we were most likely once again in the driver's seat. No way the freeway would be allowed to continue on its present course: bulldozers would be stopped in their tracks like dinosaurs during the ice age. The find also meant Dad and Mom were less likely to move to Prescott, didn't it? And that perhaps even Joseph, Mary, and Matthew would reconsider their plans. Could it possibly even lead to some sort of reconciliation between Joseph and Mary? Indeed I was imagining a sort of trading post or even an historical museum at the site, which would put to use the various talents and expertise available within the family.

Yes, I'm afraid my mind ran out before me like a Calvinist contemplating pre-destination.

I don't know what exactly the others were thinking, perhaps many of the same thoughts. Surely it also dawned on them as it did me that if it wasn't for the yard sale we might never have made the discovery. Furthermore, if it wasn't for Joseph's actions, his suggestion that we hold a sale, the unearthing of the ruins might have been accomplished, if that's the right word for it, by earth-moving equipment, parked as of now only a half mile down the road, slumbering monsters waiting for daybreak, for destruction. Oh, a timely find it was.

For the time being, though, we didn't do more than just look, Joseph insisting we not touch anything even remotely near the unearthed top of the structure, knowing that if we did so we might mess up our discovery. Furthermore, as Joseph pointed out, what we had found might be, to some, sacred ground.

"It would be a kind of sacrilege," he said, "to taint it."

"Making the country safe for democracy by destroying it," I said, knowing even as I said it, that my analogy was none too precise.

"Not bombing them back to the stone age!" Matt said, exhuming some of his Vietnam lore, and compounding my mistake, though none of us, as I've said, wanted to hear jokes right then.

"What's up?" Mary said, arriving late, in her swimsuit.

But soon Mary also saw the significance of what we had found. And so it was the six of us Wilsons stood there, in a little semi-circle around the barren spot, awash in feelings of elation and one might say, pride. We felt chosen, as no doubt any family would under such circumstances. Apparently, we were the legitimate (if colonial) heirs to an archeological discovery. We were sitting on buried treasure. Possibly we were rich, both chosen and rich, the eye of the needle notwithstanding. A yard sale to end all yard sales loomed.

We repasted at Randy's that night--Mom didn't join us but Mary did. We were, of course, all dumbfounded by the turn of events; not one of us commented, as was de riquer when eating there, about how bad the coffee was. We were virtually swimming in a new sea of possibilities.

But for the moment, at least, we had to go on with our lives; weeks, months, years, even the millennium might pass before resolution to the backyard find could be brought. We didn't, in fact, know what exactly it was that we had found. Perhaps we'd soon be living off the fat of the land—but no one had a job to quit—or perhaps we'd soon be rousted from our home at government orders.

After dinner, I attended a poetry reading with Matthew. I felt good that he'd invited me, though perhaps he couldn't have invited Mary without also inviting Joseph, or Joseph without Mary. We left directly in the van; Dad, Joseph, and Mary walked home from Randy's-across the wash and then just a couple blocks down Cattle Track.

Matt and I drove through downtown Scottsdale—the West's Most Western Town, a kind of movie version of a real town—to Tempe, where the university was situated. Changing Hands Bookstore, the site of the reading, was an alternative space, part cosmic karmic, part literary, part American pragmatist—lots of books on how to build your own adobe home. Ten years earlier, during my senior year in high school, they'd moved into this new building from the original hole-in-the-wall. I'd been there for the move, as books passed hand to hand from the original store to the new location. A human chain of people, several blocks long, had accomplished the transfer of stock. I'd always had good feelings about the place, and its co-op of owners; I'd spent many hours, while in college, on the bottom level of the store reading, paging through books, fingering art and photography volumes. Over the years I'd put together a good collection of art books, specializing in small art books, especially those made in France, such as a beautiful little volume on Picasso, with commentary in French par Christian Zervos, published in 1949 by Fernand Hazan, 35 et 37, rue de Seine.

But I'd never been to a poetry reading at Changing Hands. I'd taken in a couple in San Francisco–Allen Ginsberg at the Unitarian Church, with Gregory Corso in the back behind the pews yelling, drunkenly, "Oh, come on, Ginsberg, that isn't poetry, my friend," etc., and another at my school, the Art Institute, which wasn't far, actually, from my other school–the cable car turnaround house where my training as a gripman first started.

There was a healthy crowd at the bookstore. Matt knew almost everyone. Indeed Matt was a kind of celebrity there, highly respected it appeared, having also once studied poetry writing with the evening's featured reader, a half Puerto Rican, half British man of, Matt informed me, no little reputation, though Matt didn't seem to care for his poetry that much–"Still writing that deep image crap," Matt said, a reference which was bit over my head, although I liked the phrase "deep image." It conjured up scenes involving the unconscious (or subconscious or preconscious or aconscious), or peyote, or perhaps the Pre-Raphaelites.

The reading itself, which began an half an hour late, was not all that stimulating–certainly nothing to compare with Ginsberg or Corso. Teaching poets, or many of them, leave something to be desired I concluded–or this one did, though he had a pleasant demeanor. He was short, tightly built, his face highlighted by a thin little mustache and a goatee; he was also young; in his mid-thirties, I guessed. Quite young to already be a full professor at a major university.

"I wanted to do something very personal for tonight," he began. "Especially with so many friends and colleagues present, and former students." I looked at Matt.

"I've put together a new chapbook of poems I wrote while visiting the Lake District in England last summer. Growing up in Puerto Rico as I did the English side of my background, my mother's side, was always rather remote."

This unaccountably brought a laugh.

"But traveling through England last summer, with my mother–and I want to thank the university for a grant which made it possible–I could see the missing link in my personality, so to speak. So I sought for something—something personal—to represent the experience and came up with, after a fair amount of searching, the idea of producing this chapbook, which will only number fifty copies, forty of which are being made available tonight, to make it, the cover that is, from the clothes I wore during my English sojourn."

I looked at Matt.

Matt looked at me.

"He's gone inside," Matt said, with relish. "I mean, insane."

Still, afterwards, after the reading was over, everyone shook hands and sipped punch and enjoyed themselves.

But no, not enough for one day, was it. Late that very evening, upon our return from the reading, an anthropologist whom Dad had contacted at the university, an Emily Kunter, had come over to the house, and, remarkably, had been able to carbon-date the backyard find just like that. In fact, she'd just finished the scientific miracle as Matt and I were arriving.

"About the time of Christ, some five hundred years before the date generally associated with the beginning of the Hohokam," she said as she sat sipping sun tea on the back patio, her face reflected in the lights from the pool.

All of us Wilsons encircled Professor Kunter, except Mary, who remained at the far end of the pool (Huey and Luey, their feathers shiny as pearls, slept beneath her chaise lounge). I had my eye on Mary; I'd already begun to visualize the nude she was expecting me to do.

Professor Kunter was an University of Texas Ph.D. and an accomplished woman, especially for someone in her early thirties—more accomplished than any of us siblings, though my path as an artist, for instance, was necessarily crooked and strewn with obstacles, if not as bad as, say, Vincent Van Gogh's path. Professor Kunter was also attractive. She wore long, loose Southern belle pastel dresses and made an entrance like Loretta Young. Her blond hair was cut short, perhaps a little severely, but it had a nice curl to it. She had arrived just before sundown, I learned.

She was anxious to see the ruins right then, though she was also skeptical of our claims. But, according to what Mary told me later, Professor Kunter seemed to dilate, her eyes did, when she realized what it was we had there in our back-yard. Between 10,000 and 25,000 years ago, the first people arrived in Arizona. About 2,000 years ago, the Hohokam, or "Those Who Have Gone," began an irrigation and agricultural economy along the banks of Tonto Creek, the Gila, San Pedro, Aqua Fria, Verde, Santa Cruz, and Salt rivers. Maize, beans, squash, and cotton were cultivated by the Hohokam. They produced craftwork, developed far-reaching trade contacts, and built ball courts. Traces of ancient canals still exist today, as do their petroglyphs, their shrines, their burial grounds.

"A rich find, I believe, though we'll not know the extent of it until we excavate," Professor Kunter said, as Dad poured her more tea.

"We?" Mom said.

Of course nothing is so easy, and wonderful, as it first appears; Mom was already several steps ahead, playing chess with Ms. Kunter.

"Well, you'll want experts. This could be a significant discovery. Something important to both history and archeology, not to mention the university. This has the makings of large research grants."

Mom said, "What's in it for us?"

"I don't know exactly what you mean, Lillian?" Dr. Kunter said.

It got a bit catty then. Mom wouldn't stand for being patronized. Wilsons in general didn't suffer insults with impunity. I also think Mom, her Irish eyes glistening like an angry dog's, was somewhat jealous of this young Emily Kunter.

"I mean, Professor, this is our property."

Mom had counseled against bringing in someone from the university prior to securing an attorney. But Dad—not terribly streetwise—felt Emily could be trusted to keep our secret, until such time as we were prepared to publicly divulge it, and the rest of us, like dunderheads, didn't object to this approach. Furthermore, it would be necessary to go outside the family for an attorney. In the past Mom had held out the hope that one of us would become a lawyer—and one a doctor, one a professor, one a business person, etc. (we would have resembled the undergraduate population at Stanford)—but we were not only an attorneyless family, we soon found it was not so easy to locate any lawyer who specialized in such claims as we had found in our backyard. Although we also soon learned that there was, as of 1979, no law prohibiting our claiming the ruins as our own. Indeed the Antiquities Act of 1906 had designated American Indians as archeological resources.

Mary had apparently also had enough of Ms. Kunter, for, after disappearing for a few minutes, Mary, upon her return, held in her hands a painted wooden box, found, she claimed, just below ground level.

"Artifact #1," she said, smiling like an innocent girl.

The reactions of the gathered were multiform but of similar nature. Ms. Kunter and Dad gasped, near simultaneously. Joseph abruptly stood up, as if someone had put a tack under his seat. Mom put her hands out, imploring Mary to hand her the container. Meanwhile I, though somewhat taken aback by Mary's actions, could only shake my head at her effrontery—her precipitous decision to violate both Dr. Kunter and Joseph's orders about not disturbing the site.

But it was Matt, laughing, dieseling air through his teeth, who spoke first: "'Tis a heart, a heart, my lords, in which mine is entombed."

No one, Professor Kunter included, had the least notion of where Matt had dredged up that particular quote.

Fortunately, the box did not contain a heart—there was no solid evidence of Aztecs having been in Phoenix (White Mountain Apaches, yes). The box did not contain human remains of any sort. This particular wooden container was empty; but it was the first indication that we were indeed owners, or caretakers, of something special. It was no Dutch masters or Royal Crown box, no old Cuban cigars were inside: the delicate red and buff-colored vessel was evidently a medicine box—from the time, though of course not the place, of Christ! Or before!

"I can't believe you did that, young lady," Professor Kunter said to Mary—the wrong thing to say, especially the "young lady" part. "Promise me you won't do anything like that again." Apparently Emily already felt a strong propriety sense with regard to what we'd found, outflanking even Joseph's possible primogeniture claims.

"I can't believe you're sitting here with my family, LBJ," Mary said, tendering an obscure yet recognizable insult. But the sudden arrival of Abelnaby put an end to the exchange. Ihab greeted us all very cordially (though his chauffeur remained outside, in an idling black Cadillac). Mary introduced him all around, even to Ms. Kunter.

It wasn't until I stood to shake his hand that I noticed the powerful smell of liquor on his breath.

"Well, Ihab's man is waiting for us," Mary said.

I looked at her closely. I didn't recognize this woman who spoke such phrases as "Ihab's man." Was this my sister? Or some blond harlot? Some shapely ghost?

Mary left with Ihab almost immediately. It was strange to think she wasn't more curious about the ruins. It's not everyday you find something so extraordinary in your own backyard.

And it had all begun with a simple yard sale. A yard sale which had taken place that very morning, but now seemed to belong to a much earlier chapter in our life.

Chapter 8

KUNTER USED MARY'S actions as justification for informing both the university and the state offices of the "Wilson Find." The Salt River Indian Community also was apprised of the discovery. Astonishingly, late that very same evening, Easter Eve–it was near midnight–Professor Kunter's own husband, Tom Kunter, also an anthropology professor at the university (I learned later from Dad that she had gotten him the job in a blatant display of nepotism which was par for the course in backward Arizona) arrived at our house with a letter signed by himself and Emily indicating their concern, and speaking also for the university, that the site be kept in pristine condition until experts could be brought in.

I had accepted the missive from Mr. Kunter, although Matthew was also still up. Tom Kunter was almost as bad as Emily herself. Nothing was hidden or sugared over with this guy. No one could spend ten minutes in his "company" without becoming aware of his Prussian need to exert his will, to control the conversation, to shape it all to the narrow gages of his ideas. If you locked into the man's eyes you saw how little registered from the outside, how little he actually heard.

Soon the whole family, minus Mary, was aroused, both awake and indignant, as a result of the late night visit.

"I was wrong to trust Emily," Dad said. We were sitting in the living room.

"The university has been taken over by ethical midgets. By careerists."

"Texas Rangers," I said.

"Amen," Joseph said, although he refused to blame Dad for bringing Emily into the action.

Mom was somewhat less charitable, believing Joseph was going out of his way to protect Dad as a way of compensating for the past.

"Oh, Sherwood," Mom said, "you've lived your whole life in a cocoon."

"Yes, especially when I was nearly swept overboard during the war from the deck of a destroyer," Dad retorted.

"You were?" I said, taken by the image of Dad–Ensign Wilson–coming from below the deck, the sea raging round like a tiger. And thinking about had he been swept overboard he wouldn't be sitting there in the living room telling of it–nor would I be there, nor anything of us.

"Your father cares more about what strangers think than his own family," Mom said, not letting up. What she said was untrue, although Dad did have a Midwest, 50's sense of fitting in, of being respected by your community. When we were kids Mom sometimes called him "Casper Milquetoast" or "Mr. Don't Rock the Boat."

But all of that, and all since, I was thinking, belonged to our pre-ruins past.

So Kunters notwithstanding, we greeted Easter morning with a renewed sense of life's unpredictability. Of vista. The landscape itself was in bloom. The outer edges and tips of the patio aloe vera had turned pink, and from the heart of each plant grew a purple, tensile shoot-- two, sometimes three-feet high; little pouches of flowers, the color of creamsicles, dangled from the stem. Bees climbed into the split petals, leaving only their bronze, ringed tailends hanging out. When a breeze blew the bees would fly off, and the stems would move in the wind like a thousand tongues.

I'd slept little, thinking and dreaming of our backyard cache, of how history had been waiting there in that curious depression once covered by the trailer. As it turned out, an entire round house, used by later generations of Indians as a garbage dump, was buried on Wilson property. We were chosen indeed. Lottery winners, it seemed.

Matt was soon up, too. I watched him climb unsteadily, and slow moving as Abraham Lincoln, up from the lower part of our split level, as though, in keeping with our new find, he were returning from the dead and/or spirit world. With his cup of coffee and his pouch of imported Drum tobacco, and wearing an old black and gold Purdue sweatshirt, he sat out on the front patio and slowly awakened, his hands just poised enough to roll a cigarette. Matt embodied a central secret of both artist and Indian: the task was not so much to speed the world up but slow it down; not so much to make life more dramatic as ritualistic. For that, the artist required a healthy case of indolence, which Matt, to his credit, possessed in spades.

Upon his coming back in the house for more coffee (I'd been joined in the kitchen by Mom), he declared that we should try to make it to nine o'clock Mass at Saint Maria Goretti. "We have much to be thankful for this morning, wouldn't you say."

Joseph, coming downstairs an hour later, immediately agreed to Matt's suggestion. "I've missed the Church and maybe it has missed me. Or at least wondered where I've been," he said, the last part a joke.

Dad, despite having never felt comfortable in the Catholic Church, was also amenable, his nature being to go along with things—although he admitted that he held to hopes of getting us all out to the lake for Easter. Mom, who never went to Mass despite her, and our, Catholic upbringing, appeared anxious to attend as well. Only Mary was unaccounted for; presumably, she had spent the night with Ihab.

I was wondering if she would be home in time for Easter dinner. It crossed my mind that she might not return at all, that she might decide to depart early for Alaska, fearing the backyard discovery would postpone her leave-taking. Concerned, I intrepidly slipped up to Mary's room after breakfast, and looked in her closet and drawers for signs of her...elopement? But I found nothing missing, nothing askance, nothing that might indicate she was already gone. All her clothes were still there, right down to her panties.

"What about the Easter egg hunt? And our baskets?" I asked Mom as the family was starting to dress, though I too felt a keen desire for Mass or at least some sort of religious service. "When we come back, Peter," she said.

"Won't the eggs be rotten?"

"They're in the refrigerator."

I started to get dressed myself, but as I put on blue jeans and my bola tie I realized that the rarity of an empty house, or rather a house empty of everyone but me, provided the opportunity I sought regarding the old movie tins in the book room. My increasing knowledge of the Wambat incident had further piqued my interest. I wasn't sure, and indeed it appeared quite unlikely, that the old movies would provide any additional clues, but it was worth a shot, I thought. Mom had recently stacked up some more books, further complicating the search, and I also wasn't sure if I could find our projector, yet I felt it was time, perhaps even high time, to seize the moment. I was downstairs polishing my black loafers, and was nearly dressed, when I begged off, saying I'd go to High Mass later.

"The point is to go as a family, mon frere," Matt said.

"I know, but I won't be ready for Mass until this afternoon."

Such a cryptic and unintelligible response seemed to do the trick, and thus I was left to my wiles. I stood before the living room picture window and watched the four of them, Dad, Mom, Joseph, and Matthew drive off. Apparently someone had made a joke because I could see, as the car swung around the cul de sac, all four faces suddenly and simultaneously erupt in laughter.

Prior to heading for the book room I couldn't keep myself from going out back for a quick check of our Hohokam stash. Maud trotted along at my heels, happily. I took a broom with me, and, in a further violation of Kunter's orders, and Joseph's, and now the university's, I carefully brushed away a small section of desert soil around the coal-colored, seemingly charred remnants of the round house and within minutes I'd completely unearthed a beautiful, though slightly broken, five-inch-high clay deer, its little ears pricked upwards as though it were alive. I was so astounded by the ease in which I'd recovered the object that I returned to the house shaken and, one might say, befuddled, stupefied. One day your house is about to be demolished and the next day you feel connected to eternity--to those who are gone.

Yet there was other work to be done, too, and quickly. Some of the new additions to the book room seemed to have a particular focus: thrift. How to Prosper During the Coming Bad Years by Howard T. Ruff was one such thrift-oriented title. How to Profit from the Coming Devaluation by Harry Browne and Napoleon Hill's Think and Grow Rich two other volumes I came across. Mom's Depression childhood was having its revenge. I wondered if our new found luck would alter her thinking, or if, as I suspected, such attitudes were too ingrained, too deep- seated. She would no doubt find an element of insecurity and a source for disagreement in the ruin revelations—indeed, she could already point to Emily Kunter as a case in point. Anyway, I wasn't so naive as to expect a completely new life for us Wilsons. People hold on to the past so as to be able to recognize themselves in the present, and no amount of good fortune radically alters that pattern.

One item I unearthed—the 1952 Golden Jubilee issue of the Superstition, the Mesa High School Yearbook—actually brought tears to my eyes, tears of laughter that is. Rapidly glancing through it, looking at the pictures of students I'd never known, I felt I was in the midst of a surreal dream. Someday my own children (and Jenny's?) might inherit the book and wonder what it had to do with their own heritage, wonder if perhaps they were somehow related to someone in that annual, little knowing that their grandmother had seen in it only its collectibility. Perhaps it being the "Golden Jubilee" volume had, for Mom, increased its value.

Fortunately, the tins were just where I'd last seen them. The brown eight millimeter projector was harder to find, but at last I did locate it, hidden behind crutches of various sizes (no explaining this--I couldn't remember a single broken bone suffered by a family member). As long as I could retrieve the right reels, the so-called "First Five Years with Joseph," I was set to go. In fact, within fifteen minutes the films were rolling, my machine phobia and incompetence somehow magically overcome. I closed the family-room curtains and sat down to watch. However it took a while to find what I wanted: I tried three different reels--flashing back and forth in time from roughly 1957 to 1962 to 1955, Mary and Joseph in all these pictures--before succeeding. For at last I came across what I wanted: Joseph, a little (though large-little) toddler, waved, walked toward the camera, and generally sported around on the grass in front of our one- story Indiana house, his image, while somewhat obscured by the snowy quality of the old film, unmistakable, projected as it was at that moment on the south wall of the room. He was two years old, I guessed. Later in the same reel, he was perhaps three.

The bombshell fell in the following movie (no bomb shelter in sight either): Joseph was easily four, maybe five, and yet, Mary was nowhere to be seen! I couldn't make head nor tail of this, at first. Mary, who would have been two or three, was not in the picture, any pictures, as if she hadn't come along until later, as if she were—why had it taken me so long, why had the light bulb never clicked on?—as if she were, you guessed it, not our own, but adopted!

Mary? Adopted? Was it possible? Her blond hair and green eyes the genetic heritage of some strangers, and, conceivably, non-Irish, non-Scottish, non-Dutch, non-Welsh parents? Or had she merely been away for a couple years? Ill. Or, and this seemed even more unlikely, had she all along lied about her age, making herself two years older than she actually was? Which would, oddly, make her my age.

Well, I hurriedly threaded another reel, skipping ahead a couple of years--indeed so hurriedly that at one point the brown film strip began to pour from out of the projector, as though the machine were a living thing, as though it were expelling a double helix. But once I'd rethreaded, Joseph reappeared, clearly six or seven now, and Mary, as I now expected, made her entrance, obviously not more than three years younger than Joseph. In one sequence Joseph and Mary were having a foot race, running from a turnpike rest stop to the base of a huge water tower, and Mary was bigger and ran faster than any two-year old possibly could. She was clearly three or four. Zounds, it was incredible, earthshaking.

Adoption was the only explanation I could come up with, but I also found it nearly impossible to consider such an exegesis of the past. My sister, not a blood relative?

Even more unentertainable was the idea that next crossed my mind: Had Joseph, unconsciously, given in more readily the night of the assault because Mary wasn't blood--wasn't, in some sense, family?

I poured myself a drink, a gin and tonic. And, with Maud again at my heels, walked out once more to the backyard. To my left was what we were already beginning to call the "ruins" and out beyond the block fence to my right stood the Superstitions, shining brightly in the Easter morning sun. Suddenly it all seemed too much; I felt a strong sense of anxiety, a mix of anticipation and agon.

My thoughts again returned to the trip I'd taken north with Mary those many years earlier.

"I don't think I can watch," Mary had said. She was talking about the branding, the castration. Mary, Rick, and I were standing near the fire while the cowboys, and one cowgirl, worked the cattle. The mesquite and coals fire was housed in a tin drum. It was an overcast and windy day, flames whipping back and forth as though in torment.

Some of the land was the usual high desert, lupines and marigolds in bloom as I remember, but other parts were similar to Indiana farmland. Black and white Holsteins grazed in bright green meadows, a stand of sycamores ran alongside the creek, and farmhouses, in two- dimensional relief as in the work of amateur painters, stood out against the backdrop of valley and distant hills.

Several irons—some with a square brand, one heart-shaped, one curly-cued—were heating up in the glowing fire. The owner, a short, stocky guy, was waiting on the inspector, who was walking around with a clipboard making sure all the calves belonged to the owner and his fellow ranchers. If the inspector had some question about a calf, he'd insist that it be "mothered-up." The mother cows had been separated from their young ones, which resulted in a nearly continuous chorus of ugly-mouthed bellowing by the parents, a mooing that rippled across the little valley.

Rick was taking pictures. He considered himself an artist of sorts, a photographer; later he gave Mary prints. But I felt he was not worthy of her and too old (a position I revised as a result of my meeting Jenny).

A dog nipped at the heels of the calves. Then a young cowhand, son of one of the ranchers, let several calves down the chute. "It's got to be one at a time," the owner called out. So the first calf, a heifer, was sent down along the slatted fence, the young cowhand yelping behind as it ran. At the end of the chute waited the men and a rust orange contraption for branding. When the calf was housed in the contraption, they turned the whole thing on its side, the calf's feet kicking wildly, like those of a man just hung from a tree. The heifer was on its side, its head in a metal halter. Each calf, I learned, had its own inimitable moo of terror. This one had a low, melancholy, yet insistent moo, like an out of tune French horn. All the while the chalk white tongue lolled outside the mouth. It was all a bit unnerving. The clouds seemed to have grown closer to the hills. I felt for a moment as though we were all in some far away land, some far away time.

One cowboy grabbed the calf's feet so that the owner could slip a noose about them. Then another rancher, a tall, slim, wizened fellow, grasped a branding iron, the one with the heart on it, and applied it to the heifer's lower flank.

The skin sizzled. He touched the iron to the calf three times just to make sure the mark was deep enough. This was followed up by lacquering the branded spot with a black disinfectant. The smell was horrible, a mix of lacquer and burnt skin.

The owner, Rick's friend, did most of the ear trimming. All with just a sharp little pocket knife. They needed to tag some of the heifers, so they cut off a part of the ear. Fluffy little brown and white ear corners piled up on the ground. The bulls were dehorned; a glistening red but short-lived stream of blood issued from the two clipped spots on their heads. Then the calves were given a steroid shot. The castration of the males was also quickly done. Just a swipe of the knife and their little balls were gone. The dim-witted bulls suffering one further reduction. The owner piled the bloody balls in a pail.

Mary had watched it all and, despite her earlier protest, she had watched with evident interest.

"Amazing how fast they seem to forget what happened to them," she said, once we three were back in the van. Mary and Rick were drinking rum and coke. "They scamper off like it was nothing."

"No brain, no pain," Rick interjected. He was sitting next to Mary. I sat facing them. "Amazing how fast one can lose one's manhood," I said.

"Aren't you glad we don't sleep in the same room anymore?" Mary said, a very uncalled for and strange thing for her to say, and reveal, I felt. I hadn't slept in the same room with her for ten years.

However Rick and Mary laughed, and continued to drink.

"Wish we had something to eat," she said.

"Want some Rocky Mountain oysters?" He smiled. I noticed he had bad teeth.

"Cows ruin the land, foul the streams, and drive away the wildlife," I said. I'd learned this in my science class.

"I couldn't find anything to shoot last time I came up here. Maybe you're right," Rick responded, missing my point. I wanted to slug him. I was jealous, I suppose. I was glad when the day was over. Mary, as it turned out, nearly married that dude.

Back once again in the house I replayed the film. Then the doorbell sounded. I left the projector running, and, peeking out a window, saw, to my astonishment, a policeman standing on the front porch, a clipboard in his hand. My first thought was

Matthew, that he had done something wrong, or at least that the police were following up on some report related to Matthew. Then I thought of the ruins. The find in the backyard was not yet a regular part of my consciousness, but once I did think of the ruins it seemed likely to me that the officer was summoned as a result of some action on the Kunters' part. Momentarily I thought about not even opening the door, but I quickly figured that would be a mistake, being that it was a cop and all.

"Mr. Wilson?" he said.

"Yes."

"Are you Mary Wilson's husband?"

"Her brother."

"Is her husband home?"

"She's not married. What is it, officer?"

"Her parents?"

"They're at church. May I help you?"

He paused, obviously unsure of what to do next. Then, looking down, he read. "I regret to inform you that your sister, Mary Lillian Wilson, was in an auto accident this morning at three a.m."

At first I didn't respond.

"Is she dead?" I said at last.

"She's at Scottsdale Memorial. In critical condition, I'm afraid. We weren't able to contact you before now. She's unable to speak and her purse wasn't recovered right away. And her companion--the other occupant of the car--fled. Unhurt apparently. Are you expecting your parents home soon?"

For a moment I just looked at him. The world had stopped spinning, not merely slowed but stopped altogether. Then I felt myself shudder, like a cold engine.

"My parents? Yes," I said. "They went to early Mass. I'm sure they'll be back soon. Oh, my God, there must be some..."

I didn't go on: I knew it was Mary, our Mary. I felt as I'd never felt before how terrible it was being close to and intimate with another person. One's heart is a terrible beast.

"I'd be happy to wait here if you want to run up to the sanctuary," the policeman said. "Or I could drive you there."

But again I didn't respond right away. I couldn't believe the little girl I'd just watched dance across the family room wall--I could hear the ticking sound of the old projector even as I spoke to the officer–the girl I'd just learned was perhaps not my biological sister, and who'd told me only the other night of Joseph's "love," she said, for a boy who'd raped her, that girl, our Mary, was near death. What else could possibly happen! All that and the ruins, too, unbelievable! As though time were collapsing all around one! As though, like branches of a sycamore, everything overlapped.

"Saint Maria Goretti," I said.

I hopped in the white police car. The officer turned on his siren.

"It's the first time in a long time we Wilsons...," I started to tell him, but stopped, thinking about how nice it would have been if the entire family, Mary included, had gone to Mass–almost believing that if I had gone, even with Mary absent, that the accident would not have occurred the night before.

And if not that–if there was little or nothing I could have done to prevent Mary's destiny–that I had never returned from San Francisco, never attempted to reintegrate myself into family life. And if not that, that we'd never left Indiana for Arizona in the first place.

EPILOGUE
The River People

I CAN'T RECALL much of what followed. Mostly we were stunned, numb. Mary lingered. The doctor, a short, Asian man, with kind, black eyes, sat us down in his office and explained the trauma involved in the injuries. He didn't have any information about the whereabouts of Ihab Abelnaby. Nor did the police.

Mom wept wildly, preternaturally, upon first hearing the news—even saying to Joseph at one point, when we were back home: "Why did you have to return? What are you doing here? Who are you anyway?"

In response Joseph, devastated, immediately drove off in The Nimitz, only to return a couple of hours later with a new, shorter haircut. In fact, he'd gotten a blade #2 buzzcut. He looked like a boy, an old man. He looked like the 50's, and the future. All his finger waves were gone. What had possessed him to cut his hair, and do it right then, who knows--it was a strange thing to do, but our minds were presently on other things. My own thoughts ran toward both Mary and Abelnaby. His vanishing as he did made the whole episode, the tragedy, seem less real, and strangely miraculous.

Matthew insisted on a traditional wake. I'm not sure he'd ever insisted on anything prior to that time, but he was adamant about the funeral. Dad supported Matthew's wishes, although at first Dad didn't know what Matt meant by an Irish wake, nor did I.

"At all times someone remains with the body, someone always stays with Mary," Matt said.

"But where do we bury her?" Dad said.

"Here," I said, raising eyebrows all around. The five of us sat at the kitchen table, the surreal sunset darkening and coloring the windows. First orange, then red, then blue, a bleeding palimpsest of hues.

Mary had been moved to a morgue; Easter Sunday was nearly over and we still hadn't decided on a grave site. The Wilson family plot was back in Indiana, and the Flanagans and Kittredge had scattered hither and yon.

"What do you mean, Peter?" Dad said. It was clear that Dad was in charge now. "In our backyard. In the ruins."

"Do you think Mary would want that?"

"I don't think it's legal," Joseph said.

"People move out to Arizona in the first place so they can do as they please," Mom said, which was true but didn't really address Joseph's concern.

To my surprise Dad was actually considering my suggestion. Once I saw that he was listening, I made the case.

"We've lived here just as the Hohokam and their predecessors lived here. Perhaps we found the round house for reasons other than buried treasure. We should leave something behind. Some part of us. And Mary, adopted or not, will always be part of us."

The adopted reference caused an uproar.

"What do you mean 'adopted'?" Matt said. "What are you talking about?"

I turned to look at Dad, and Mom, and Joseph, waiting for them to answer. Dad spoke, but haltingly, tears starting to fill his eyes. "Mary was adopted, yes."

"After Joseph, we didn't think we could have another child," Mom said, trying to explain.

"Did Mary know she was adopted?" I asked, calmly. There was no need for recriminations; Mary was gone.

"Yes, she knew," Mom said, then abruptly stood up, went to the refrigerator and set some food and Coronas on the table. "We have to keep our strength up."

"How come I didn't know?" Matt said. "And Peter either? I can't believe this. Sick, sick, sick."

Matt was livid. His hands started shaking uncontrollably, like crabs just pulled from the sea. He appeared to have suspected nothing at all when it came to the truth about Mary's origins. And I must admit Matt's ignorance caused me to feel that perhaps I wasn't so totally out of it after all. Interestingly, Matt didn't reach for a beer, either then or during the following two days, when Mary was at last laid to rest. He took this particular tragedy straight.

"Why didn't you tell us?" I said.

"There wasn't any reason to," Dad said. "Would you have loved her less? Mary knew. She could have told you, if she wanted."

"I just don't get it, Dad. Why all these goddamn secrets?" I said, a little less calmly that time.

For some reason, my question seemed to provoke Joseph, who up until then hadn't said anything. He looked at me like I was some sort of leper.

"If you weren't so fucking blind--and I'm not referring to your injury--you'd have known long ago. You'd also have realized, Peter, that you were half in love with Mary yourself."

The way Joseph said this, with a kind of braying confidence, much annoyed me; but such confidence, or arrogance, that he did display at that moment was undercut by the awkwardness of his usual gesture of running his hand through his hair when there was no hair to run it through.

Still, I was angry. "Say what?" I said.

"You heard me, didn't you? Or do you now pretend to be deaf, too."

That was quite over-the-top, I felt. I abruptly stood up and pushed Joseph off his chair. His lumbering body crashed loudly against the wall. A stack of boxes tumbled down from the corner, landing on him. One of the boxes opened up and spilled on the floor, revealing travel and tourist-spot brochures from all over the country: Yosemite; Mt. Rushmore; Hannibal, Missouri, where Twain hailed from...as well as somewhat more obscure destinations like The House on the Rock in Wisconsin, which tourists prefer to Frank Lloyd Wright's original Taleisin, in nearby Spring Green.

"Fuck you, Joseph," I said.

Joseph rose, prepared to fight, but then abruptly stopped himself, taking a more defensive posture. And like Dad, he was crying. Matt had immediately stepped between us anyway. So Joseph just stood there in the kitchen for a few seconds; he looked like he didn't know what to do next. He was obviously distraught, confused. His face matched the dim parlor of the sunset. In the end, he just walked out of the kitchen—and, soon, he would more or less walk out of our lives again.

"Coward," I called at him. "Pervert," I yelled (oh, I wish I could have that word back!) But Joseph simply climbed the stairs, his broad back hunched over. He spent the night in his room, alone. He didn't allow anyone in; he wouldn't even respond to Mom's entreaties.

"I can't understand why you didn't tell us," Matt said, but he didn't wait for a reply. He too walked out, retreating to the screened-in porch. Maud followed him. Maud had cringed and slunk away when Joseph and I got in to it, but now she appeared all right, unbowed. Matt turned on the tv: hymns--the Mormon Tabernacle Choir, perhaps--could be heard issuing from the back room.

I sat down once more and looked at Mom and Dad, realizing they'd carried that secret with them all those years. Though probably, after a while, they rarely thought about it: Mary was just one of the family and that was the end of it.

"Did Mary know her parents?"

"No. The records were sealed," Mom said, "that's the way they did things then. Her father died in the Korean War, we're sure of that much."

"Before Mary was born," Dad said.

"And her mother?"

"We don't know," Mom said. "We think she was from Quebec. French. When we first brought Mary home she spoke French. Only French. But not Parisian French."

I thought about the little bump on Mary's nose, which I now associated with her being of French heritage.

"'Salut,' she'd say. 'Salut, Daddy.'" Dad was weeping openly now, tears flowing into the lines in his face. "I can't believe she's gone already. I don't think she ever knew how much I loved her. Did she?" he said, looking at me.

"Of course she did, Dad," I said. Mom, Dad, and I were sitting in near absolute darkness, I noticed.

The next morning, when tempers had cooled and sorrow began to overwhelm us, with Easter all over, the colored eggs back in the carton, and the baskets unopened, it was decided that Mary would be buried in our own backyard.

"Mary always believed the freeway would be built on the reservation, that Scottsdale would pay off the Indians, that our homestead would be preserved," I said. "Anyway, I think the ruins permanently bring a halt to the road, at least in terms of it coming through our house, if not those of others."

The following two days were the most painful our family had ever experienced, more painful, I imagine, than even the somber days of the Wambat rape, which besides, only some of the family had weathered.

Unfortunately, our feelings of loss were compounded by the fear, as yet unsubstantiated, that Mary had actually willed her life away—that she had committed suicide, driving herself and Mr. Abelnaby off the road. Obviously Abelnaby, a man who'd more or less exploited Mary for years, had survived the crash (it turned out that he hadn't even suffered a scratch). His Cadillac, which Mary was driving, hit a light pole and then careened some hundred yards off Pima

Road, coming to rest on the reservation, in the midst of the brown, harvested fields. Mary had died instantly, the authorities said. Her body, disfigured, rested limply against the seat. She'd been thrown forward and then back, the seatbelt still wrapped around her when the ambulance arrived. I read the accident report, noting one odd detail in particular. Mary had Type O blood, as all Native Americans did, but none of the rest of us Wilsons did, despite our Canarsie lineage. Perhaps some Indian had mixed with the French Québécois.

So, while I took some solace, as we all did, in the knowledge that Mary had died without suffering, the possibility that she had brought on her own death gnawed at me. Had she drunk too much? This seemed unlikely since the reservation was dry. Still, she could have been drinking after leaving the bingo hall, which she had apparently left about midnight. Oddly, only I knew she'd taken up the bottle again; for a change only I was privy to certain information. More oddly still, Mary had—unintentionally, I hoped—kept her promise not to reveal her renewed drinking to Matthew. But a more likely motive than Matthew for her death, if indeed she had sought death, was an unwillingness to herself face a life of alcohol dependency again.

I was apparently also the only one who knew that Mary was planning to go off to Alaska, and that—this too was hard for me to acknowledge—she might have been on her way out of town, leaving without even saying goodbye, visions of a new life in the great north stretching out before her, when she wrecked.

"What does it matter if she took her own life?" Matt said, when I brought up the subject later that day. Mary was laid out in her casket in her room upstairs. "This isn't a mystery story, Peter. It's far more absurd, and maybe even evil, than that."

But I cared. The manner of Mary's death was tied in with everything that concerned the past. And there was something more: that Mary was killed on Easter morning, that she was driving along Pima Road (even if she was headed out of town), such "coincidences" as these provided, for me if not Matthew, reassurance and comfort. I believed these events belonged to some sort of larger meaning, some sort of design. A design I didn't entirely understand however.

I wanted to speak with Abelnaby; he was the best source for determining Mary's state of mind at the time of the crash.

We kept the vigil of the body. I took my turn with the others: Dad, Mom, Joseph, Matthew. In fact, late Tuesday, after midnight, after Matt had gone to bed and before Mom had risen to make soda bread, I was able to fulfill my last promise to Mary. The candles encircling her open casket were sufficient: the light was warm and radiant on Mary's remarkably unmarked face and her white, Irish-lace burial gown. I undid one button. The tattoo, a blue anchor—related to Anchorage?—rested on her sand-colored breast. I painted her thus, demi-nude fashion.

The picture was done in minutes. A rush of votive adrenalin and inspiration overtook me. And it was during those moments alone with my sister in her room, a place I had seldom tread, that I fully realized how much I loved her and how much I would miss her. And how much I'd failed to pay attention to when she was alive.

Early the following day we gathered outside--the morning cloudy, and cool, as is often the case in the desert. Joseph stood in the center of the ruins digging a grave. No one stopped him from digging there. It was as if he was answering Emily Kunter or her band of scholar thieves. Joseph worked on, bending, rising, stretching. His hands were soon raw, bloodied; his breath distilled in the sky that hung low overhead. He had been vociferous in expressing his belief that we shouldn't disturb the site until it could be done properly, but now he was removing dirt shovelful by shovelful, not even stopping to examine the Indian artifacts that were exhumed as he worked. The old question, If a museum was burning down, should you save the workers or the paintings? seemed to me suddenly relevant. The dry desert climate preserves prehistoric materials: polychrome pottery, aboriginal utensils, spindle whorls, copper bells, ceremonial relics used in fertility rites, and human and animal bones would all emerge. Our ruin was soon revealed to be a three-room dwelling, which indeed predated the Hohokam. But no one cared about that that morning Mary went to her grave. How quickly, and meanly, our joy over finding the Hohokam stockpile had turned to sorrow.

Only family attended the funeral; we hadn't invited anyone else. We didn't know any of Mary's friends or colleagues, except Abelnaby.

"Joseph can't even let her alone when she's dead," Matt whispered to me, as Joseph neared the six foot mark.

But I couldn't be concerned about that right then (surely we Irish are the most opinionated people in the world). What mattered now was that our sister was gone. "You wanted a traditional wake, didn't you," I said to Matt.

Matt's eyes were red from crying instead of drinking.

The Virgin Mary bathtub shrine was unearthed and used as a headstone. Joseph conducted the service, saying at one point that Mary belonged on Wilson land.

"No one deserves to be buried here more than Mary," he said.

Even in sobriety Matt offered a few words from Shakespeare.

"Remember the 'vicious mole passage' in Hamlet," he began. Continuing, from memory:

That for some vicious mole of nature in them,
As in their birth--wherein they are not guilty,
Since nature cannot choose his origin--
By the o'ergrowth of some complexion,
Oft breaking down the pales and forts of reason,
Or by some habit that too much o'erleavens...

But Matt broke off, broke down, without finishing the speech.

We spent the rest of the day at home, indoors. The house itself felt like a tomb.

Joseph slept in my room that night, in the other twin bed–left over from when, in childhood, I had shared a room with Mary. Joseph had come into my room to talk; he didn't want to be alone. He didn't act like himself. I think his mind wasn't quite right. He kept bringing up all the things the family had done when we were kids: camping trips, parties, gymnastics meets, catechism classes, etc. He was crying a lot of the time. But sometimes, when he came to a certain story, he would laugh, or he would grow strangely lucid, as though he remembered every detail, as though he were reliving the episode at that very moment. I was little unnerved, but I listened quietly. Joseph lay back on the sheet and stared out the window.

"A full moon," he said.

"Yes," I said. The moon was blazing overhead and Joseph was talking a blue streak. "Leslie brought the marijuana to the river that night. I'd known him since grade school.

He was always one step ahead of everyone else. I remember the day he first came to school in a white trench coat. It was fifth grade. Soon we all wanted one. Leslie would turn the collar up, James Dean style. Mom finally got me one—Dad didn't make much back then, as you know, but somehow Mom got me that coat. The next morning it was a perfectly sunny day, and warm, but I still wore it to school."

"I remember him," I said. "Leslie."

"He was the first to deal drugs. I mean, he'd make deals at Dairy Queen. First grass, and then...."

"What was the attraction of being a Wambat anyway?"

Joseph thought for a moment.

"Belonging to a secret society, I guess. That's part of the appeal of the Church, too. Secrecy, privacy. A different world. Makes one feel important, I suppose. But everyday American life is not that interesting. Has there ever been a country with such a meager sense of aesthetic beauty?"

"I don't know. There's jazz, for instance. And Frank Lloyd Wright. But you know, when I went to Mary's club, the Bush, I got that feeling—the thrill of a secret life."

"God forgive me," Joseph said, abruptly recalling again the fateful night along the Wabash. "I felt mummified. I know you'll never be able to understand why I didn't do anything, Peter."

"It's all right," I said. "That was a long time ago." I realized I didn't have the heart to ask if Mary being adopted figured in the equation. Or if he feared losing Leslie.

Joseph didn't say anything more. Every few minutes or so his body would convulse, he'd choke on sobs. Finally, he fell asleep. He turned over on his side and soon was fast asleep. His feet hung off the end of the bed.

After a while, he started snoring. It was terrible, that snoring. But I was awake anyway. I lay there wide awake, in what felt like a strange house—a strange house, in a foreign land, in an unknown season, I was thinking.

The next morning as we got dressed, Joseph said: "I'm going back to New Orleans, Peter. Not to the Church, though. Something else. The ruins will be held up in litigation for years, you know that, don't you?"

"I suppose you're right," I said. "Did you know the ancient Pima symbol is the Man in the Maze? If you walk out on the reservation you'll see it at the gateway—a circular symbol, with concentric but interconnected lines, and the little figure of man in the middle of it all. Once and a while I walk out there, usually at twilight, and stand in the open land and look back at our house, barely distinguishable from those that surround it."

I was thinking about the last time I ventured out to Pima lands: at sunset an owl came flapping by, nearly scared the wits out of me.

"So what will you do?" Joseph said. "Remain here?"

"I'm not sure—maybe go to San Francisco. Or maybe I'll stay on here for a while. Anyway, don't forget us, this time. Let us hear from you," I said. "Epistles, anything."

Joseph smiled and then hugged me.

"I've never been a very good correspondent. But I was always thinking about the family."

"I'll miss you," I said.

"After a while you start missing everybody," Matt said, coming into the room. Matthew and Joseph also hugged.

Joseph flew to New Orleans that very night. His new haircut only reinforced the feeling that so much—too much—had happened during his brief return. I also couldn't help but think about Mary never making it to Alaska. Dad, Mom, Matthew and I drove Joseph to the airport. Already there was a hint of the hot summer ahead.

The following week Mom and Dad moved to Prescott. It was as if everyone in the family had always had an alternative plan ready for just such eventualities as Mary's death. Within the year Mom had opened a country store, selling antiques and odds and ends. "That's why I collected all that stuff," she said. "I've always wanted to go into business." She again told me the story of Great-Grandma Polly O'Ryan, who would sit out front of the Coney Island nightclub with her rosary, apparently counting the beads but actually keeping track of how many beer bottles the delivery men brought in and out. "A smart, tough old bird, Polly O'Ryan was," Mom said. Mom never admitted to any sort of collecting addiction.

As for Matthew, he didn't marry Lacey, nor the Beer Girl. Instead he moved to the Midwest to attend the Iowa Writers' Workshop; they gave him a Teaching Fellowship.

"Artists are Indians," he'd said to me one night prior to his departure. "De Tocqueville inadvertently describes the artist in his chapter, 'The Three Races in the United States.' He says of Indians: 'The wild enjoyments that formerly animated him in the woods painfully excite his troubled imagination. He contrasts the independence that he possessed among his equals with the servile position that he occupies in civilized society."

I thought back to our childhood days in Happy Hallow park: living so close to a woods and a river formidably shaped the imagination of myself and my siblings. Interestingly, the original name of the Pimas was Akimel Au-Authm, The River People. Visiting Spaniards gave them the name "Pima," because when the Spaniards spoke to these people in Spanish, the Indians answered, "P-mac-n," which means, "I don't understand you."

The River People were reasonably happy on the reservation, which was formed in 1874, until they woke up one day in the 1880's to find the Salt River dammed up before it reached their farms.

Perhaps the violence that visited our family, at the Wabash and then on the reservation, was to be found in earliest reveries and excitements.

A bout of pancreitis, suffered his first week of school, forced Matt to give up booze for good. He'd joined AA, as well as Impotents Anonymous, though his impotence, he wrote from Iowa City, disappeared with the end to his drinking. He also liked being back in the Heartland.

"A lot of nice, bland people," he said. "What I like is that they are all the same."

The freeway was stalled—no one knew what to do about the ruins. I found it amusing that the caterpillars were parked at night almost directly behind our fence, their silhouettes huge and skeletal. I also found it satisfying to escort Emily Kunter to the backyard to show her Mary's grave, smack dab in the middle of the site.

"I know this has been a hard time for you," she said, "but we must think about how important this find is to an understanding of American..."

"What was your maiden name?" I interrupted.

"Kunter."

"Your husband took your name?"

"Yes."

"What was his maiden name?"

"White."

"Bob White?"

"Yes. Is that relevant, Peter?" she said, standing there in her flowing dress.

"I see why he changed it, that's all," I said, enjoying myself thoroughly.

"Well, you're wrong to think you can get away with destroying this site, Peter. You Wilsons will hear from us," she said.

"From you Kunters?" I said.

"From the State. There are limits to private property, you know. You can't win. And the health department will be interested to learn that your sister is buried in your backyard. Good day."

"Texas wasn't big enough for you, eh?" I said.

I'd read somewhere that only Texans brag more about their state than Hoosiers.

I went to my reunion in May. A few people asked me about Mary. They remembered her as a cheerleader. One woman was even curious about what happened to Rick, the college guy Mary dated.

"She didn't marry him, then?"

"I don't know what became of him," I said, only to learn later that day from a classmate of mine who knew Mary, Susie Askin, that by the time Mary was able to get her birth records from wherever–Quebec, I guess–Rick had gone off and married someone else. Susie knew more about this than I did, of course. But considering Mary's experiences with men it was perhaps not all that surprising that she became a "dancer."

I helped Mom move her things out of the house. It took all summer. It was the hottest summer on record; the streets were desolate. Red ants claimed the alleys. The heat was like a virus in the air. As it turned out, Mom didn't throw out anything, or virtually anything. Still, she seemed relieved to be out of the house, to put some distance between herself and all the memories.

Dad made an interesting comment one day.

"I've never looked at you kids as being mine, or in my image, as much as being yourself. Each person is an individual. At least that's the way I've always felt."

Matt wrote me a second time. He'd started teaching. "Light out for the territory ahead," he said.

Perhaps he is right, I thought to myself. The ruins would, in the long run, take care of themselves. But I didn't believe I could take off alone. I'd never been as independent as Matt or Mary and, above all, Joseph. If truth be told, I didn't think I could go anywhere without someone by my side. And there was only one woman I wanted, now, Jenny. I wanted her twenties. I guess it was Joseph who made me realize my thing for Jenny was a little out of the ordinary, but then again she was only ten years younger than me. I felt perhaps I was the last Wilson, the last to carry on the male line, I mean. Matt seemed married to literature and Joseph to religion, or something. And so I decided I should write to Jenny, test the waters. I'd tell her my eye had healed; I'd tell her I held no grudge against her father, etc. Of course the eye thing would be a bit of a fib.

But I felt I was regaining some use of my right eye. I no longer wore a black pirates patch and I felt, at times, an increasing sense of perspective, of three-dimensionality, especially when painting. My picture of Mary was not so flat, so modern, so foregrounded as some of my other work. Mary's body was a solid form—this I had learned from P. Cezanne—but it was also shadowed and surrounded by space, by a kind of depth. The point of focus was not so much Mary, nor the Superstitions in the background, but rather some obscure point in the middle distance.

So for a time I didn't do much but hang around the house. Sometimes I moped around the house. One night I inexplicably found myself going from strip joint to strip joint on the West Side. I'd told myself I'd go out there and see what I could find about Abelnaby, but after few beers, a few more than regular, I was driving—dangerously—from titty bar to titty bar. I also made a sojourn back to the Salt River gambling venue. I not only didn't learn anything about Ihab, I lost a lot of money. At last I was informed that Abelnaby had gone to Alaska. The police had tracked him there; they required that he file a report on the accident, and were trying to charge him, at the very least, with leaving the scene of the accident. His police report was inconclusive—deliberately confusing it seemed to me. Apparently he'd left town the day after the accident. I had thoughts of seeking him out myself, of going to Alaska (the scenery there would be great, and I was thinking that Jenny might choose to join me on such an adventure as that). In

Alaska I'd pin him down, find out about Mary's actions that night, etc. But truth is I feared both what the truth might be and that I'd never know the truth. And what did it matter after all? I was beginning to agree with Matt, I was ready to drop the whole thing, when, out of nowhere, a break in the "case" came.

The morning headlines read: "Bush Owner Extradited–Alaska Sends Man Back to Arizona."

I felt a surge of joy as I sat at the kitchen table, fry-bread-less, reading the story. I felt as Clovis Point anthropologists must when they come across evidence of some connection between the first Americans of the Great North and those of the Great Southwest (though of course the analogy is more emotionally than logically exact). Fortunately the newspaper article was written in traditional inverted paragraph style, important information first, so, despite the length of the piece, detailing Abelnaby's extensive and nefarious activities in both Alaska and Arizona, the reason for his extradition was contained within the first sentence. And to my surprise it was not for his role in the accident, or at least not directly that.

> Ihab Abelnaby, owner of the recently closed down nude
> dancing operation Great Tundra Bush Company, was returned
> to Arizona today to face charges of allegedly selling stolen
> ancient Southwest Indian artifacts to Phoenix's own world
> famous Heard Museum. Police are still not saying where they
> believe Mr. Abelnaby obtained the artifacts...

Obtained the artifacts? To my sorrow, and discredit, Mary was my first thought: Could she have given Ihab the medicine box from our ruins in exchange for a ride to Alaska? On the other hand I was thinking that maybe he had forced her to. And maybe she knew nothing about it--that too was a possibility. He could have snuck in our backyard on his own. Or his operatives could have.

Thank goodness the next sentence put to rest speculation involving Mary.

> ...but reliable sources have told the Republic that Professor
> Emily Kunter, chair of the Anthropology Department at
> Arizona Tech University, has been implicated.

I was flabbergasted—coffee came spewing out of my mouth. How possibly to understand why someone so set up as Professor Kunter would stoop to such activities; but of her I ultimately cared little. What was important was the desire to comprehend the strange, special fate of my family, and especially, the odd, tragic, yet extraordinary story of Mary's life? In sum, Mary was a girl who'd never known her birth parents, been raped at fourteen, spent most of her adult life as a stripper, and now, was mixed up in, and perhaps dead as a result of, the greed of two business people, Ihab Abelnaby and Emily Kunter. Indeed I couldn't help but think Ihab's empire was not so much different than Emily's: weren't they both involved in stripping away the last vestiges—erasing the last footprints—of a life where body and soul were not commodities to be sold to the rich and powerful.

Within the year, as 198_ came hurtling toward us, Ihab would be convicted and sent to prison, down the road in Florence, Arizona, just south of the Gila River Indian reservation (the Gila River was also dry). As for Emily, she would lose her job at Arizona Tech (though her nepotism-blessed husband still had his) and would also go to trial. She would be given a suspended sentence since it was her first offense.

I never received a letter from Joseph. But Mom did. Joseph was living in Key West, working as a gardener. He was hoping to return to the Church someday. He sent his best regards to me, Mom said. "He sounds pretty happy," she said.

The big country had claimed us: Joseph in Florida, Matt in Iowa, Mom and Dad in northern Arizona—and me? I kept thinking about San Francisco; I kept turning it over in my mind. Except for me, everyone in the family had found a new driveway to pull into (Mom and Dad had taken the van and truck, leaving me The Nimitz). At last, like many other families, we were spread out across the country. Were we still recognizably a family? One star of the constellation was missing, and those remaining were realigned—that was one way of looking at it. Perhaps only a certain eccentric, even neurotic, character had kept us together so long in the first place. And yet, deep down, we were not merely eccentric, we were wild. Wild Irishmen. Wild Scotsmen. Wild Dutchmen. Wild Indians. Our attachment to the family was, I believe, a last if impossible and paradoxical attempt to hold on to something undomesticated. Isn't family a primitive thing?

Wasn't Mom right when she said "blood is thicker than water"? Wasn't it all about family? That special feeling. The Wilsons, including my sister.

Each morning after Mary's death, I rose to place fresh cut sunflowers on Mary's grave, or rather along the barbed wire fence that, at the Attorney General's orders, had "temporarily" been placed around the "Wilson Site." Time would only tell what would become of the ruins as well as Mary's burial mound, though I was determined to fight for both as long and as hard as I could.

I owed it to Mary, and to the rest of my clan. It was true, I suppose, that I never got to know Mary, nor anyone else in the family, very well. And I may, as Matthew suggested, been naive, or as Joseph suggested, a little in love with Mary myself. I may have been distant and cold sometimes, and blind. But, in the end, I would never consider Mary to be anything less than blood--nor Joseph anything less than my brother.

REC PARK

A Small-Town Romance

PART ONE

Prologue

DUE TO THE cool weather, the newbies' homesickness, and Christina's morning sickness, Dick and his new family generally stayed in and watched a lot of kids movies. *Mulan*—perhaps you've seen it—is about a Chinese girl way back-in-the-day who takes her father's place in war against the Huns. I thought the Huns were some sort of Germans, but it turns out they're Mongols. The Mongols in this movie are evil. There is no son to fight, so Mulan pretends to be a boy and wins the day, at some cost to her counterpart young leader's manhood. But in the end he stays to dinner. The theme of the story, beyond the obvious feminist angle, I take to be that individualism serves the greater good.

Tinker Bell has a similar theme (with some complications—more along the lines of be true to yourself), but despite Dick's recommendation (we were at Frank's) I was a bit skeptical at the outset, thinking it would be just a Peter Pan spinoff. Is there a *Wendy?* We do get to hear Tinker Bell speak for the first time. I don't know if *Tinker* is true to the original—or *Mulan,* for that matter, though it appears to have some historical resonance—that is, I don't know if the "Tinker" part of the her name originally applied to "tinkering," i.e., making and fixing things, but in the movie Tinker is not happy to just make clay pots all day and wants to do something more along the lines of her four best fairy friends, like helping the wind or the sun, or helping birds to fly, both because she thinks such work would be more interesting and because it, helping spring to arrive, would allow her to go to the mainland (which for us, here in El Camino, is Los Angeles). I only saw the movie once so I'm not sure why there's no spring in Pixie Hollow, but the thing I liked best was, at the beginning of the movie they described the mainland as having all four seasons at once and certain fairies only served in one season, one section of the mainland—I think I just answered my own question.

Dick (between hands, Mike dealing) said that they watched half the movie and then took a nap—all three of them—and then watched the rest. His step-daughter had wanted to watch *Tinker Bell* the afternoon before, hopeful that it wasn't as scary as *Mulan* was in parts. "There's no crying in *Tinker Bell*," she'd predicted, but that turned out to be only generally true. It does end on a happy note. Tinker accepts, finally, that her talent is for tinkering not something else and in the end uses her talent to create something beautiful and astonishing, out of old used or broken parts from the mainland. The movie had a quasi-Irish feel and Irish-like music. I think they wanted the misty joy of Irishness but also wanted Pixie Hollow to be only a place in one's imagination.

It was about four p.m. Dick said they'd finished watching. The light was pixie dust in the blinds, which prior to their arrival he'd always turned downward but his new wife always turned upward. So you could have light but not be spied on by the neighbors. Though he knew they were talking.

He'd sent Christina and Mya to the library to return the videos and pick out a couple of more. He'd needed time on his own, he said—he's a professor—and had been trying to get them to venture out more on *their* own. Since their arrival from the Philippines, he'd scarcely, if he thought about it, had two minutes in the house alone. Mya was already in school, but Christina was always home, with little to do. She'd start books, cook, wash. Dick guessed it was an Asian thing to lie down a lot, like you're in an opium den. She liked to listen to music—Rock and Roll (but eighties while he preferred sixties). They'd known each other for four years online, but this was something else again.

Thirty minutes later, Christina and Mya were to return. Mya liked to ring the doorbell—where they came from there were no doorbells. She pushed at the door. Dick saw her face through the six-inch opening the door chain allowed.

"Okay, okay," he said.

"We couldn't find it," Christina said, laughing.

"How could you miss it? I said one block east, Richmond, and then five blocks north. It's right next to the pool and the high school. Did you ask anyone?"

(After using up Richmond, Concord, Franklin, etc. as street names, the town turned to Midwestern States, Indiana, Illinois etc; meanwhile cross streets are tree names—the town so small there's no need for numbered streets.)

"Mom was too shy," said Mya.

"Christina?"

She hadn't shown the least interest in finding her way around.

Ours is generally a friendly (if perhaps a little self-regarding), sports-oriented, conservative town. (When a culture is physical, and outdoorsy, the more right-leaning it is likely to become, if you think about it). It is a safe town. The schools are good. Mya attends Concord, an elegant, low-lying two-level structure, white with marine-blue fluting, circa 1936—the schoolrooms and offices rather small of course due to the era of construction. You can walk pretty much everywhere. The four borders of Sepulveda Blvd., LAX (where Big Mike works), the massive Chevron refinery, and the Pacific Ocean serve to limit growth—there's not even room for a cemetery. The town has a slightly surreal feel to it, I guess, as if a (brick) Midwestern town had been set down right next to Los Angeles. El Camino is about as close as you were going to come to a Pixie Hollow, in California—our civic and business leaders trading on the small-town charm.

Christina's nose had been running for two weeks straight, as she adapted to a new place. Just the day before a strong wind had blown away the pollen, and her nose had cleared up. Dick had bought her Claritin. He finally convinced her to use nose spray. Actually there was no morning sickness yet. Just fatigue. She slept sixteen hours a day, like an animal. Her small body curled up under the covers, the cover over her head to block out the light. She didn't want the baby. She wanted to work. She'd spent six years as a single mother raising Mya.

Mya generally kept occupied. She played girl games online: "High Tea Hotel" and "Kids Cooking." She worried about "customers," meeting their needs, which Dick assumed was how you won the games, or scored high. She liked to paint—watercolors. Blue, green, red, and often a DeKooning yellow. There was usually a house, a church, a sun, a tree, grass, water, animals, a bamboo plant. She wanted a brother or sister—Christina reported her saying, "I'm always alone." Back where she was from most everyone had two or more kids (in Manila, Mya has half-siblings apparently—her birth father was already married when Christina got pregnant by him; Dick, the current father, the only other person she's ever had sex with). Dick came from a family of six boys. The Starlings were taken for Catholics or Mormons but were neither though his mother, as a child, had been sent to Catholic schools. Christina was Catholic. She and Dick were saved from a tough decision by the miscarriage.

I won't be here for dinner, Dick had said, and decided to take a walk. (The fog just beyond the city limits, standing there like a flower.) He liked to walk around Rec Park–always liked having a park to walk around. The park is in a swale in the middle of town, off Eucalyptus.

He'd only been gone a short while when Mya was to call. "Papa, what do want for dinner?"

"I won't be home for dinner," I told her.

"I'll be home after dinner."

"Can I have ice cream?"

"Yes, after dinner."

"Where are you?"

"Starbucks."

"Okay."

The movies hadn't been returned. Christina and Mya were asleep. Mya slept with her hand on Christina's breast, a habit Christina was trying to break but had let go that night.

"I wanted to watch *Tinker Bell* again," Dick said (his father was an engineer). Said if he thought about it he generally couldn't recall watching kids movies with Marie, his grown daughter, when she was young (I suppose DVD's weren't so readily available). He recalled, further, taking her to *Roger Rabbit* when she was eight but walking out because the movie was too violent. And how also a few times since the arrival of Christina and Mya, he'd called out "Marie" to Mya. Once even calling out "Cheri" upon hearing Christina working in the kitchen (in the kitchen he at times imagined each of his ex-wives walking in, alive and young, softly calling). Marie says, said Dick, that occasionally her mom will call out "Dick" when she means "Pete."

Because of the shortness of time–he was feeling fatigued–Dick just watched the extras: The *Tinker* trailer, the Magical Guide to Pixie Hollow, and how the people on The Mainland created Pixie Hollow. By the end he was in tears.

I

WE KNEW HE had been thinking for some time, as he was thinking that day at the pool, that S.K might be interested in attending his alma mater—and that he had pull. Earlier in the day at the library he'd run into her and felt the connection between them strengthen. Our library, like our pool, is attractive, the whole Main Street area of El Camino rather beautiful in fact—both art nouveau and art deco, and Romanesque, mostly of stone and brick. The library blends into the landscape, the lower level for children and the upper for adults. Sweet-smelling eucalyptus trees stand like giants just beyond the big picture windows, suggesting a place steeped in history, yet a place that seems to have never really changed, never quite entered the 21st century. He coached M.K., the little sister, and was hoping S.K. might be by to pick her up after swim practice.

One reason Dick had chosen El Camino in the first place was the presence of "The Plunge," its Olympic-size pool one of the first in the region. Its art deco facade features two stone swimmers, a female and a male, in swimsuits, hers a one piece and his like a Speedo, both holding towels, hers spread behind her, his at his side, the figures looking at each other and standing in relief on either side of the entrance. The locker rooms are small of course, accessed by a ramp going down to below the pool level, the floor slippery gray concrete, the showers behind a curtain, that area small too, and reminiscent of the old stadium at Purdue, where as a kid Dick swam with his buddies. Early on it was clear that he was a strong swimmer; and reportedly (I've made a small study of him), he worked hard at it in high school, placing second in freestyle at the Hoosier state meet—Dick intimating that he might not have been accepted at Chicago sans swimming credentials. In any case, he'd needed the scholarship. Yet even at an academically- oriented place like Chicago participating in college athletics was a big commitment, and Dick in the end had felt compelled to quit. Only doing so however once it was clear his history professor, who'd taken "a shine to him," could get him an academic award, ensuring matriculation.

The encounter with S.K. had occurred at the town library, bemusing to his way of mind since he was a college professor and she a top student (a senior) at the high school. The previous Friday, she had performed on the flute during half-time—it had been a warm, feral fall night (I took some pictures for the benefit of the high school, as I'd become a decent amateur photographer due to my work as a real estate agent). S.K. was deemed the second-best performer in that entire (award-winning) ensemble. Of course Dick understood the library incident itself was nothing to make much—or perhaps anything—out of, and knew his anticipation of such a moment occurring at some point probably colored his thinking un-reasonably. He'd been standing at the book bargain table and she had said—he had not known her voice could be so...polite-sounding, respectful—said simply, "Hello, Dick," smiling. It was unaccountably revelatory, especially in the context of her usual affectlessness. She happened to be with her boyfriend, her third recent one by his count (all three of which she had met in the band, which she later realized was an inconvenience, as there was no avoiding seeing them after a break-up), but the boyfriend somehow didn't dampen the effect, perhaps even enhanced it, for Dick.

He had been caught off guard.

"Hi, S.K.," he responded but didn't fully turn to her: a few minutes earlier, when parked in his car outside the library, she had walked by with the boy-friend, a lanky, red-headed fellow—the Flynn's boy—and had waved and before Dick could realize that she was waving to someone in the car parked next to his, he'd cheerfully waved back, only to immediately lower his hand, like the ball-player who too late pulls back his bat. He, Christina, and Mya had taken M.K. on a weekend trip to Las Vegas over the summer. (M.K. had no qualms about walking around the hotel room naked, and said as much: "I don't really care if people see me naked." She was small, like her older sister, possibly as smart; her parents having posted online a while back that she'd gotten a perfect score on a recent standardized test.) Maybe S.K. was just offering pleasantries based on family friendship.

The Kims are Filipinos, though the father's heritage is Korean—the extensiveness of "The Filipino Community," part of the changing dynamics of our domain, is hidden under their Spanish surnames. When the community got together, which it often did, the kids were expected to put in an appearance, though S.K was old enough, now seventeen, that she rarely would. Truth was, she didn't feel any particular need to be friendly to Dick because he was friends with her parents. And not for a minute had it gone unnoticed the way he looked at her, and tried to make small talk about high school and everything.

"Saw you running today," he'd reportedly said to her at one of the many birthday celebrations held by the community at Recreation Park, one she did feel obligated to attend.

"Oh, awesome," she answered.

Whether S.K. liked him or not—and truth was she wasn't at that point aware of any feelings whatsoever—she didn't like being seen so grubby. Her running outfit was baggy as night clothes, her hair damp with sweat—sorry as a rooster in the rain was how she imagined she looked. If not running with the school team—they thunder through town—she liked to head out at evening time and run along the shore, the ocean usually a striking tattoo blue at dusk, the waves an unending text, only seagulls and a few odd walkers as company (Filipinos generally choosing not to be alone, such a desire suggesting something wrong with you).

Like most kids with Ivy League dreams, S.K. needed a sport to complete her resume, so she'd joined cross country. The Ivy's professed that they were looking for well-rounded types, not just eggheads, her parents pushing for Stanford so she wouldn't be so far away from home. Her father pushing quietly, her mother not so quietly. Her mother talked a lot generally.

Of course she was not aware—or if so, only vaguely—of the effect the "Hello, Dick" had had at the library (she didn't call him Mr. Starling or Dr. Starling, or Tito). Not aware that it had made him feel better about himself—and more strongly about her. He'd assumed she didn't like him, or found him to be somehow sketchy, professor or no, so he was pleased by the acknowledgment. (So many beautiful, talented young people, and of all ethnicities—like some sort of Ellis Island—passed through his college classes that it was curious that he'd focused in so on S.K., we felt, in retrospect). Dick went out of his way to not make

S.K. feel uncomfortable. He never quite met her eyes. People go off the rails a bit at forty, but that's no justification for misconduct.

She was not, as it turned out, to make that day an appearance at the pool. Yet, as it was November and was rainy that week–everyone driven inside like into a barn–he knew if he so desired he could ferret out her favorite haunt, should she indeed have one. However there were so few places in town that if she indeed had a favorite–it wasn't Starbucks (Dick liked the wooden taste of the coffee)–it would be awkward to show up there, or do so too often. Our local police have little to do which is good for our kids' safety here west of Sepulveda, if not so good if you like liberty. (In its first hundred year history, recently commemorated, El Camino hadn't a single murder).

It was not until the following swim practice, also on a Saturday, that he was to again come across her. Dick enjoyed coaching, and still liked to swim, enjoyed the whole ritual of it: stripping down, sitting on the tan wooden bench and pulling on his suit, showering on the way out to the pool, emerging from the underground tunnel into the bright, flickering, heavy-aired stadium. And afterwards, there was the familiar smell of chlorine, the gingerly walk to the showers, the ritual of rolling up your suit in a towel. At times he worried that he pushed his little swimmers too hard. Mya said: "It's alright, Pa. We can take it." (When Mya talked to others she'd generally refer, American-style, to "my dad.") Even after all those months of coaching, he loved to watch the girls–his daughter, M.K., the bunch–move through the pale blue water, at different lengths, intervals, their sleek, small power on display. It looked like an electric grid.

S.K. had arrived but was accompanied by the boyfriend., our Hal.

Still, there was, for Dick, a new "Hello, Dick" (again not just "Hi"), even if he figured she was probably just happy to be with her new boyfriend and thus was generally feeling generous toward the world.

She felt a bit self-conscious, we know. She had noticed before of course that he was powerful swimmer, was powerfully built; noticed the strong haunches and strong legs, the shapely, and at that moment still wet, swimmer's back, the skin nearly as white (especially in contrast to the dark hair) as the towel around his shoulders (Hal's skin was a rose color). But S.K. felt it was normal enough, in no way outside the box, to notice and admire a powerful physique, and, at the time, thought there was nothing more to it than that.

"This is Hal," she continued. "He's on the high school swim team."

"You are? Good for you. You are lanky."

"I'm in the band, too."

"An unusual combination," Dick said. He did think it a bit unusual, but he was well aware that he sounded like an idiot.

"I guess it is," the boy said.

Hal was handsome, his face almost as delicate as a girl's, as if swimming had worn smooth his skin. He played trumpet. At the games, Dick enjoyed listening to the sections of the marching band—brass, woodwind, and percussion—as they wove together and then separated again on the map of the field, the colors all the while unchanging. It had been warm the night of the home opener—September surprisingly often our warmest month, early September, at any rate. At the same time the night had had an end-of-summer feel to it, the game starting at dusk, in a kind of fisherman's last light, though the stadium lights created a halo high above, or you could say it looked up there like an alien craft hovering, the grass below an emerald green. The teams shouting as they ran onto the field. There was a fair showing on Hawthorne's side (the town is located just east of Sepulveda)—if nothing like what we see when Manhattan Beach shows up, for example, with their huge (award-winning) band and bevy of cheerleaders and dancerettes and boatload of fans (three large yellow buses parked outside when we played them last year).

There had followed a bit of an awkward pause, Dick almost hoping M.K. might interrupt, that she was dressed and ready to go.

"Have you started to think about colleges, you two?" he asked, as filler—yet not simply filler.

"I have," Hal responded first. "I'll probably go to Cal like my parents. S.K. is getting some pressure, right, babes?"

"Since fifth grade," she said.

The three were laughing when M.K. appeared.

It was cool out and windy so S.K. bundled up. She had Hal with her to keep her warm, but with M.K. there too she couldn't be overly affectionate (she liked to link arms, at a minimum—PDA's not commonly seen in our town however).

Filipinos I understand are not that shy about displaying affection, nor was she, nor shy about dressing sexy, if tomboyish, or joking around about sex even in M.K.'s presence, even if they were all Catholics her family–semi- regular attendees at St. Anthony's– though admittedly the Korean dad, K..K., was a bit more uptight about sex, although one time joking around he'd pulled down his pants and showed them his butt. That was funny.

She'd had a bit of argument earlier with Hal. He was off to Ireland for Fall Break and they hadn't parked in a while (usually in the salt-sharp air under the stars out by the airplane fields). She'd tried to assure him that they would find time. An hour was usually enough.

Parking, she'd would go down on him–so far not asking for the same, not yet comfortable enough to do so.

Dick walked home, too, Mya by his side, the Chevron refinery standing in the black night up ahead of them like a lighted frigate. ("The Standard Oil Payroll City," was how our town was first advertised.)

Dick wished right then he were alone. Alone with his thoughts, I guess. However disappointed he was in S.K. having been accompanied by the boyfriend–and it wasn't all disappointment because it helped him imagine what they did together–he reminded himself that she'd spoken to him, said that "Hello," the slight echo around the pool providing a nice soft layered if sort of distant quality to it. Still, Dick felt there was something in it, her talking to him, introducing her boyfriend, if not as much as he had speculated as there being earlier in the day. Earlier in the day he was pretty sure it was love he'd felt, or love of a sort, even though he couldn't know what she had felt. Should he call her when he got home, after his wife and daughter were asleep? He'd have to have some pretext, of course, something to do with swimming, as regards M.K., or perhaps even Hal. His daughter had S.K.'s number. One thing he would grant, S.K. had been nice to Mya. Friendly, generally. There was, true, one occasion when she had a little too forcefully said that Mya didn't know how to clean up after play. They were a little too disciplined, or organized, those two K's. Dick wondered if they'd give X.K., the baby boy, more latitude.

He didn't call. More days passed, rainy shroud-like ones. He was reminded of Chicago, although back there the wind blew harder and a November rain could quickly turn into snow (diapers on clotheslines freezing into the shapes of dead chickens). Meanwhile, he had research papers to grade. Dick had taught for fifteen years at the college in Santa Monica, the last five of those at the branch campus near the Santa Monica Airport (only the other day coming to realize that the campus building—it has a pale green diaphanous tower in the front—was meant to look like an air controller's tower, though the airport was scheduled to be shut down and the school building would soon stand there without a referent).

As it happened he didn't see S.K. over the week, parading around with her boyfriend or otherwise. And the football team was on the road. There was again Saturday swim practice, and that thought buoyed him. But Saturday arrived and she didn't show. Dick had sat with M.K. in the stadium bleachers after practice. Deigned to ask her to stay behind for a minute, ostensibly to discuss something about swimming, about the upcoming meet. She was shivering a bit. He put a dry white towel over her shoulders. M.K. had a short, square body. She herself had said that people called her "cute," intimating that she knew she wasn't especially pretty. Neither maybe was S.K. as far as that went, though Dick found her attractive. She had gotten what the kids called her "glow up." Dick liked her slim, willowy body (M.K figured to thin out), and her soft, husky voice.

A pool of water had formed at the girl's feet, the water dripping off her ankles. (Her skin a pale coca cola color, a half-shade darker than S.K.'s., surprisingly)

At first they were to discuss her times, which had dramatically improved. She was now ahead of Mya, in freestyle and backstroke. Dick had the feeling it was sheer intelligence—or intelligence applied to technique and training—that had caused M.K. to advance so quickly, her solid little body now like a torpedo in the water.

"No S.K. today?" Dick asked.

"I walk home by myself now, Mr. Starling."

He would have never let his daughter do that. But he'd learned that Filipinos were used to hardship and were realists, practical, driven by necessity. Christina said girls in the Philippines needed to be tough. "Men will look you up and down and whistle." Dick liked tomboyish girls, like Christina, and S.K. But he was beginning to think, that in addition to other issues they had as a couple, that Christina was perhaps a little too masculine, for his taste. In the Philippines she had wanted to join the army, like her older brother. But Mya had come along. Was Christina's toughness the chief problem they had? Dick thought maybe it was. That maybe it was even more important than their intellectual incompatibility. And that he was, too, despite his sculptured physique, too polite, not rugged, macho enough for her.

(But it might be easy to be fooled. James Dean was a polite boy from Indiana, the most polite state in the union, but no one should be surprised to find out that he was not, privately or for that matter in front of the camera, so reticent, so polite. The shy, dreamy quality was always there, but it suggests to me a need to be careful, overcareful, not to stir the beast. As if it were necessary to keep tabs on his emotions.)

Or was the fifteen-year age difference at fault?

"S.K. is out of town with my dad, visiting Stanford," continued M.K.

"Stanford, huh. I went to Chicago."

The professor who had taken a shine to him (had a thing for him?) at Chicago was gay, Sicilian, a Renaissance scholar—with a yen for Hollywood movies—a native Chicagoan. In addition to the scholarship rec, he had hired Dick as an assistant—mostly it involved putting bookplates in the professor's vast personal office library. Dick began to see the words *Ex Libris* in his dreams. He also had access to the professor's library cubicle (which one time he used for a rendevous with a coed).

M.K. didn't appear to want to talk. "Can I change now, Coach?

He felt (as had Frank post his coaching of fifth-grade basketball) that contemporary kids were self-absorbed. Even sullen, as was S.K., at times. Was he starting to hate the young, even as he was more drawn to them?

He did manage to glean some further information about S.K., from one of her classmates, a Filipino boy who'd only recently immigrated, at last reunited with his mother, and who was now attending the high school—Jason was his name. His mother was friends with Christina and it was from the wife that the information wound up in Dick's hands, although Christina was certainly unaware (she told me as much) that what for her were passing remarks were not so to him. The boy's mother, Maribelle, had mentioned to Christina that her son was childish.

"He saw S.K.'s boyfriend in the urinal at school, he was standing right next to him. 'He has a big penis,' he said."

"He told his mother that?" Dick said.

"The other day he also said to her that he saw them kissing, S.K. and the boyfriend, at the park, lips to lips, he said." He's so immature, Maribelle had said.

Dick would often see Jason playing basketball at the Teen Center, next to Rec Park.

Filipinos love basketball–the NBA games coming on there in the early morning.

S.K. liked the park and also being out of the house, in her case from a two-bedroom apartment where she shared a room, and a bed, with M.K. (X.K. slept with the parents.) There was a small living/dining area and an alley-style kitchen. One bath. The piano took up a good portion of the living area, the rest of it largely swallowed up by the TV and couch. The sisters shared a small desk, although more recently S.K. would head to the library at night to study, often with Hal. The Kims lived directly across from the library and the high school. They were so near LAX, that at night–especially for some reason at eleven p.m. and two a.m.–the sound of the planes would rattle the windows. The girls' window faced north and in the daylight the huge planes would appear before it, slowly rising, scraping the sky, seeming for a moment stationary before the window, like painted cutouts, or even imprints on the glass. The city had mandated new sound-minimizing window installation for those who lived close to the airport, but so far it hadn't reached their place.

Hal (Dick was unable to get the image of his penis, of both boys actually, out of his head) was a wealthy kid. His mother and father were lawyers. He wasn't, S.K. felt, a smooth lover, but she'd already had a couple of the smooth ones–or smooth as might be expected from band geeks–the previous two wanting her to put out (she'd let them fondle and kiss her breasts, that's it). She'd been boy crazy since middle school. One time in middle school, caught by her parents sneaking out of the house early to meet her then boyfriend, she'd been punished with a slap across the face and grounding (if only those who'd been there to see her win the top student award at middle school graduation had known that). Her father, who was the one who slapped her, had said mysteriously that she wasn't free to get in trouble like other kids. But it didn't stop her.

Hal was, however, a good kisser. He was also super smart, a surprisingly good swimmer, and had that brilliant exotic red hair, which his mother said, he said, was the color of fall maple trees. S.K. had never seen a maple tree, having never been east of Riverside (I'd at one time lived in Boston and was astounded to find a lot of the locals there had never been west of Providence, Rhode Island). Hal's mother, like Dick, had grown up in the Midwest, a land of friendliness, Dick persisted in believing–a place where kids did say hello to their elders, at least so back-in- the-day. Have I mentioned that I sold Dick his home, that beautiful Hollywood Bungalow circa 1936, on Concord?

Hal and S.K. were sitting atop one of the concrete picnic tables in the half-dark of a certain group of coast trees, when Dick saw them. He had on a hoodie, running pants, and tennis shoes. The path took him up the incline and passed the picnic tables. There was a nice computer- like blue light at that time of the night. Dick too, of course, liked getting out of the house.

Hal's hand reportedly was on her knee. It was cool out, clear and cool, and she snuggled up against him. They kissed playfully. He moved his hand to the inside of her thigh. She was wearing jeans and a blue school sweatshirt. "The Knights." She put her hand between his thighs. It was warm there, like a bird had been nesting there.

"Hello, Dick," she said when she saw him.

Dick had apparently planned to just keep walking, to not look up, give them some space, privacy–not tamper with their young lives.

But now he slowed. "Hi, S.K.," he said. "Hi, Hal."

It was rather thrilling. Maybe she doesn't dislike me after all, thought Dick. Maybe she doesn't like me, or doesn't think much about me, but maybe she doesn't actively dislike me, he now felt. (It is true Dick was beginning to think people in the town–even us his card partners–disliked him. In any case, word travels quickly.)

He was, or at least felt so at the time, satisfied with a simple "Hello, Dick." S.K. would be off to college soon anyway, and in her case off to a prestigious college most likely. "Hello, Dick" was enough for him. Even Hal had chimed in "Hi, Dick." Dick probably wouldn't have known what to do with it anyway, had any interest been shown. And there was his family, his wife and daughter, to think about. He was content to see S.K. happy, smiling, even to see her with her new young man. Dick walked on, his breath coming rapidly. (He needed more time in the pool.)

Meanwhile S.K. watched his figure, his silhouette, disappear around the corner. She wondered if he would be back on other nights. For her too it had been a bit thrilling. Maybe, she would later surmise, because I was caught doing something wrong in public. Or was it because M.K. had said, in passing, something about him wanting to talk to her about Chicago.

II

ADVENT SUNDAY LAST Dick was once again cross paths with our S.K.. He was an irregular church attendee; but Ally (Mike and Cynthia unable to attend) had wanted Mya to join with her in a dance class at the church and now they had performed a liturgical dance. Ally and Mya were not as close as previously (friendship among preteens migratory). It wasn't until the closing prayer just before the benediction that he was to notice S.K.. Earlier he had noticed a shock of orange-red hair but for some reason had failed to connect it to Hal. Her head had been bowed, exposing the nape of her neck, the color of our sand dunes and a shade lighter than most other parts of her body. S.K. had been concentrating on the unfamiliar liturgy. Like virtually all Filipinos, she believed in God, but she wondered about the efficacy of praying in a non-Catholic church (Hal's family Irish Protestants) and she wasn't in any case sure what to pray for. She wasn't feeling it.

Dick didn't care much for the church building. Despite it being a house for Methodists it was of Spanish-Mission style (and at one hundred years old, nearly as old as El Camino). He had grown up, in Indiana, in a rather different sort of Methodist structure. The roof of the El Camino church was of red terra cotta tiles, and the walls, inside and out, were adobe white, the sanctuary cavernous, its ceiling high and curved, the stained-glass windows two stories above the church floor. On any given Sunday the two long seaman's galley-like wooden pews were largely unmanned. How lonely it must be, Dick had once openly surmised at the card game, to in these palmy pagan days still be a Christian, to but sit in a broken pew with a few stranglers (as if it were A.A.), while others were out enjoying play and destruction—even if to be among the remaining few, a sort of Shaker, might in some respects be bracing.

"Weren't the Shakers the ones who didn't have sex?" Mike laughing.

But Dick's comment about the empty church most likely hit a sore spot with Mike (as it did with me). Mike, a El Caminoian native—he'd only been away for college and during his stint in the Navy—had attended a Brethern church five or six times a week as a child and now was in the process of rediscovering his faith, the Brethern having a few years back merged with the Methodists.

Mike had even been around in 1969, if but a child then, when a B-26 bomber on test drive suffered engine problems and plunged into an apartment on Eucalyptus just behind the church, killing all four on board and two on the ground—Donna Meyerson and a Mr. Hood—the accident, along with the fire that burned down the bowling alley on Main, the worst disaster to befall our modest hamlet if potentially much worse as the heroic pilot had veered at the last moment to avoid crashing into a baseball diamond full of families enjoying a carnival in Rec Park.

Admittedly the Methodist Church, the first church built in our town, was now almost exclusively a church for older, middle-of-the road white people. immigrants now flocking to either Catholic or, increasingly, evangelical churches (Christina's friend Zhenia was always asking Christina to come with her to Hope Chapel in Hermosa). Millennials meanwhile generally eschewing affiliation

Whatever Dick's misgivings, he'd always enjoyed singing hymns—and felt calmed by the familiar rustle of the hymnals and clothes as parishioners rose to their feet. Following the service, he noticed Miss Marge forward at the chancel. Earlier in the month she had expressed disappointment about Mya having given up piano, and now Dick was looking forward to telling her that she would return. "The Asian students usually continue," Marge saying at the time. "S.K. and M.K. Jordan. Michelle. C's Lia. I wanted to recommend S.K. for a local scholarship, but for some reason she didn't have a social security number"—information Dick stored but didn't really think much about until later. Mya had talent, more natural talent than M.K., to his mind, but M.K. practiced more and recently had passed Mya up, just as she had in swimming.

S.K. ran forward, school girlishly, to speak with Marge, Dick not joining them—keen not to provide the grapevine with ammo, already unnerved by the mere mention of S.K. by Marge. He believed that no one other than S.K.—except maybe to some degree Christina, me and Mike, or, God forbid, Hal—was aware of his interest in her, whatever sort of interest it was; but if the gathered saw something now, if it registered, however unremarkable it might be, such as chatting at church, they might at a later date add that, connect it to other observations and, like Dick when it came to S.K.'s social security number, begin to put two and two together. If S.K. were to come outside and speak to him, fine, and if not, then it was generally for the best.

On the way out of the sanctuary he was to speak to Pastor Smith, keen to let her know how much he'd enjoyed the sermon. She had preached, rather eloquently, on the incompleteness and openness of "The Gospel According to Mark," leading her to equate this to the ongoing nature of the Christian story, and to mention the role each person, each Christian, plays in the unfolding mission of the church. This ongoingness had led her—Dick couldn't quite recall exactly how—to suggest that Jesus goes out before each of us, and awaits our arrival—a theme, it occurred to him, not unlike one Walt Whitman had presented his variation on: "Failing to fetch me at first keep encouraged, Missing me one place search another, I stop somewhere waiting for you." Dick often included *Leaves of Grass* among texts for his American history classes apparently. Mike, Dick now also recalled, had on one occasion mentioned being keen to find out, in death, "What was on the other side." But how to respond to such a statement? Surely it was wrong to think of death in human terms, to think there was such a thing as some ghostly "other side." Yet it was not for him to say what Big Mike should believe. Just a couple of weeks earlier the two men with their daughters—Mike having been given some tickets by a friend of the city council—had traveled down to the Disney Concert Hall, Frank Gehry's latest creation, the curved, sheeted metal reflecting, like waves, the gray, evening sky before them (the hall's wood interior the light-brown color of violins). Dick mentioning, to me, that when Mike stopped at a red light near the hall—which was across from the courthouse and the new cathedral—he had wound down his window and handed out a "penny bag" to a homeless man (what a dolorous thought what America has come to, all the money funneled to the top!)

Dick wondered to Mike where had he gotten the bags.

"We made them last Sunday at our church."

"Ours?" Dick was thinking.

(During jury duty downtown a couple of years earlier he had checked out the cathedral. There was something new in the architecture, he felt. The entrance to the church—I've been there, too—is indirect, down a long swale that leads to the rear of the sanctuary. In effect one arrives as if from an inside to an outside, to a kind of picnic area, as if parishioners—some solitary, some in two or threes, or families—have come in for noon meal. The stone walls have the appearance of balsa wood, or ply, but on a huge scale, and blond, fitted, not unlike something you might plane in high school woodshop. Dick said he didn't genuflect but rather merely sat in a pew and watched those at prayer, their hands folded—on the way out it's difficult to avoid the eyes of those protesting child abuse, however.)

The "penny" bags contained a shaver, a toothbrush and toothpaste, and some snacks. Dick felt that should he himself at some point return to religion it would be to the Methodists. He applauded their emphasis on feeling over doctrine, and their willingness to minister to church and unchurched alike.

He was a little put off however when the minister seemingly took his compliment as an example of mere perfunctoriness. "Good to see you—and your family, too," she said. (But a couple of days later a letter was to arrive at his house welcoming them, despite his previous if irregular attendance, to the church and letting them know the church was there for them.)

Outside it was a lovely shirt-sleeves day, "another day in paradise"—the California breeze that rushed high through the treetops reminiscent of his youth. He had been glad to get away from the narrowness of the Midwest, yet at the same time he was glad that El Camino was a simulacrum of sorts to his hometown. Dick was sentimental about Cam, perhaps precisely because it was not his hometown.

S.K soon appeared, but sans Hal—something unanticipated.

"He needs to pack," she explained. "He's off to Hawaii for Thanksgiving. I'm cat-sitting Leonard. Once in the morning and once late afternoon. At ten and four."

"Can you handle it okay? They live up on Whiting, don't they?"

She looked at him more closely, skeptically, now. Did he come on to his students, too?

Would he risk his reputation, even his livelihood, just to follow her, visit her there?

"I like to walk up there, up the hills, toward the dunes, when I'm not walking in the park," he continued.

This sent a deep thrill through her, just as on that other occasion at Rec Park when he'd come across her and Hal. Was it that he was an older man? Or just the general sense of transgression? Or something else?

El Camino is truly one the hilliest towns in all of America—have I mentioned that previously? Whiting, a wider street than most as it was not part of the original city plan, is at the top of a hill and beyond the dune near the cliff that hangs out, like an airplane hanger, above, and about a half mile from, the ocean. Most who live up there can see the ocean from their house's second-floor, if they have a second, or third, floor.

The parishioners had dispersed. He liked seeing S.K. in a dress, the lavender color a nice contrast to her tan-colored skin and mink-black hair. It was a tableau, as it were: she stood under the eucalyptus tree, Library Park as backdrop. Previously, he'd pretty much only seen her in jeans, or a running outfit. (Yes he liked tough, free-range kids, but also in girls, and boys for that matter, he liked to see something of the feminine, too.)

They were joined shortly by Christina and Mya.

"Can I go with S.K. and hangout with M.K., Papa?" Mya pleaded.

Mya was very social, but she sometimes tried too hard, and had acquired a bit of a weirdo label. The two girls didn't always get along, Mya considering M.K. to be too "judgmental." But being with friends was paramount now, Mya rarely home. Dick missed seeing her more, missing as well being witness to her interaction with her friends, who also didn't come around much now. (He'd always regretted not getting to see, due to his divorce, Marie interact with her mother.)

"If it's okay with Mom, it's okay with me," he responded.

He'd scarcely had an opportunity to talk with S.K. But college did briefly come up.

"I might be able to arrange a visit at Chicago. See what your parents think."

"I will!" she responded—uncharacteristically enthusiastic.

Before parting, she spoke to Christina: "Tita, you passed the driving exam, I heard."

She had passed on the third try. It was surprising that it took three tries, considering she'd previously ridden a motorcycle, bombing around the narrow, crowded, polluted streets of her small native city in Mindinao—Mya dangerously dangling off the back like a flower.

"She had a good instructor," Dick jibed.

"But he won't ride with me!" Christina complained.

Dick was thinking he'd call Marge later about piano.

S.K. was surprised to learn her father was amenable to the idea of a visit, despite the fact that she would traveling alone and for three days. More surprised that he would send her there as a Christmas present. She had run into Dick at the Blue Butterfly a few days after the meeting at the church just before Christmas day, delivering then the news. Sometimes she went to the café to study with friends or with Hal (there was a blue butterfly preserve out near the ocean, west of LAX, where, as I've said, she'd sometimes park with Hal, but she hadn't ever seen a blue butterfly in town—they're tiny, the size of a fingernail.) At the café that day she'd been alone and so chatted Dick up about the trip. Rather breathlessly: "I can't believe it. My dad is usually so strict. Maybe because it involves college."

At Dick's request, she'd promised to "debrief" her trip upon return, although she didn't altogether understand what he meant by that. "We can meet in Manhattan Beach," he'd said, a bit mysteriously. She acknowledging meanwhile to herself that it was a sort of odd investment he appeared to have in her future, but he thoroughly understood the ins and outs of academic life and was a resource not to be overlooked. (Teens of course have such conflicting, ambivalent responses to things.)

She'd also promised to visit the Robie House. The house—home—was a few blocks from the university. She had never known what it meant to live in a house, having gone from apartments in the Philippines to the one in El Camino. The facade of the Robie House was plain yet terraced, with one cantilevered roof that winged out above the patio area—the word "cantilevered," which the tour guide, Lance, had elaborated on during the tour, new to her. The long horizontal planes of brown brick, with stone trim (brick a common feature of buildings in Cam) appealed to her, too. There was an enclosed garden and adjacent trees. The real surprise, other than the private garden in the rear, was how the "unobtrusive" entrance opened out into the unbroken flow of the interior–living area, dining room, library–though that aspect of living together in a single space she was rather too familiar with.

The hardwood floors of Lance's fifth floor place looked like leather. Young professionals moved around on the street below or at dinner in glass-front restaurants. There was a park for kids, with swings and a teeter-totter, and their voices echoed up from below. More than anything else, she was struck by the pale yellow lights–the color of a legal pad–that spread across the square, mixing generally, or so it seemed, with a late day blue light off the shore.

"It was the wine maybe" (she'd only had sips, before then, at parties) and the jazz music, like right out of a movie, and there was the way he talked about Chicago and his Midwestern niceness–so foreign yet not so foreign (she'd had a taste of it with Hal. And Dick, too). The sex happened in his small double bed, the same size of bed she shared with little M.K. Lance was a big guy and their lovemaking took up the whole bed, he both tender and forceful, at once–she had let him take her, strip off her jeans (half of sex is power). It was over overall fairly quickly.

He had pulled out quickly, suddenly, and then come outside her ("thank God"), actually above her, like he was watering a plant–but still it had been great, she had come to, for the first time in the presence of a man.

For the debriefing, Dick was to arrive early, and turned to some reading (on Federalism).

He sat on the patio, women flashing by for the most part, shopping or off to the beach. Starbucks, he felt, was the most egalitarian of American institutions, expressing key aspects of the Revolution, not the least of which was commerce. The Manhattan Starbucks was roomier, nicer than El Camino's. Dick smiled when four middle-aged Asian woman passed by lamenting the heat–they themselves laughing upon realizing that they were all wearing cashmere sweaters. Indeed the weather that day along the coast was very nice–so predictably so is the weather such that we scarcely need pay attention to it, free to concentrate on ourselves. Even if he could afford it Dick wouldn't have chosen to live in Manhattan Beach though–it was crowded, and a bit snooty. There was however a beautiful new county library, all glass, a box of light that looked out on and reflected the sea. But even then the experience of the library was tainted by the addition of three sculptures on the terrace behind it, facing toward the hills. The sculptures, the work of a local commission, were truly horrible, he claimed–I haven't seen them–apparently the worst of them a monumental blue and gold steel sailboat sculpture, rivaled by that of a fanned- out pelican representation. (The third was a rusted-metal fish sculpture.) He was particularly put out by these sculptures because he knew (what didn't Dick know?) that one of the founders of Manhattan Beach was, ironically, a fellow Hoosier, an Impressionist painter named Albert "Pops" Conner, who'd made his way out from Richmond, Indiana (itself an arts center) in 1887, when the coastal town was barely more than sand dunes. The experience of passing by the sculptures nearly ruined the experience of the library, Dick claimed. Do the rich, he wondered, especially the *nouveau riche*, especially perhaps in California, live so much among themselves, in a solitary social class (not counting maids) absent of diversity, that over time taste atrophies?

Taste becomes only a black BMW or accent pillows? Is there after a while a nearly complete absence of an infusion of new ideas and experiences? Dick ruminated thus, to our amusement. He feared El Camino was next. Houses were being torn down and replaced one McMansion at a time: "They build a big house, ruining the modest character of the neighborhood, and then hang an American flag outside."

But Dick also, at times, took a jaundiced view of El Camino, believing it too small and rather too middle class. He sometimes felt judged, watched there (understandably enough, as we were to learn–Mike's gambling habits also no secret).

"What's your drink?" he said to S.K. "Mine's Americano."

She smiled. It was the smile he'd first seen in our library, a closed-mouth, bemused, intelligent smile. To her, it was almost as if he'd asked, "What's yours?"

S.K. didn't know the drinks well. There were girls at school who would go to Starbucks pretty much everyday–"like white girls," they'd joke. There was no country club in El Camino–no room for one–but there was a country club set, of sorts–increasingly so.

She'd settled on a mocha.

Returning to the table, he said: "Did you have good weather?"

He knew already she had, having followed the weather in the paper each day she was gone, worried that bad weather might cause her to cross Chicago off her list. (This is as good a place as any to acknowledge that Dick himself wondered why he was so invested in S.K. attending there. Yes, he was proud of the school and his degrees. Her youth was a factor of course–she was young, unfinished, "living history," as it were. It is always fun to watch human growth. But other or deeper reasons for his interest had so far eluded him. Even his voyeurism didn't seem to fully account for it.)

S.K was smiling inside now. How exciting and pleasurable the big so far unsaid event had been (after a certain discomfort).

"The Robie House was cool," she offered.

"Yes, it's wonderful, isn't it."

"Did you notice there are no billboards in the city?" he asked. She had seemed to drift off.

"Now that you mention it."

She hadn't noticed, but now in her mind's eye she could see it. From now on Chicago would be a reference point.

"The tour guide was a student in the architecture school. Enamored of Louis Sullivan.'"

"He doesn't like Wright?"

"Yeah, Wright too. But he seemed to think Sullivan deserved more credit than he'd received."

"I think he's right there. ...Or Frank Lloyd Wright there. Or right behind."

S.K. smiled. "You mean close behind."

Dick enjoyed S.K.'s intellect and wit. Christina lacked knowledge of artistic movements and social issues. She hadn't even had a TV growing up. She had grown up on a farm, only her older brothers for playmates. However, her being a farm girl was also part of her appeal.

"Then he invited me to go to Spring Green." S.K looked down. She wasn't a shy girl, but at that moment she was.

"Just like that?"

She looked up. "You didn't tell me people are different in Chicago. So friendly!"

"They are, but not normally like that. You didn't go, I trust?"

"Not to Spring Green."

Dick took a closer look at S.K., this young but clever girl. "And?"

"I'd gone to hear music in the Blues Quarter the night before. I think it affected my judgment!"

We can say Dick was nonplused. She couldn't mean anything other.

"You?"

"Yes."

She recalled how she'd moaned, "Yes, Yes," with Lance. Now it was all like a dream. She'd scarcely visited on campus.

"Your first time?" asked Dick.

She laughed narrowly, reportedly. She hadn't wanted her first to be a high school boy—perhaps because everyone at school, Hal included, expected it, as if she had no more imagination than that.

"You're okay with it?"

"I'm good."

Privately Dick shook his head in amazement. It was like he had sent her on some sort of errand, or mission—as if his hand had guided her somehow.

"You won't tell, will you?" S.K. said, almost pleading.

"Who would I tell?"

S.K. sipped her frap. "Your wife? Then it might somehow get to my mother. Filipinos gossip. They don't talk about their own family, but they talk about other people's families. My parents would kill me."

Somewhere between helping each other and being rivals a lot does get said among Filipinos. A lot of feelings get hurt. The mouths of Filipinos move like chicken butts, he recalled Christina saying. (But of course Filipinos are scarcely the sole purveyors of gossip.)

"It's different for us," S.K. continued. "Our parents love us, but they love us for performing well. For representing the family well. Not for being ourselves. That's why they're always taking pictures."

"The pictures aren't of you?"

"Of our best selves only."

He thought there was some truth in her observation. Pictures of a child's accomplishment was quickly posted on Facebook. The picture, though once removed from the actual, was somehow the greater reality. Asians generally, he felt, tended to want to display their success publicly in a manner not in line with the prescriptions of his own upbringing. Although in other respects the deep concern for public image was not so very different than his Midwestern heritage (or my Buffalo one, for that matter), basically a belief that one's standing in the community matters. And hadn't his own mother encouraged him to push forward. To always put the best foot forward.

"It will be our secret," Dick assured S.K., in reference to her new status.

"Thank you." She took him at his word.

"It's not my business anyway," he added.

But truth was, now that it had happened it was impossible for him as much as he tried to not make something out of it, to think of it as just a random event unrelated to his life. He couldn't–or wouldn't be able–to think of it as just one more girl losing her virginity, as much as it was, in itself, just that.

III

MEANWHILE CHRISTINA WAS wanting to see snow. Dick already believing he'd more or less wasted the first day of his Christmas vacation—waiting at the Philippines Consulate as she renewed her passport—and also that she'd strategically made her request once she'd already secured the passport chore out of him. She wanted to see snow even though she'd seen it the previous winter, if for the first time—a first for Mya, too—in Big Bear. It was such a simple wish wanting to see the snow—absurdly simple to his way of thinking to be almost profound. Christina was basically simple, having interests but not what he considered to be intellectual interests. She had a deep love for nature. A silver sunset at the far horizon of the ocean was beautiful, snow tinged with blue arguably even more beautiful, but Dick held the opinion that nature lacked any intrinsic meaning—unlike culture, which took on the meaning of its time and place and thus was universal (this a bit over our heads).

More broadly, Dick claimed marriage itself was but a series of demands, mostly women placing on men (we demurring this time). And even as Dick acknowledged male sexual demands, he argued that ours decrease over time, increasing theirs which are already increasing—another demand.

Dinner on the table?

They like to cook, or they use it, or rearranging the furniture, as a release the way we use alcohol or sports—Frank interjecting, half-jokingly, some people just shouldn't be married. Mike that them cooking was a good thing whereas our drinking not so much.

Dick said: "I suppose Christmas is getting to me. Something is. It's basically masochism, modern Christmas is. We've been bad all year ('Speak for yourself') and so punish ourselves, with Christmas."

Does anyone stop to enjoy it, he asked? With all that shopping and all those memories of other Christmases?"

At the table there was a push. No one had both pairs. Big Mike dealt another card. Dick downed his beer. Frank was drinking whiskey. Big Mike nothing. I don't drink. The receding afternoon sun was like water, I'd noticed.

She'd apparently gone with Maribelle to Big Bear, Mya going along, too, the snow level unusually low at the time.

"But the reason I bring it up—keep this between us," Dick said, "is that our argument was so bad, not just about seeing the snow of course—though later I adjudged that Christina, not only as a nature girl but also as a visual artist, had probably a very deep need to see snow, even though she'd already seen it—but also about her claim that she'd never been anywhere, that I never took her anywhere."

If she had her druthers, they would camp and travel—and she looked long-ingly, he knew, at the weekend bonfires on Dockweiler Beach (Mexican families for the most part). There'd been a time, in his childhood, when Dick too had lamented the indoor hours and spent whatever time he could in Happy Hollow with friends (often coming across arrowheads), or playing sports—"You were so rough and ready," his mother once saying, he wondering to this day what had happened.

He'd reminded Christina however that if not for him she would have never seen America.

But even the bit about not going anywhere wasn't, he thought, at the heart of the argument. It's no fun being married to a scholar a little closer to the truth. As for his part, I think it was already, too, the matter of S.K. (who herself had never seen snow).

Frank, the Southern gentleman, suggested Dick might regret saying more things about his marriage.

"My mother," Dick said (cracking open another beer), "one time got drunk at Christmas."

He and his brothers were already in high school so it wasn't like she was doing something really mean—but apparently she walked through the dark liv-ingroom holding a candle, the room lit otherwise only by the tinsel since the

Christmas tree lights were off, walked around saying "Santa Claus is dead! Santa Claus is dead!"

Dick said how many Christmases had his parents pretended for the bene-fit of the kids–his brothers and him–that everything was alright? "Just think about families who know they are getting a divorce but pretend through Christmas, and maybe New Years, so they don't ruin it for the kids. Or may-be one of the two parents knows she's going to seek a divorce, maybe she has already filed, and pretends for the sake of the kids–even for the sake of the spouse, not wanting to ruin *his* Christmas. My first wife had sex with me the night before she had delivered to my office at the college, on Valentine's Day no less, divorce papers. The thing that really gets me, that gets me all these Christmases and Valentines later is on that night when we had sex she let me do it anally, which is something I like to do, on occasion, but she didn't like. She offered up her butthole one last time knowing that it was the last time for anything!"

He wondered if she enjoyed the sex that night. Couldn't recall if she came. Probably not, since it was anal. He thought it was probably an insult more than anything else.

"Think of Mya," Frank cajoled.

"She's eleven."

"Christmas is still very important to her."

"I haven't bought a tree yet."

"No tree?" Big Mike said.

"Some people don't."

"Even some Jews get one." I said. But I didn't think Dick capable of an act of sadism, if that's what you could say not getting a Christmas tree was. I offered to drive him, help him. "They're cheap right now," I joked. "Even an ugly, scraggly tree is better than none at all."

He had, we learned later, walked by the Boy Scout House, near the park (the Scout House tree lot began in the 1950s, according to Tom Shanks, co-chair of the tree-lot committee). They sold blue spruces, no less, but were already sold out. Their prices weren't great but people felt they were making a donation to the Scouts.

It was a dark, deep, drizzly night, a Dec. 23. Earlier in the week, the rain had been harder, like medicine coming down, everything nearly brought to halt. (Although Dick and I had kept to our usual Thursday happy hour at Tex-Mex; our two umbrellas stuck in the corner next to each other like a pair of slain pheasants).

The darkness in town is standard, due to the sparse array of street lights and the absence of starlight, which Los Angeles, which seems far away but isn't, blanches with its lights. Dick, who didn't want to drink anything more as he was thinking of driving across Sepulveda to Home Deport for a tree, was sitting in Starbucks. He almost always had a book in his back pocket and that night it was Alain-Fournier's *The Wanderer.* He'd read the book some twenty-five years earlier and sometimes would tell people it was his favorite novel, or his favorite novel of adolescence, but most people hadn't heard of it, and in any case he had read it only that once. Had he been afraid of being disappointed upon reread-ing it? A few years earlier he'd bought a translation he didn't like and stopped reading after twenty pages or so—though he was left wondering if the problem was with the translation or the novel. Now he was reading the translation he'd first read as barely more than an adolescent himself. (Christina had said she was astonished he could read in Starbucks. She said when you were in a café in the Philippines you were always worried about your things being stolen or some such occurrence.)

But he left off reading. He was enjoying the book so much he didn't want to devour it.

Mya, who now had her own cell phone, had called to see where he was, un-derstandably worried since he hadn't come home for dinner.

The drive through the rain felt cleansing. He preferred rain to snow. Rain had sound, reminded you of where you were. The question is, not what I am do-ing here, Dick believed, but what am I doing here right now.

The attendant at Home Depot was an Hispanic youth, maybe seventeen. "We started with a couple of hundred trees," he said. "Now we've got only these two."

Due to hour, the date, and the rain, no one else was shopping for a tree. It seemed a forlorn place, as though Christmas was already over, the horse race already run. Not even a spotlight shone on the two trees. They seemed mere silhouettes. Dick had floated the idea—to Mya not Christina—of an artificial tree but Mya had objected, vigorously.

The boy was slight, about the same shade of light brown as Mya—and S.K. (though Asians even brown ones have a yellow tinge, I've noticed)—rather nondescript otherwise. Friendly though. And it was a job to him, a job he was probably happy to have no matter how cold and rainy it was that night. Dick felt Hispanics, especially those recent of Mexico, tended to lack a strong education ethic. The males especially were told to get a job and support the family, whether as a son or a young husband and father. They did seem to have a strong work ethic. But he didn't know really, from the inside, how deep it went. He'd had, however, a peek at Filipino culture, and they had much in common with Hispanic, including a love of food and fun and alcohol and family, right down to Catholicism and, to varying degrees, Spanish roots. In his visit to the Philippines Dick had seen how the proverbial "other half" lived. He remembered that he couldn't face, for instance, a cold bath so had had Christina heat some water in a kettle.

He still wasn't sure he should buy a tree. Was all the pretense, sham, really good in the long run? Was it not part of the masochism? But with the rain—a bit heavier, turning from a drizzle to something more intentional-seeming—and the hour, and the date, it was time to shit or get off the pot (that metaphor coming to him even though it didn't quite fit). Besides, the attendant was presenting things as a choice of trees, a simple choice between two trees, not between a tree and nothing, or between rain and snow.

PART TWO

I

THEN THE UNEXPECTED befell the little group that is the subject of this chronicle. All hopes of S.K. attending Chicago–Dick still in the dark at that time–had been suddenly and cruelly dashed; more importantly her general sense of happiness (sexual satisfaction) and sense of freedom was impacted. Would the words of her father ever truly sink in? It had all come out of left field. A huge hole was blown open in her life. Meanwhile other words, words she had often heard–"illegals," "undocumented," "alien"–filled in the spaces. Could it be so? Were all those birthdays really for some other girl?

She thought it almost a blessing there being so little time right then, there in the kitchen, for discussion, as her dad needed to get to work and she to band practice. Had he chosen that moment to tell her because there was at that moment so little chance for discussion? (Her need to get to band, as if nothing had happened, made her think of "The Metamorphosis," the Kafka story they'd read in AP English, how Gregor, despite being turned into a bug, was primarily concerned with finding a way to make it to work, and to make it on time).

"Why didn't you tell me before now, Dad?" she wanted to know.

"I meant to."

"Then why?"

"Maybe I thought some miracle would happen," he said, pausing a moment beside the refrigerator before leaving the room.

Oh my god! it did, Dad, S.K. said to herself, off-topic, rather bitterly–if losing her virginity could be considered such a thing, a miracle–but of course it was not the kind of thing she could bring up with him, then or later. And it wasn't, sex wasn't, as important now as it had been just moments earlier (how totally funny to think she was in Chicago at that time under a false identity–as newly minted American girl).

Certain pieces of her past did suddenly coalesce–the slap and warning in middle school, for instance. She understood now–at least to some extent–why she been left with her aunt and uncle when her father and mother immigrated, her mind swimming back to that year. Two visual pictures came to mind: the lush tropical greenness of their place in the mountains, and the unremitting poverty. The two-toned sound of the bubbling river the main aural memory. Her aunt and uncle and her cousins led rather truncated lives, the conditions and circumstances difficult, which she'd got a taste of that year in the forest–and now perhaps would taste once more! S.K. had worked hard, studied so hard, spent four years since her arrival in the U.S. assimilating, achieving–and now she feared she was to once more be outcast, she was on the outside looking in–yes, "undocumented," "illegal," "alien." A ghost–ghosts something her superstitious relatives always feared. But why was she illegal and not M.K., who likewise was born in Manilla? S.K. stopping herself from asking her dad, right then, fearing the answer.

She went off to band, needing if nothing else a distraction, unable as well to think of any other action to take at the moment. She merely had to cross the street to get to the high. The marine layer was in, the football field dewy–almost ghostly. S.K felt helplessly alone with her secret, but she was determined to keep knowledge of her new status private (an un-Filipino-like gesture). Marching band had been a key part of her identity and she would try to trust in the possibility of continuing in the same fashion as she had previously–dismissing as some do, when a virus attacks the likely truth that life would never return to normal, believing the virus will miraculously disappear, that from such a nightmare they will wake, or even that there has been just some sort of mistake.

The fact that she was perhaps not an entirely unique case, even in our small, mostly white town didn't cross her mind, nor would it have made her feel better, understandably. But if there were any at the high school in the same boat, they too would most probably be Asian, as there were few Latinos west of Sepulveda–only two in the marching band. (We might here add that it is just the sort of challenge S.K. now faced that generally brings out the best in people, and we had faith in her. One might even go so far as to say that in losing one's self, in becoming a stranger to one's self, one may find a deeper self, as Christ teaches.)

She was happy not to run into Hal in the band room. She didn't want to break down, a definite risk should she stand near to him, look in his eyes. The only person in the room as it turned out was a lone trombonist, a freshman male, a fat kid, who'd she never spoken to but knew was a good player. He could make his trombone talk. Never had she come across a female trombonist though she knew of course that they did exist. Everyone else was already gone out to the field. Once on the football field herself, S.K. tried her best to concentrate on the music, on movements and formations—on such configurations she had performed so many times and often found sustaining joy in. There was nothing quite like belonging to a group, a company.

Of course she could hardly avoid Hal altogether—nor did she want to, however hard proximity would make keeping to her resolve. She was already, once again, scheduled to watch Leonard. For $100 a week, money she needed—and no doubt would more so now. Hal was going to Ireland for two weeks with his family at Christmas (they were always off to some exotic locale or another). She had agreed to meet him that evening at The Plunge, after his swim—and her run—at which point they planned to go to the library, something she felt it would look awkward, even suspicious, to try and avoid.

But would he want her if she were illegal? What about his parents? There were just so many questions to consider now. His parents were way conservative, like so many in "Don't Tread on Me" El Camino.

We know too she felt she bore some responsibility for the situation, even though of course she shouldn't have felt thus. (Yet how often children, of divorce, for example, harbor such thoughts.) She even felt that somehow she'd let her family down.

Unaccountably, Hal was not there when she arrived back. She saw it was past seven, their usual meeting hour—her run had taken longer than it generally did somehow—and the pool was now empty—eerily so—light whipping snakelike on the roof, the high windows on each side already gone dark. Yet at the same time it was oddly comforting, the solitary pool, the ghostly, dark otherworldliness.

Some sort of repressed childhood memory related to her origins appeared to have prepared the ground for such loneliness.

Maybe Hal had gone to the library, but there was no response to her text. She herself would generally shower at the pool, after her run, and she had decided she would do so as usual this day—but then the obvious occurred to her. He was already in the shower, the Men's. S.K. smiled at the thought of surprising him—it was a bit risky, of course, in case someone else was in there, too, yet she felt there was less to lose now anyhow.

So it was, we know, that she rather fatefully walked down the (rather slick) concrete ramp to the Men's and peeked hesitantly (or so we might imagine) around the corner of the door.

"Hal? Hally? You there?"

It was not Hal but rather Dick, our Dick Starling, poker-game partner, who was in there.

"Tots, sorry. Sorry," S.K. was heard, gasping. She ran, a third "Sorry" echoing in the hallway as if the sound itself were chasing her. "OMG, what will he think?" Then rhetorically: "What else could possibly happen to me?"

There was additionally the question of what had she seen? She wasn't in fact totally sure.

He'd been suitless. Had he turned around? Had she seen his "dick"? She thought not. It was almost amusing. He had called out, "Haven't seen him. Hal." She was pretty sure she'd heard a chuckle, too, or the distorted echo of one.

Nonetheless, S.K intended to shower—Hal might be waiting at the library—but as it happened, before she had a chance to strip down, in the Women's, a voice called down to her. But this time it was neither Hal's nor Dick's.

"Miss? Miss? I've got to lock up."

Everybody knows Smiley.

"I'll be right out."

Dick waited for her topside. Curious, for one thing, to see her new haircut, which he'd caught a glimpse of in the shower.

S.K., as it happens, had cut off her long, straight, black hair which she'd worn the same almost her entire life—done so in response to the immigration news, I guess. A kind of punishment if also a new lease on life. She was to appear before Dick once again sweaty and disheveled—and now sporting what can only be called "a boy's haircut." Or, a swimmer's.

"Like the Roaring Twenties," he said. "I like it."

"Thanks."

She'd read *Gatsby*.

"Is everything okay?"

"Everything?" Did he somehow know about immigration?

"I mean Hal? You expected to meet him here, that's what Smiley said."

"He texted." That was a lie, but it was in keeping with her new resolution not to spill the beans. Finding Dick at the pool was unexpected (she'd begun to wonder if luck had indeed turned against her). Her sister's swim season was over and S.K. had not come across him otherwise at the pool. And when did he speak to Smiley?

"You're okay to walk home?"

"I'm going to the library."

"Oh."

The library is only a half a block from The Plunge. To Dick, S.K. seemed now a bit distant, cool again, almost like the old S.K., before they had befriended each other. Maybe it was because of what had happened in the shower, he speculated—it had been fun for him but maybe embarrassing for her (the blame falling on her).

But she turned and waved as she left—tenderly, even softly, innocently, or so it seemed to him.

Hal meantime was nowhere to be seen, wasn't even answering texts. S K. ran not merely walked home. She wanted a shower and quickly dropped her running outfit on the bathroom floor—I imagine her standing there before the mirror forlorn as a striped stalk of corn. She got under the hot water, making it, the water, a few degrees hotter than usual for good measure, the steam rising hot-springs-like off the contours of her body.

In the shower, both what she'd seen at the pool and her new life status, or the one in the context of the other, was to suddenly hit her with full force. She'd seen Dick naked, that in itself was something, but also, she'd had an inspiration, or what she was to take for one. S.K was not the type to marry someone for reasons of convenience, we know that—she felt she could make her own way in the world–but, that being said, she would most likely do what most others would do in similar circumstances. Get pregnant, as a way to stay in the country. It probably would prove necessary–her mind was swimming quickly forward now–to give the baby up for adoption. That would be hard, blasphemous, but what was necessary was necessary. She was not Filipino for nothing.

S.K. was thinking, too, that there was not only Hal, and possibly Lance to consider, but also–she just couldn't prevent herself from thinking it–perhaps Dick as an option, even if he were, as he was, married. Wasn't he a fine specimen of a man? She knew that fact even more now–and so as she washed she found herself reviewing the situation, thinking about his attributes. Obviously he was intelligent, he was tall and fit, was white, all things that recommended him to her. Dick, she pushed further, had a biological daughter, evidence that he could have children. Taking in the balance everything about him, and about Hal and Lance, Dick gained stature (comparison a primary mode for decision making).

Not that S.K was totally unaware of how strange and generally appalling it was to be thinking as she presently was. Suspect as well was that the harried baby-daddy thoughts had come upon her so quickly. Could she really be thinking about having a child, even with the idea of adoption–or especially with the idea of adoption? Perhaps she wasn't handling the new knowledge of her immigration status that well–but who could blame her? It was so new, novel. She was only seventeen. When you're seventeen everything is dire, even for someone as level- headed as S.K. And in any case, in this case, it was serious business.

"S.K., you're wasting water," her father called in.

"Okay." She shut it off.

II

THE FIRST THING to go—other than her long hair—was running. She missed being at the shore at twilight, and of at the end of her run turning back toward town to see, in the marine blue sky, a half dozen planes or so floating seemingly stationary like ships in a second sea. But to her surprise didn't much miss running itself. It seemed almost an affectation now. Her mother's fears of darker skin and missed periods also assuaged. Hal had asked about her defection, and she'd said simply, "I don't want to run cross country anymore" (not her country).

Hanging with Hal the other night, she hadn't even wanted to park, begging off as best as she could.

"But I'm leaving Monday for two weeks," he'd protested.

"We'll take care of it one way or another before you leave."

"Take care of it?"

"Yeah."

"How many ways are there exactly by your estimate, K?"

"There's phone sex. We haven't tried that!" she retorted.

She no longer went to the library. She often didn't respond to texts from her friends, which everyone took as total weirdness, Judy, her best friend, particularly hurt and confused. However on a Friday at the end of the school day she'd run into Judy and Hal as they were coming out of chemistry.

"Come on, K," Hal said, "Judy wants ice cream. Cold Stone."

"We all scream," Judy put in.

They took Hal's car, a black "Beamer" passed down from his father. It was a hot car but small and called for gymnastics when they parked (his groans usually drowned out by the planes overhead.) Judy reached from the back seat and turned up the music, blasted it, something simply not okay in El Camino. When some outsider would drive through with rap thumping, heads would turn, a federal case made out of it. S.K. turned the music down a bit, almost reflexively.

"I beg your pardon, girl," Judy joked.

"Dude, start begging," said S.K., with a bit of an edge.

"I think I'm the one who has to beg," said Hal, in front of Judy.

S.K. did at last do it with Hal, was fucked royally by him, by all accounts. "At last," we say, because S.K. and Hal had come so close to doing it many times previously. It turned out to be a different experience than she'd imagined it would be the first time—first time with him, that is. While less romantic, it was oddly powerful, or more powerful than it had been with Lance (she lacked a wider basis of comparison). In the context of her and Hal's recent quarrels, it was of course make-up sex. But S.K. attributed the difference from her expectations regarding it, and also the experience with Lance, largely to her strong feelings for Hal, as well as to her feelings for Hal in conjunction with the possibility that they were—sans protection—making a baby. Their baby. Who would have thought that baby-making sex would be such a powerful elixir? Perhaps Dick figured in the equation as well.

One wonders if Hal got the fact that she wasn't a virgin. (In any case, the prospect of another generation of El Camino Flynns was cheering, to us.)

She'd received a text from Hal upon his landing in Ireland. She was at his house cleaning the catbox when the text came through.

"Missing you. Haven't seen a leprechaun (or anyone who looks like a ghost of you), so I guess we are in the clear, Love," it read.

Perhaps he'd been drinking when he wrote it, S.K. ventured. To say that the message was cryptic, if not simply random, would not be saying too much. Judy was out of town too for the holidays or S.K. might have seen if Judy could make heads or tails of it. Of course S.K. knew she could simply text Hal back: "Say what?" But she was half afraid to do so—for reasons, or half- reasons, she couldn't fully identify. Was it that upon fucking him, her interest in him had diminished a little? Already she was nostalgic for the solemn innocence of their experimenting days.

There *was* Dick, but certainly she couldn't ask him, his superior close-reading skills notwithstanding. What anyway did it have to do with him and why should he have any idea what the text meant, even if she were to reveal, to him, that she'd had sex with Hal?

But at three on the same afternoon that S.K. had heard from Hal, the sunlight spreading like butter across the top of the bluff ahead of Dick, the windswept trees oddly two-dimensional against the sky above, he had set out for Hal's parents' place. Of course he needed a pretext for stopping by to see her. He'd honestly always be intrigued by the Flynn Craftsman. His own was built in 1936, as mentioned previously; theirs in 1925. His was a modest bungalow and the Flynns a large American Craftsman. He had an old brown couch on his porch. Theirs had a swing, the house being inherited from the father's side of the family. Dick had purchased his fifteen years earlier, after being hired at the college (Dick a Ph.D.–Chicago–at twenty-five). His had seen two of his wives–and a daughter and a stepdaughter (his Irish Catholic grandfather–never met–married four times, Dick joking that he was thankful to be "a quarter Irish".) The Flynn's house had served three generations.

It was warm for December. The great pleasure of a hill town is the sudden appearance on the horizon of an unseen steeple or house, and almost as fun its disappearance upon ascent or descent, as the case may be. That day, if Dick were to have kept going straight, he would have run into sand dunes, and then, beyond the high tension wires, across the roadway, come upon the sea–that sea that he'd crossed in order to visit the Philippines, to meet Christina four years prior, ironically. Twice he'd visited there, first in Cebu, and then later Christina's rural Mindanao.

Almost immediately, in Cebu, he'd sensed something amiss. But he found himself unable to put his finger on it as first. The three of them, Mya six at the time, had taken a trip to a resort on the shore, whence it hit him: the women weren't showing any skin–even flat young girls sporting t- shirts. When he ventured a year later, along with Christina's three brothers and Nenita, their mother, up to the hot springs of Mt. Apu–second highest volcano in the world, did you know that?–it was a similar story. (At the same time there's a thriving sex economy in Manila, a paradox Dick wrestled with.)

Perhaps his living so close to LAX had provoked the adventure in the first place.

S.K, enjoying the open space, the luxurious home, spent more time there than was required by her duties. It was a fairly steep climb for Dick, four blocks up the hill, an armada of white clouds overhead. But he walked at a brisk, determined pace, sweating, houses seeming to slide by each side of him. He generally felt invigorated. Was that S.K.'s silhouette there in the house? It could hardly be anyone else's, but the bright, now near-blinding thin light from the west caused her figure to appear (not unlike the trees), etched, abstract–like an Oriental painting, but a living one.

He waved. She cautioned herself, again, against telling him of her newest exploit, or of immigration issues. Certainly it would be enjoyable to replay for him the sex, to be in the same room, the same house–in Hal's house!–with Dick, thinking about this new experience with Hal, and the other one, with Lance (she was double-fucked now). But perhaps Dick would think her a slut.

He wore blue jeans and a t-shirt, looking like a teenager, if a stalwart one. He, too, was hoping to keep control of himself. If he thought about it, and he was almost forced to now, he had always had a second interest, another desire, when he was involved with someone; he was never, except perhaps for when he was young and first encountering love and was totally focused on one person and mad about them...but even then it was brief and not complete, he recalled.

"Come in, come in," S.K. said. She'd almost called him "Tito."

He hesitated. Wiped a droplet of sweat from his chin. "Wouldn't want to violate any house rules, stated or unstated."

"Because of your love of houses?"

The ceiling in the kitchen was lower than in the rest of the house, just as it was in his own, the architect's desire being to make people aware of the space, and spaces, they entered. Theirs, like his, featured corner windows.

"Have a beer. House rules," S.K. boldly insisted. If she were going to have sex with Dick, this was her opportunity. "I'll find an opener."

But it was twist off. He learned against the porcelain counter. "Cat treating you well?"

She laughed. Dick was his general charming, dry self. Had she noticed before how long his neck was, especially compared to her fellow Filipinos?

"I don't like cats. Dogs. In the Philippines I had a dog," she said.

"I hated seeing the way they were treated there, chained up all day long."

"They're guard dogs."

"I know. Funny, even a dog's life is not the same place to place."

"I treated Pilo well. Took him for walks."

(Dick recalled all the barking dogs that had plagued him when he'd briefly lived in Hollywood–Hollywood not what people imagine it to be, if not as seedy as formerly.)

The Flynn house was the second house he'd been in with S.K.–the second Craftsman, too. She had briefly one day come over to his place with her mother. It just so happened that she came over on a day, a Saturday, in which the paperman, a Hispanic who lived on the East Side (men now doing boy's jobs), had unaccountably delivered the same paper for a second day in a row.

"Look at this, will you?" he'd said holding up the two copies, "Friday's paper delivered twice." They perhaps found it not so astonishing as did he.

"I told him he should report it, but he's curious to see if it will happen again tomorrow," Christina put in. She had come down from the shower, black strands of her hair having left wet imprints on her robe.

Dick had been a paperboy in Indiana, every paper strictly accounted for, the stack smelling of fresh newsprint and tightly bound with twine, which he would cut with a pocket knife. Sometimes folks would forget to put a "stop" on their paper, should they be gone for vacation, and the papers, the slap on the concrete serving notice each day, would pile up on their front porch or steps as if at an abandoned house. What was he supposed to do about that? It was difficult to think of another job with complaints so built into it.

He was counting up the places he'd now been with S.K.: the library, the park, the Methodist church, the pool, two different coffee shops, two houses. As for her, she might be inclined to add how a sense of his presence had also definitely colored her Robie House tour. Both of our protagonists were now feeling the thrill, the power of being together in a lived-in house, in their shared town, our town, a house that excitedly wasn't either of theirs, and also because it was Hal's house. And also perhaps because it was temporarily vacant and they felt the thrill of trespassing.

There were three bedrooms: the parents, Hal's, a guest room. S.K. felt she should use the guest room not Hal's room for sex, if there were to be sex. Even more so than to Hal, she felt she was being unfair to Dick in not revealing her motive, beyond the feelings she had for him.

(She'd gradually come to admit to herself: she liked him, and not just as a friend, she told me later.)

Along with feeding the cat, and cleaning the litter box, she had to make sure Leonard didn't get out. It was a large calico Tabby, about the same coloring as Hal, comically.

Hal had been eager and powerful; Lance forceful and expert, and also tender. Had she been different with each of them? She couldn't say. With Lance she'd thought of herself as an American, if an alien in Chi-town; with Hal, no longer an American, but still an El Caminoian.

Not that she could tell exactly how this difference played out in her performance—or even in her feelings. Both "experiences" had been real and unreal in multiple ways. She wondered what knowledge of Dick—sexual knowledge—would contribute to the mix, what might get highlighted, should she have him.

When they got to Hal's bedroom, the last of the tour, so to speak, Dick and S.K. acknowledged each other in ways they previously hadn't. Hal's room was minimalist, the decor green, perhaps a nod to his Irish heritage. The furniture was modern. The bed, well, was the elephant in the room.

"What to go for a swim?" Dick suddenly suggested.

It took her aback, it was so not what she'd expected, or generally fantasized.

"The Plunge?"

"No, the ocean."

"I'm not a good swimmer. Besides, it's December."

"The water's not that cold yet. It will be fun."

Still, she was hesitant.

"What will I use for a suit?"

"Just go in your shorts. I'll borrow a suit of Hal's."

"You would do that?"

"Better that than his bed."

This also took her aback.

"I don't get you. You just didn't happen to be passing by."

"What you're referencing is a big step. You might regret it, afterward. And for me, if not for you, it's illegal. Isn't that funny? The person on the top might be legal while the person on the bottom illegal. Or vice-y verse-y."

She laughed. S.K. was close to confessing everything. Especially with the word *illegal* in the air.

"A swim then?" he continued. "Before the sun goes down."

"Let me pee first."

She closed the bathroom door. "Doesn't he want me?" The thought depressed her.

Dick tried on the trunks she had provided him. Our boys, the kids, wear long, patterned trunks, while our girls generally, like girls everywhere, wear skimpy bikinis. Our local boys, many of them, will even shave off most if not all their body hair, which the girls apparently encourage. Is it a masculine gesture, a feminine one, a metrosexual one? It didn't escape Dick's mind that Hal too was a swimmer—and reportedly a good one. He'd qualified for State during the fall. The trunks were a tight fit.

Minutes later, the two were walking toward the ocean, up the dunes (as a child he'd gotten lost in the Indiana Dunes when his grandfather had let go of his hand). Down the other side was El Camino Beach, the sea's horizon red at the moment, as if a battleship were going down.

Dick had taken a beer along to drink as they walked. She carried her cell phone.

"Now I've got to pee," he said, as they neared the road.

"Go ahead," S.K. said. "I've already seen your butt!"

"That's all?"

"I wasn't quite sure what I saw that day."

"Well, it was only the second or third one you'd ever seen, right?"

He could see her blushing now, dark skin-color or not. They were stopped, for him to pee.

He turned his back to her. He had a view of the alligator back that was Palos Verdes.

"Third. I had sex with Hal." Yes, she'd blurted it out, that part. We don't know why then and there. Maybe it was the intimacy, maybe the landscape and the sea, maybe just the natural progression of their relations, hers and Dick's. And he had his back to her. "Sunday. Before he left," she continued. "Do you think there is something wrong with me?"

Finished, he turned around. "Truth is, I don't know you that well, S.K. I like you but I hardly know you—unless thinking about you a lot is knowing you. But I don't think what you did with Hal is strange, or wrong—if nonetheless rather striking coming so soon after the other one. Hal is your boyfriend, right?"

She took this to be a rhetorical question.

"There's something I'm missing? Something more you want to tell me?" he continued.

But it was unfair to dump the whole thing on him. "Let's swim," she said, trying to sound cheerful. The despair, a despair born in part out of having gotten so close to happiness, now circled back to her.

"Yes. Race you," Dick said.

She took off ahead of him. She was, at least at this point in their lives, faster. The beach was virtually abandoned, the sky almost dark. It was generally the time of day when she'd used to go for her run. Only at the far horizon of the federal blue water was there light to speak of. The ocean grew louder as they approached. The waves shimmied. And the hint of salt, now revealed, filled their nostrils.

S.K. removed her top, and was bare-chested (her breasts the color of tangerines), but she'd kept on her shorts. "I'm going in," she shouted.

Thursday, in our weekly, *The Herald*, there was no mention of Dick's heroics, to his relief, no doubt. But by the weekend the story had spread—apparently due to the paramedics—and Dick was being hailed, in *The Daily Breeze*, as having saved S.K.'s life. The article detailed her strange antics, the inexplicable decision to swim out and keep swimming, and how Dick, who it was thought just "happened" to be at the beach, had swum out to save her. And also how lucky it was that he was such a strong swimmer—even his early days competing in high school and college were mentioned, ironically. He'd given her CPR. And then, with her cell phone which she'd left in the sand, called for help. He wasn't carrying one, a cell phone. The fact that she wasn't wearing a bathing suit contributed to the rumor, increasingly circulated, that she had been there not to swim but to commit suicide. No one had thought to ask if he was wearing his own bathing suit. Surprisingly so, since everyone knows our little Mayberry by the Sea is also a regular Peyton Place.

III

IRONICALLY, CHRISTINA HAD been preoccupied with the little house she was building in the Philippines. In her hometown. Progress was slow but steady. She would show Dick pictures of the house, ask his advice at times I understand, and generally keep him abreast of developments. But she was using her own money, not wanting to further burden him, who seemed unduly burdened, though due to what she was unsure—he'd said little to her. He tended to be old school when it came to masculinity she'd discovered, not macho exactly, just reticent. She'd learned it had also something to do with growing up in the rural Midwest, a place she'd never been of course.

He was to return to the Midwest, to Indiana, a little over a month after the beach incident, for sadly his father's funeral, to fly into Chicago and drive down in a rental. His dad was buried that wintry day next to Dick's mother in a Navy cemetery—the sadness of her passing also hitting him hard that day. But she had died, abruptly, many years earlier, in fact soon after his post-grad- school move west—there being however no link at all between the two, I'd learned, even if Dick couldn't always convince himself of that. It turned out to be a very cold day for the funeral, trees half-bare, the brown leaves like rags. But four of his five brothers were there (one, a poet, having died rather young) and Dick en- joyed the brief time with them despite the circumstances. In part because of the circumstances.

Visiting S.K. maybe wasn't the best idea. But perhaps the old Chinese say- ing about being ever responsible for the drowning person you saved applied. On the way back from Indiana he'd hit Chicago rush hour, a piece of real estate even more crowded than the 405, and even slower due to the ice. Dick and S.K.

had shared a secret, forged a compact, an almost religious one, to not reveal the truth, any truth–athough even S.K. didn't know if she'd been intent on suicide that day (which seemed now a lifetime ago). While it was relatively safe to meet in Chicago, both also knew that any contact between them had the potential of raising more questions about the nature of their contacts. Speculation had grown since December–Hal especially skeptical. More than once, when S.K. was still in Cam, he'd brought up certain details, suggested certain contradictions. For one thing, he couldn't imagine her choosing to end her life, especially as he felt they were in love. And of course he wondered what had become of that pair of swimming trunks. But on the whole Hal had been tender, solicitous–almost as if walking on egg shells. He hadn't pressed her to have intercourse again (was it that he thought of death when he thought of her?)

She'd not discussed her desire to leave El Camino, start fresh elsewhere, with her parents or anyone else, including Judy. And so on what was a full moon night, having texted Lance, she hiked the two miles to LAX–he, as promised, there in Chicago to meet her, just as a few months earlier (O'Hare a beautiful airport, the exposed steel tubes of the archway shining in the morning light like medallions), he'd been there to see her off. "This is the first day of the rest of your life," she told herself upon that second arrival in Chicago, cliches rushing to her mind now that she was under duress ("There's more than one way to skin a cat," another).

Lance was gone at work when Dick appeared.

"Come in, come in, Dick," she said, eschewing formal address.

They hugged. That felt good, to both of them on many levels.

"I'm so sorry to hear about your dad."

"Thank you. He was great fellow. I'll miss him," Dick said.

"I know a little of what you mean. I've been missing my family."

(Not Hal, thought Dick?)

The two had yet to sit down.

"Nice apartment," Dick said. "I see his love for Louis Sullivan."

But he was actually looking more at S.K, the beauty of a woman perhaps the one thing he appreciated more than a beautiful building. Beauty such a snare, ironically.

He could see right off that she was pregnant, a baby bump visible under the tight purple v-neck sweater—sweaters so much a part of the erotics of his Midwestern youth—and also her face was now rounder, her skin shinier, her expression less remote.

They wandered into the small kitchen. "Beer? Lance likes beer. A Midwestern dude at heart, I guess."

"Oh that's his name."

"Didn't I tell you before?"

"Don't think you did."

It was thrilling to be there, for Dick, in the way it had been at Hal's house that time—before things had taken that turn for the worse. S.K., too, feeling the pull of the forbidden past.

She held out the beer. "Twist off!"

Dick drank. "Hits the spot. I don't guess you're in any condition to join me?"

So he knew!

"I'm not eighteen until next week."

He laughed. "That's the only reason?"

The repartee—foreplay?—was fun. Christina liked long comic stories, and pratfalls, but Dick liked wit, wordplay. Yet if this was foreplay, it was a week too early. (He couldn't help but muse that a week later she would be legal in one sense but still illegal in another.)

"Sit."

S.K. sat across from him, like they were about to play cards. The deck shuffled.

"You know then, I guess. M.K. told you?"

"I know."

"You're protecting M.K.'s reputation?"

"Even at twelve years old it's important."

"You know about immigration, too?"

Even if he didn't, she was ready to tell him. After all, she was already pregnant and it was no longer necessary to keep the other from him.

"So it's true?"

"The eponymous 'undocumented.'"

"Just you? Not the rest of the family?"

"Right."

"That's strange. I wish you'd said something. I wish I'd known. It would have helped to explain certain things."

"I felt ashamed. It seemed a shameful thing. Like I was a total imposter...or intruder."

Dick had finished off his beer.

"How many months are you?"

"About three."

"Hal's?"

"I'm pretty sure. I've heard that backdating is possible, that the gestation period can be older than the act—but I know it's Hal's. He doesn't want anything to do with it though, isn't that awesome? What a loser he turned out to be."

Dick didn't say anything. Certainly Hal not wanting any part of it was part of the shame she felt.

"I wish *we* could go to bed, Dick."

He looked at her. "Bedrooms are nice...but I like kitchens, too, the way the light glances off the appliances and tiles and stuff, like at a pool. I'll have one more beer, if you have it?"

Dick didn't know if she was actually suggesting they go to bed. But there they were again, together, close to the act. After a tough weekend, he could have used a release. When had he become so cautious?

S.K. realized more deeply that she had missed him. Was it because he had saved her life? (She'd thought she'd seen her last, there under the salt sea, her eyes burning with the salt, her body suspended among the sea life—until Dick, like a different sort of fish, huge, wavy in the sunlit, sloshing water, had swum toward her.) She couldn't understand, again, him not taking her up on her offer. Was he rather more guardian angel than lover?

She had to ask at last: "You don't want me?"

"I wouldn't put it that way. I don't think it would be for the best. I'm trying hard, lately, to do what's right. The Christian thing generally, if you like."

"Oh, I didn't know you were about that."

Was he? He didn't have an answer to that.

"Another beer coming up."

"In the Methodist Church we used to only get grape juice at Communion."

Dick thought about his father. He would drag them, his six sons, to the Wesleyan Methodist Church each Sunday, each of them having shined his shoes. Each boy had a suit, with two pairs of pants. Sunday in effect was his mother's day off (she had, contrary to Catholic teachings, let her boys be raised Methodist). Dick had objected at a young age to being farmed out to the Sunday school class, so was to sit with his father, and his older brother, Bryce, in the mahogany balcony pews, peering down at the minister in his purple robes and at the shiny altar.

S.K. served the beer. She liked serving men and missed serving her father. Serving men was a way of demonstrating loyalty. Her values were similar to Victorian ones: propriety, restraint, loyalty. Or at least those were the values she was taught. As to sexual prudishness, another Victorian virtue, there was a split in the Filipino character just as there was in the Victorian.

"Has Lance taken you to Spring Green yet? I mean, in a literal sense."

"He says when the weather breaks."

"When will you tell him?"

"Soon." She sat back down.

"I saw right away."

"You were looking for it."

"What will he say?"

"Don't know. I suppose I could get away with saying it was his—at least for a while. At least until the baby is born. And maybe even after."

"The baby will make you legal."

S.K. eyed him. Was he making a judgment?

"Yeah."

He noticed it wasn't her usual "Yes."

"Where is Lance now?"

"At the Robie House."

"Can we join a tour?"

Dick thought it best to exit the apartment. One more beer and he was pretty sure he'd fuck the daylights out of S.K., pregnant of not, underage or not. (But can you be underage if you're an expectant mother?) She looked, to him, so ripe and lovely in her new state.

The two grabbed their coats. She wrapped a red scarf around her neck—having quickly learned the local tactics, he also noted.

His rental was a Buick Regal. There were more real cars in the Midwest. Thank God the President had bailed out Detroit. Thank God they had a decent President (who had cut his teeth in Chicago). But his harsh deportation policies were questionable. Dick was pretty much of two minds when it came to immigration. He felt for the families, yet he hated seeing the country change so much. He was a student of American history, knew full well that immigration was part and parcel of the American experience, but the new levels of immigration were unprecedented— and in any case, they were the first he'd experienced personally. Personal experience brought history alive even as it also altered (distorted?) it.

Transportation for S.K., and Lance, was the El. Sometimes she'd ride it just to get out of the house. She particularly liked how it snaked through the old, brownish neighborhoods, passing by the second-story apartments, the people inside cooking, showering, at leisure, etc., the rooms lit up like little theaters.

They parked a couple blocks from the Robie House. The walk in the cold carried Dick back to his college days, days when he didn't have a car. S.K. was about the age, and size, of his college girlfriend. Janey.

It had started to snow. S.K. had never seen snow prior to moving to Chicago—her family never having ventured up to Big Bear or really anywhere. Snow seemed to her to come directly down from the sky, not slanted like rain, touching everything below equally.

The center piece of the Robie House interior was, fortunately on a cold day like that, the fireplace, S.K. surprised to see it was lit.

Lance was a tall fellow, nice-looking, but with a different mug. Polish?

The fire, crackling now, was lit on special occasions, this day a meeting of the University Board of Trustees. She was to quickly hug Lance, but had felt him stiffen a little.

"This is Professor Starling, Lance. A friend of the family, from El Camino. He went to Chicago, too."

"Dick," Dick said, holding out his hand.

The three of them stood near the fire, shadows from the flames flickering on the brick wall opposite, almost ominously. But at that moment Dick felt primarily the thrill of again being inside of a Lloyd Wright building. He himself had made the pilgrimage to Spring Green many times.

S.K. tried again. "Dick was on the swim team."

Lance blinked. "Oh really."

"Many moons ago that was. Go Maroons!"

It was then Dick was to notice Lance eyeing him, in a manner not unlike had Hal recently. He'd encountered Hal at the pool, a few days after learning from M.K. that S.K. was pregnant. The two men were alone in the locker room together, our Hal sitting down, about to swim, Dick standing, done and showered (Hal's back, smooth and muscular as a violinist's). Dick at first had controlled his urge to address him.. Surely the young man knew of the child by now, and surely M.K. would not have spoken to Dick, on S.K.'s behalf, if Hal had generally been there for her, been supportive (now, of course, Dick knew this to be the case). It occurred to him, too, that day at the pool that perhaps Hal still didn't know of S.K.'s immigration issues, Dick himself only beginning to put two and two together—no doubt, Hal didn't know; S.K. must have kept that secret, knowing the recriminations would have followed fast and furious were he to find out she had slept with him primarily out of a desire to get pregnant.

Dick had dressed and was ready to leave. He had something on Hal, but also Hal possibly had something on him—for conceivably, he had figured out, as others were beginning to, including us, that it was highly improbable that Dick had been at the beach with S.K. that day by accident. Rumor had it that they were lovers. Mike believed as much, though he admitted to having no hard evidence. Yet Mike, whose on the city council, knew the cops were reviewing the incident, the matter; but he'd chosen not to warn Dick, out of disapproval of the carryings on with S.K. perhaps. One thing is indisputable though: Dick saved our S.K.'s life that day at the beach. He acted heroically.

Hal was the one, suited now (his dick like a slow-moving slug in his Speedo), who chose confrontation.

"Dr. Starling."

"Hal. I thought that was you," Dick responded.

"None other."

"For a second, from the back, I thought it could be your father." (The father, too, was a swimmer.)

"Any news of S.K., Dr. Starling?"

That time the "Dr." sounded sarcastic, aggressive. Dick looked around the clay-gray locker area to see if anyone had come in through the tunnel. He flash backed (a flashback like a flood) to S.K sneaking around the corner to surprise Hal, only to find himself instead—in all his glory. He was aware of how voices traveled there, like in a concert hall. And no one generally knew when Smiley might pop up.

"I don't know anything that I suppose you don't already know, Hal," Dick said, firmly.

"Try me?" said Hal.

Dick believed he saw Hal's salmon-colored face redden a shade or two. It would be a pleasure to throw it, the immigration issue, in that red face, but there was a value in maintaining the pretense of ignorance. The more knowledge of S.K.'s doings he were to confess to, the easier it would be to tie him to her. Still, it was odd to carry on a conversation in which the two people involved didn't acknowledge what they both knew—namely, that S.K. was pregnant, and additionally that he, Hal, was likely the father.

But he must be careful, vigilant. He was aware that Hal brought out in himself something disproportional. Some sort of rivalry for S.K., was it? Middle age against youth? Newer resident against a family of long standing, one that had made El Camino home for generations?

Competing Craftsman householders? Swimming competitors?

"I've got to go," Dick said, attempting an even tone. "I suppose we'll run into each other again. It's a small town. And swimmers are relatively a small subset."

"With its own code of honor."

"Precisely. Not to let someone drown."

"Or pull another down under the water with you when you are going down."

"Even non-swimmers like S.K. may practice that."

Dick stuck out his hand for Hal to shake and he, perhaps not knowing what else to do, took it.

"You saved S.K.'s life, I have to thank you for that," said Lance.

"She told you?"

"I did some research on my own."

S.K. looked stunned.

"I just happened to be in the right place at the right time, that's all," Dick offered, but it sounded fatuous, and falsely modest, as if he were talking about a successful career. In any case, it was a lie.

"Yes, that's what the news reports said."

"You didn't tell me you read the news reports," S.K. inserted.

Lance ignored her comment. "I'm off at four, we'll get dinner."

"I'm afraid I'm flying out in a couple of hours. But thanks, in any case."

"We thought we might follow along, if you don't mind?" S.K. suggested.

"I'm scheduled to take the board members on a tour."

"Oh, no problem. I've been here many times before. I need to hit the gift shop though."

In the fog of the funeral—and now S.K.'s situation—he'd forgotten all about his promise to bring something home for the girls. Filipinos were gift-giving people. A gift meant you cared.

S.K. joined him. "Maybe we shouldn't have met. I'm sorry," he said.

"As long as he doesn't contact anyone in Cam, no harm done. I'm happy to see you. It's a burden, isn't it, keeping a secret?"

Dick just nodded.

He found a Sears Tower key chain for Mya and a Frank Lloyd Wright pendant for Christina. He was missing the girls now.

Perhaps Christina's charms—her prayers—were working their magic. Filipino women had a way of getting what they wanted. And getting a man to help them get it, qualities he grudgingly admired.

As for S.K. and Lance, they ordered in Thai that night. Barely spoke during dinner apparently, he quickly downing two beers.

"Did you have fun with your friend?"

S.K. didn't like the insinuation, despite her half attempt to seduce Dick.

"He's more than twice my age, for God's sake. A friend of the family. Get a clue, Lance," she protested.

He was not mollified. "When were you going to tell me that you're pregnant? I've been waiting, you know. It's either your professor or Hal."

S.K. gulped. How long had he known? Also thinking: Shouldn't I do the right thing by him, he who had taken her in when she needed someone? Could she do the right thing? Do right by Lance, if perhaps in so doing not generally right by herself or the baby.

"Can I have a beer, Lance?"

"Get one. But you're not supposed to drink during pregnancy."

She got up and went to the old Frigidaire. She glanced around the kitchen and into the next room—it all seemed like a bit of dream, her life there. Perhaps she'd decided to go home the moment she had seen Dick. She was determined to face the music now. Her parents could either accept the baby or not ("Not," she was thinking). She believed Dick would be there for her if all else failed. Was she being naive? Or did she see that something in him we too saw? Dick was not a bad sort. Who were we to judge anyway?

IV

S.K DIDN'T DRINK the beer. In the morning, when Lance was gone to the university, she packed. That chapter of her life was finished for good. And whatever was in store, she was determined to make the best of. Everything fit in a single suitcase and backpack. She left the gold necklace he'd bought for her, and a note, on the dining room table.

The morning of her return—on a red-eye, a day later—LAX was scarcely visible through the fog, the main terminal appearing like an ocean liner at sea. Since our town is up on a bluff and a half-mile inland, and has—now as she saw—a brick, magical-realist, also Midwest look to it, at times it's easy to forget that it's a coastal town, if a coastal town on a bluff a half mile from the ocean.

S.K. walked in the marine layer down Sepulveda the two miles to El Camino, her face and neck wet from the invasion, her red suitcase, which she'd bought secondhand, in tow and growing heavier by the minute. The sun was dishwater yellow in the distance. It was no hour for a young girl to be walking alone, even if Sepulveda was already noisy with people and traffic.

Second City had provided her with some street smarts, she felt, and, in any case, she would need now to do things for herself, for the foreseeable future. We might guess that S.K. was trying to cheer herself up—what a strange few months it had been, her whole world turned generally upside down. And yet was it not all, also, that pilgrimage to the self that each and every one of us must make at some point? The crossing lights ahead of her were like maritime signal flags.

She was not headed to her house however, not going home—not yet at least. Her parents were in fact unaware of her return, likewise others, including M.K. and Dick. She had found an apartment on the East Side where the rents were cheaper, through an ad, so, for the time being at least, she could operate inde-pendently—and anonymously. Sepulveda was a dramatic divide. No one on the East Side would be likely to recognize her. She wasn't going back to the high school. She would need to get a job, something, anything, soon. Perhaps at some point she would contact Hal, see if he would at last man up. But she wasn't hold-ing her breath.

Soon she would find out if it was a boy or a girl.

At the intersection, a Starbucks beckoned. Starbucks had commandeered many of the best corners (just as churches had succeeded in doing in earlier de-cades). She'd rest there, warm up, before making the rest of the trek. It was what it was. She was determined to be okay.

Still, there was a strain, hidden by the fog perhaps but not to be dismissed, anymore than the real world was. It was not one emotion but ambivalence that predominantly caused the strain. On one level she was happy to be back, happy to be home—if not quite home—and on another level fearful of facing it all, the disappointment and recriminations. Nor did she look forward to witnessing the untouched lives of her classmates, when the time came. Would she go to gradu-ation if Judy invited her to—despite Hal being there to graduate, despite every-thing? Well, that was still a couple of months off.

Then she thought: But you'll be five months pregnant then, S.K.

She had contracted—sending on two months rent—for a studio. It was part of a duplex, near an elementary school, a location which she figured might be safer than some other parts on the Eastside. (During S.K.'s abscondence, El Camino had been subject to a murder-suicide, it occurring however on the Westside, in Rec Park, this in a town, as I think I've mentioned, never in its hundred-year his-tory having had experience a homicide. Frank it was who'd gone to the park one day to shoot baskets, only to find blood "the color of berries," he said, still visible on the pavement. That the young couple were a Hispanic man and his girlfriend, and both from Riverside, i.e., not locals, provided I suppose some solace, but it all still was gruesome. Frank described parking his car in the lot under some trees by the basketball court where but 48 hours earlier a man had shot a woman, in their car, and then left her body there on the pavement, drove back and shot her again before, as they say, turned the gun on himself. Frank had seen two plainclothes officers there filming the crime scene, attempting to recreate what happened. It was ghostly, he said. On his way out he noticed a make-shift memorial to the girl—votive candles and red Valentine balloons. "I'd only thought of them as a couple," he confessed. "Sort of passing over her individual identity.")

S.K, walking, taking her bearings, thought then of calling Dick, to see if he was available to meet up with her—but resisted, believing it was important not give in, at least not so quickly, to dependency. And she was, strangely enough, enjoying the solitary walk, perhaps fancying herself the prodigal daughter returning to the village, which so abruptly, stealthily, she'd left three months earlier. Now, she was abrupt and stealthy in return, if not the same person in many respects. And carrying another person inside her. A person whose existence was intended to save her from deportation (what a way to enter the world), but a little soul whom now she was starting to love.

She set to work on the place almost immediately. The studio generally was nothing to shout about (I have no holdings over there), but it looked out on the school playground, there was a palo verde in the front yard, and her duplex neighbor, a man in his fifties—Hispanic—appeared friendly. If quiet. She'd observed that Hispanics when among friends were loud and playful (like Filipinos), but when alone were quieter than any other ethnicity. The nearby houses were modest, older, and had the benefit aesthetically of not having garages at the front—Dick having suggested to her that garages were the chief bane to contemporary house design. About eighty percent of the residents around her were Hispanic, S.K. figured. And a lot of them seemed to be riding the same bicycle. She was aware of standing out, as a Filipina, and as a young, single women.

S.K. managed to turn the place into a home of sorts. It was already furnished. There was a little round blond kitchen table, a twin mattress, and a small desk—all from Ikea and all, to her mind, redolent of her first doll house. There was even a TV. She'd washed the walls, wearing only panties and finding it somewhat erotic therefore. She'd washed the cabinets and the floor, too, even though the apartment was reasonably clean. Keeping busy was a necessity—and then there was an element of punishment in the work, too. She knew there was an Asian side of her that liked sacrifice, and feared freedom. That found pleasure in the lack of freedom. The cleaning also helped her to focus. Generally, she found it hard to read, to concentrate, and watched movies on the TV instead. Older ones mostly. She liked 50's films best. The 40's movies were often about crime, but by the time the 50's came along teenage sex had been introduced. And color.

Splendor in the Grass was her new favorite. Natalie Wood was marvelous, Warren Beatty beautiful–the war with parents hit home despite the fact that she'd never really been at war with her parents. Although she was disappointed in her father–if he were her biological "father" and grandparent to her soon-to-be born child.

At moments of weakness she thought further of contacting Dick. What she couldn't know, even if she might suspect, was that his feelings for her had intensified, the intensification fueled perhaps by her absence, for it was an absence wherein he could picture her alone in her Chicago apartment–sitting, reading, watching television, eating, taking a bath, playing the flute, etc.–a picture by which he could take possession of her. Dick had even begun to wonder vaguely to himself if S.K. were to give up the child, if he might raise it–should Christina agree, a big if of course. He might claim that it was his child, by S.K., and argue that he had a responsibility to raise it, and that he would want to in any case. Filipinos were used to such messy family relationships. In an odd way he felt he had fathered the child. Hadn't he generally set her off, in sending her to Chicago, on the resultant odyssey? Dick tried to keep himself from imagining any scenario where he and S.K. would be together. And certainly a three some wasn't realistic.

She, meanwhile, had found a church, in Hawthorne, nearly a mile from the apartment. And found a friend in the priest. Religion now seemed to reinsert and reassert itself. Mass had previously been only an occasional thing however, even in the Philippines. It was hard to believe it was nearly Easter. But that it was a time of hope and rejuvenation–of rebirth–heartened S.K. She attended daily Mass. The walk was good for her and the baby, if not without some risk. She needed to get out of the house each day. It was funny to walk everywhere again as she had west of Sepulveda prior to her relationship with Hal. Have I mentioned she'd cut her hair shorter, page-boy short (it looked good on her), in order to appear even less recognizable?

Father Golosino–Mike knew him–was Filipino, Filipinos (to the surprise of some) the second largest immigrant community in California and duly represented among the priest class. The mile journey there, on E. El Camino Boulevard, took her under the 405, past Hawthorne High School (a one-time rival), past the auto transmission place, the donut shop, the message parlor (with its beaded curtains and neon red lights, in daylight, in the windows), to, really, in many respects, what was a treeless and different world, yet also in many respects redolent of the Philippines. Father Golosino also offered some familiarity. As did St. Joseph's itself, which was Spanish-style, like the outside of the Methodist Church in Cam. But inside, St. Joseph's was elaborate and baroque (garish even), it also occurring to S.K. that day as she entered that Protestant churches didn't have a namesake—a saint—attached to them, the exception in town St. Michael's, which was Episcopal. Modern aesthetics, or at least Protestant or Asian ones associated with the modernism of Wright, were not at all the order of the day at this old (1930) white, Spanish-style church. But, somehow, the architecture of St. Joseph's seemed more receptive and welcoming to new life, to babies, she felt—even those born out of wedlock. (Yet S.K. cautioned herself: perhaps it was just the familiarity of the Catholic Church that provoked such feelings. As well as the apostasy of the Methodist Hal. But Dick, too, was a Methodist, at least in name. So, it wasn't fair to overstate the case for Catholicism.)

The church was decorated in the violet hues of Lent—the color of varicose veins, she mused. Many devotional candles were lit. The incense—a cloying smell—was strong. But again, she felt the atmosphere to be welcoming, a place for children, and saints. A place in which being was more important than becoming. (Ironically, her own recent advances had been undermined, and she was thrust back to a state more resembling pure being.)

Father Golosino presided that particular day—S.K, during the Mass, strongly feeling that he was speaking especially to her. She recalled her sophomore math teacher had given her the same impression, in between formulas.

At the donut shop the conversation was lighter, if also—contra the intent of meeting in an open area—sort of romantic, too. She had never thought of a priest in such terms—never thought, despite the scandals, that any terms existed to think of a priest in that fashion. A priest to her was spiritual, poetic, generally neutered. But now, she saw that a priest was a man—just as she had learned that

Dick, a professor not to mention a parent and a friend of her family, was a man. A man first, perhaps.

"I chose this parish because of the donut shop directly across the street," Father Golosino joked.

"You get to choose?"

"Not really. More like you're assigned. But there's a shortage of priests, so you have some leverage. At times I think of leaving the priesthood however."

This confession surprised her. Father Golosino was bald, but only about forty. He had a habit of sticking his tongue out when he was thinking. That day he was dressed in his vestments still—creamy white, angled as boat sails. In church the vestments appeared natural, or at least familiar, but there in the coffee shop they had the appearance of body armor.

She didn't understand entirely the reason behind the chats. Just friendship and support—Christian charity—she assumed. She had told him her story. He knew the details. Father Golosino, she saw, enjoyed her company. No doubt he needed outside friends and enjoyed the company of a young person like herself.

"Do you want to talk privately?" he suddenly asked.

"Here?"

"No, no. We could go for a ride. And then I could drop you off at your home, your apartment."

S.K. hesitated but assented—she was not up to the walk back to the apartment (and was generally finding walks more taxing)—but she believed, also, that she might be able to persuade Father Golosino to drive her through downtown El Camino. His car wouldn't be recognized by the locals. She herself was wearing a sort of disguise that day, a blue Dodgers ball cap (which of course she'd removed during the service).

Father seemed happy to do as she bid.

"I always enjoy going there. The trees, the angles the hills create. Like in Cezanne. The small town charm. The big blue water tower at Hilltop with 'El Camino' in big letters. The town's such a splendid throwback. I'm often in contact with St. Anthony's."

She hadn't thought of that, that priests go around parish to parish. But of course it was a small band of brothers, a knighthood of sorts. And was she a damsel in distress?

Spring had come. They drove with the windows down (he owned a Toyota hybrid). S.K. was crying. It was traumatic. She had sent emails to her family, assuring them that she was fine, but she hadn't informed them that she was no longer in Chicago, that in fact she was living just the other side of Sepulveda. When they drove by the little apartment near the high school where her family was—just four now, not five—S.K. slunk down in her seat. It seemed cruel to carry on such a charade. But in general she felt she needed more time to think. To decide. Recently, even abortion had crossed S.K.'s mind.

Seeing the high school was equally devastating. Together the grass, so green it looked like it had been painted, and the Romanesque architecture, with its tan and red pattern of bricks and arches, made a picture—especially so perhaps because she was now seeing the high school from the point of view of someone coming from the Eastside. Inside, in class, sat Hal, the father of her child, no doubt pretending to others that nothing was wrong, nothing out of the ordinary had come into his life, at least nothing since her abrupt departure. Was he still on the swim team, still in band? She wondered what he had scored on the SAT (she had not taken it). She reflected back on hiding under the bleachers in the striped light with Hal before band practice, band members on the field tuning up while she and he made out. They'd had a running joke: "Have you read *Under the Bleachers* by Seymour Butts?" "No, but I've read *Rusty Bedsprings* by I.P. Knightly."

Certainly he'd gotten questions about her whereabouts. But she doubted many thought much about her anymore. They all were busy with high school, with studies, activities, parties, relationships, their own lives. One learns the cast of characters in one's life can change quickly, even in a small town like El Camino. She guessed that even Judy rarely thought of her anymore. One learns what it means to be ignored or forgotten. She'd learned something of the faded shirt of love.

"Can you take me to my apartment, Father?" S.K. asked.

She kissed him on the cheek when they were stopped in front of her place. It was perhaps the boldest move of all her romantic conquests, of all her exhibitionist's displays. You might kiss a priest's hand, but never his cheek.

He laughed.

"We can do this again. Don't hesitate to call me if you feel down."

"K, Father."

"And I want you to think about something, S.K."

"Yes, Father?"

"I have a round table in the basement of the church, which I use for private gatherings."

S.K. felt like Father Golosino was about to make another confession and she wasn't sure she wanted to hear it—the secret lives of men, priests too, often sketchy, nasty. (I've observed that those who enter into church service are in many cases wrestling with something, seek a place to hide and to think—that being not so unlike S.K.'s own current situation, ironically.)

But she said, "Yes, Father?"

"I want you to think about bringing all the parties together in an attempt to work through the issues toward some resolution. The present purgatory is not to anyone's benefit. Will you think about it, S.K.?"

"I will, Father. Thank you," S.K. responded.

She pictured the setting, pictured an unheated church cellar, like a bit of hell, a bit of the hell which undergirds Christian teachings.

But maybe Father Golosino knew best. Maybe the church or this priest, her friend, could work some magic. It was something to think about. Something, too, with which to occupy her mind in the interim.

V

EASTER MORNING, FATHER Golosino unbidden sent a cab. Was he in love with S.K? Perhaps so. S.K., after some hesitation, accepted the offer, only to at the last minute ask the driver to take her to the Methodist Church instead—"The one in El Camino," was her request.

"Of course, Mam," he answered.

She climbed in the back of the cab, unable to recall being addressed as "Mam."

She didn't have anything to wear, just some stretch jeans she'd bought at a yard sale and a silky yellow top, which under the circumstances caused her to look like an Easter egg. Who might be there at the church she couldn't know for sure. Not her parents of course; they'd be at St. Anthony's. Miss Marge no doubt would be, directing the bell choir. Dick and his family, probably too, although they too might be at St. Anthony's. The biggest question for S.K.—even bigger than whether Dick would be there—was of course would Hal, and Hal's parents.

Presumably his parents knew—knew they were grandparents to be—but perhaps they didn't. Perhaps Hal had managed to keep his own counsel. She could of course go the Methodist church and confront him, them. Would they say, "I knew we couldn't trust you"? Would they now fully accept her? Or even less so? Then of course there were others she might recognize—and that would recognize her. It would all be out in the open, at last. Word would travel quickly no matter if some of the principals named were not in attendance.

As it happened she was too early, there being no dawn service at the Methodist church.

The Blue Butterfly on Main also turned out be closed for Easter. The town had an odd aspect that morning with everything closed. It was almost as if she were to return to her home town to find it now a ghost town. There were yet a few pedestrians, and a car or two moving past. And surely Starbucks if nothing else would be open. She was to cross at the light, where stood Stuft's Pizza, and then to cut catty-corner—reminiscent of cutting through backyards as a child—between the plaza and the brick, low-slung Police Station and City Hall, Starbucks but a block over.

The line as it happened was half way out the door: for some, this was the primary ritual of the day, Easter or no.

Of course he would be there, Dick looking up—from *The Breeze* (which he read each day with a certain trepidation)—and quickly expressing astonishment.

"You're full of surprises. Sit, take the weight off, S.K."

As if riding in a gondola, she leaned back in the chair he'd provided from the adjoining table.

"Can I get you something? A smoothie?"

"The lines are too long, Dick."

"Well then, a little coffee won't hurt you. Have some of mine."

S.K. sipped Dick's Americano, a nice warm up.

"They say spring will return this afternoon," he to add.

But then there was a pause. S.K. not wanting to explain; he to pry. Was she living at home? Certainly he would have heard something. He had to admit to himself, with her return he generally felt more compromised. The authorities were closing in on him he suspected, but he didn't want to needlessly alarm S.K. Especially as she was pregnant. And besides, it wasn't like he'd done anything illegal.

"Where do you live?" he asked at last.

"Across town. On the other side of Sepulveda. It's okay, I've a little studio apartment."

"Since when?"

"A month."

She was due in late summer. S.K looked around, wondering suddenly if anyone were looking at them. Some of the faces were familiar. Judy's stepfather was there, but he apparently hadn't noticed her, pregnancy perhaps a disguise. Her face was bloated.

There was something he needed to ask her, he felt. Then he did raise it.

"Can I ask you," she heard him say, "it's not a nice thing to ask on Easter, especially since I'm so glad to see you again–but was I, S.K., was I next? Were you hoping to sleep with me, last December, with the idea of us having a child? Sorry, it's a question I've wanted to ask for some time."

He doubted, too, he would have another opportunity to do so.

S.K. started crying. He gave her a napkin to wipe away her tears.

"I don't know. My head was swimming..."

He laughed. She laughed.

"I liked you," she continued.

That made him feel better, that she didn't dislike, disapprove of him. And wasn't just using him. That was the concern underneath the question he'd asked.

"You're going to church, S.K.?"

"Thought I would."

"Which one?"

It was the logical question.

"I was thinking The Methodist one."

"Why are you here alone, Dick?" was something she wanted to ask. Then she did, likewise, almost wishing she hadn't.

"She found out about my visiting you in Chicago," Dick said.

"Oh my God, I'm so sorry, Dick." She didn't know what else to say. Was it M.K. that had spilled the beans?

"It was only a matter of time. I know Christina came here with great hopes, and tried hard. I feel especially bad for Mya. She'd waited all those years for a father."

S.K was taken aback. "You'd leave them just like that?"

"It's not just like that. But that doesn't make me feel any better about it."

"I feel responsible."

"You aren't."

"Christina will feel shame."

"Her mother is coming to visit from the Philippines. She might be able to help, be some sort of buffer."

"Unless that makes her even more ashamed, with her mother here."

Dick hadn't thought of that.

They were quiet then, among the holiday chatter, and sounds of the coffee grinder and blasting steam shots.

"Maybe small towns are no longer for me. Or no longer exist," Dick ventured. " When I first came here, I liked that it was something of a replica of my hometown, in Indiana. A model of what a small town should look like. But now it seems a bit too much, to me, like a toy town."

Immediately, though, he felt such comments were somewhat fatuous. (Still, I recall him saying he didn't want to wind up frustrated in a small town like one of Sherwood Anderson's grotesques.)

S.K had leaned forward. She felt like a gyroscope.

"How about you, Dick, are you going to church?"

He couldn't recall her using his name like that. She was grown up. Dick momentarily flashed back to a conversation he'd had just the night before at the Standard Station with the new waitress, whom he'd first noticed during her high school days. She'd come over to ask if he wanted another, and he'd said to her, "You've grown up." "I remember you from Starbucks, sir," she responded. He enjoyed watching her crack open his beer. There was something in watching a girl work. (He reportedly wandered up the hill to his house around midnight, turning for a moment before going in to look back over the town.)

"I was thinking The Methodist one, too," he said now to S.K. "I feel a need for prayer. I haven't prayed in decades. Even when I'm actually in church."

He'd attended Mass in the Philippines. The sanctuary was open-aired, birds flying in and out. The parishioners were solemn. There was none of American-style glad-handing and hugging. At least at the Catholic church.

"Hal will probably be there, at your church," she said.

Dick sipped his coffee. Do we go to different churches in a broader sense? He looked around. The place was packed but only a few faces were familiar. Soon, none would be.

"The young girls always wear leggings now," he said, randomly. "I'd noticed it before, but it hadn't registered that it must be taking quite a bite out of the blue jeans market."

S.K. laughed. "Totally. You know, I hated that we didn't have a mall to hang out in here."

"Where'd you get those jeans?"

"Not exactly fashion-forward. Or exactly Easter wear."

"Yes, the Methodists are quite strict, at least on the second count. You might try the Catholic Church."

She understood. "It might be too big of a shock to my parents. Tell me what to do...Professor."

He laughed.

"I can't tell you what to do."

"I miss being told what to do!"

He pondered.

"Your family would be happy above all."

"I haven't forgiven my father."

Dick had done some research—her biological father lived in Manilla. But when she didn't deign to continue along that track, he was content to let it go. The subject generally was very painful, for him as well—he would miss Mya terribly, just as he had missed Marie terribly after his second divorce (his first marriage remains a mystery).

Still, to comfort S.K., he said: "People belong to the people who raised them."

He believed that, and yet he also believed you can't have too many people that love you.

One thing S.K. did ask: "You're afraid to be seen in the same church with me?"

"It's not that. I don't care that much now about what people say here. I won't be staying, for one thing. Fifteen years is a round number of sorts."

"You've been here that long?"

"Yes, almost as long as your life! You were three when I moved here."

"Living in the Philippines."

"Yes, how odd life is. We were half way around the globe from each other."

Saying all that that way gave Dick some perspective. S.K., mother-to-be or not, was way young and of another culture, or sub-culture.

"Won't you hate to give up your house?" she asked, an afterthought.

"I will, for sure. But it's pretty much tripled in value. I'll be able to help Mya." (With college, he'd thought privately.) I might take some time to do some writing."

He passed S.K. the drink.

"It's almost time for the service."

"Would you walk me there? "

"Of course I will. I'll sit with you, too, if you want."

"I mean St. Anthony's."

St. Anthony's was close by and was, like everything else, but a short walk up the hill, in this case to the highest point in town, the aforementioned "Hilltop." No doubt both S.K. and Dick thought about how they climbed the dunes together a few months earlier–and about how providence had worked its course.

There were throngs standing in the vestibule (unlike the Methodist Church which was sparsely attended even at Easter). Everyone was nicely dressed, if not, as in our childhood, in their Sunday best. Still, what wonderful pastels belonged to Easter.

Undetected by the others gathered, S.K. squeezed Dick's hand one last time. She looked back, smiled, and then ran toward her parents. And M.K. and X.K. All the K's back together at last, Dick thinking, even if S.K. was biologically only half a K.

Dick was tempted to remain there for the service. Tempted to call Christina, tell her he was there, and get dressed and bring Mya. But was he still too Protestant, too beholden to the church of the inner self? And he didn't want to crowd S.K. on the morning of her reunion.

From Hilltop one can see across the swale to where, on a rise, sits the Methodist Church, it too but a short walk. Entering, he saw Mike was up at the front with Ally. Who was Big Mike? Had they really gotten to know each other? (News of Mike's gambling debts, the fallout from *la passion du jeu*, had hit Dick hard.) He hadn't seen Hal at first. Perhaps Hal had gone off to the bathroom. But then he was there, sitting next to his parents, the shock of red hair–his father's, too—closer to buoy orange than red, Dick now concluded. It was odd to pray there with him, with them. Fortunately the church was crowded enough, that Dick, late and sitting in the back, felt he could remain anonymous, undetected, at least for the short term.

The service closed as it had every Easter of recent memory with the bell choir, Marge at the helm. The bells looked heavy, especially so in the arms of those old women who made up the bell choir. Yet the playing was smooth, rhythmic, ethereal.

That was the last I would see of Dick.

EPILOGUE

S.K. I WAS to see again. But bear with me a moment, I need to take a bit of a long way around. You see, Mike had asked me to take some pictures on a Sunday, of Smoky Hollow (I've mentioned it previously, right?), pictures for the city council–it being a cool day, the in-shore flow like a giant spray bottle released over the town. I'd already been to an early service and was still in my church clothes when I headed over, soon finding myself alone with the buildings, something I do enjoy, just as Dick had said he did–what others must feel when they are alone in nature, he said. It was incumbent on the city council, according to Mike, to act wisely and in concert when it came to Smoky Hollow.

The idea generally is to turn the area into a fashionable enclave of office buildings and workshops to attract creatives, as a lot of people these days everywhere work to re-imagine public space on a more human scale, after a long campaign by developers to simply maximize profits. The mid-century modern buildings are one-story, small, brick, and sweep horizontally across the area. It got its name because smoke once settled there from Standard Oil Co.'s refinery, which opened in 1911 and, as you know, is now operated by Chevron Corp (the faint running-chain sound of the plant always noticeable). The area is no longer smoky, of course, and local officials once contemplated calling it simply 'The Hollow' to prevent people from getting the wrong impression." Said City Manager Jim Carpenter, in jest: "It's a state-of-the-art industrial district–circa 1955." But notes Greg Goodell (with whom I often compete for commissions): "You're a golf shot to the ocean yet very few people know about it. That's part of the charm."

The deliverables for one booking we worked on recently, for example, de-emphasizes architecture and emphasizes design principles, though of course we were only able to color just so far out of the lines (I'd spent years ironing my clothes before coming to realize it was okay to iron outside the lines). Much of the original buildings will, if all goes as planned, be preserved.

There's a mix of machine shops, artist studios, craft breweries, and start-ups–everything down there feels hands-on. One make-over, for example, is Smoky Hollow Studios, created from a warehouse on Penn St., the remodel revealing concrete floors, original exposed wood rafters, and a nice patio, "making it the perfect spot to host events, shoots, and gatherings," so claims its website.

We are witnessing whether we like it or not our industrial base morph into something quite other, "preserving" being both an act of keeping and remaking (admittedly, the law of nature is change, as my ancestors proved during the Scottish Enlightenment–Craig's Tools, Inc. right next to Online Marketing and Hollywood Branding, for example). Preserving is further an act of trading on the past.

I suppose my interest in photography grew out of, among other things, a desire to ground myself. I was carrying two cameras that day, one for close ups and another for wide-angle shots. The light, as a result of the earliness and the marine layer, was perfect, indeed almost smoky. The yellow refinery lights were like tracers through the trees. Meanwhile the low sunlight from the east had turned the brick a salmon-color. I walked down into the hollow, the cross a top St. Anthony's visible still, as were to the south the refinery and to the north the water tower–floating in the sky like a pale blue balloon. Mostly however it was the buildings shouldering me that I was aware of (that a huge metropolitan area existed more generally just beyond town was hard to imagine). I suppose some might find it surprising that a real estate guy would focus so much on the past, expected rather to possess a yen to subdivide, but I find a certain solace in the past, using photography as a vehicle for such–though admittedly I am, as already suggested, reminded of the passage and remaking of time, especially now as regard to Dick's absence. Photography is an art that in its attention to the present moment creates memories but also reinforces a sense of transience.

You'll recall, I expect, that we don't have a cemetery. Some of our dead are in nearby (generally poorer) neighborhoods, east of Sepulveda (a resolution pending to change our section of the street's name to the more tourist-friendly "Pacific Coast Highway"); some bodies have been shipped home (in most cases to the Midwest); a few have had their ashes dispersed in the sea (Mabel Smith, for example). In the absence of a cemetery, the locals began around about fifty years ago to place circular commemorative plaques in the sidewalks, like what you find in Hollywood for the movie stars, the plaques in our case being dedicated to ancestors or in some cases, self-dedicated (selfies of a sort) by families. Typical types of inscriptions are "In Loving Memory of...," or such things as "Live to Surf," or in a few cases "In Service of His Country." (One particularly painful one I recall coming across was inscribed "To Our Littlest Angel," in memory of a two-year old boy.) A few are dedicated to a business or a club. "Women of the Moose," for example. A lot of the plaques are found up the hill in Old Town, but the earliest are to be found in Smoky Hollow, especially along Eucalyptus and Indiana.

There's a "Starling." Of course I might have thought little of it had I not been thinking of Dick–and had I not found it on Indiana Street. And true, most of the names on the plaques are Anglo names (though that too is changing), and, too, even if not the most common American name, there are surely quite a few Starlings around. The plague reads, "In Memory of Rev. John Starling, 1922-1951." The dates too struck me, as the plague could hypothetically reference Dick's paternal grandfather–and, as I said, it was on Indiana Street–but it was my recent, if brief conversation with S.K. that really set me wondering.

She had turned eighteen–not to mention become a mother, of a beautiful boy (Big Mike joking that she should have named him "Pre-K"). She worked as a barista at the Blue Butterfly, her mother, having overcome the shame of the out-of-wedlock pregnancy, now the boy's babysitter. The Blue Butterfly had a new owner and is now a hipper destination, but I was to run into S.K. at the 99Cent Store (the store itself a story, as its opening provoked another town controversy–"It's so un-El Camino," as one lady said, though to me it's but another dime store).

"I'm slowly learning the coffee drinks," had said S.K. We stood near the checkout stand, groceries in hand.

She was back to her old shape–even "running shape?"–her hair short still, boyish, but it suited her. The outdoor exercise–and just summer–had turned her skin darker, now a coffee rather than a tea color. (Summer was coming to a quick close.) I had no reason to believe that she should possess any knowledge related to a Rev. Starling–but who knows what may have passed between Dick and her, especially in an unguarded moment (I knew little back then of her birth-father saga, by the way).

"I run for pleasure now," she laughed.

I was surprised I hadn't seen her running–but perhaps she was intrepid enough to return to the beach. (She and Dick's intrepid swim–gone wrong–never came out. I will take those photos to the grave.)

The baby boy was doing fine–S.K. I imagine a bit curious about my abiding interest in her, and Dick.

But I felt a need to complete the picture, wrap things up–as much as possible–Dick having left without a single word of goodbye to us remaining three card players. No one, including Big Mike who'd generally been closest to Dick, at least previously, had heard a peep from him since his departure, leaving me to believe my queries were unlikely to resolve but feeling a need to pursue them all the same. Mike's recent resignation from the city council (ultimately, they didn't want my photos) and the "For Rent" sign outside his apartment complex means perhaps Frank and I will soon be looking for a third not only a fourth. Mike is currently keeping his cards close to his vest. I've known Mike for a lot of years, it would be a loss.

Dick in my presence had never spoken of a Rev. John Starling. In fact, no one in town I'd queried–even those at the historical society or *The Herald*–knows anything of the fellow. But it would be just like Dick to fail to mention something so important (if in fact so), that is, that his residing in El Camino wasn't just a matter of happenstance.

"He had just come from his father's funeral in Indiana, when he visited me," S.K. offered, upon hearing about the plaque. "But you know that already, right? I straight up never slept with him...for the record. We were at my boyfriend's apartment in Chicago and Dick said to me he wanted to (she blushed), 'make it,' or words to that effect, but that he was trying to be a Christian now."

"He said that, 'A Christian now'?"

I'd whispered, wondering then if anyone at 99Cent might be overhearing us.

"That's all he offered. You know Dick. The dude was not forthcoming," whispered S.K.

"Yes, even when he drank–did you ever see him in that state?" She shook her head. "He was, for all he did reveal, not really, as you say... forthcoming."

S.K. had given me a penetrating gaze.

"What was it that *you* loved about him?"

"What do I miss?"

I'll admit to being taken aback, and hesitated, but she didn't hold back.

"I'll tell you what I loved, sir."

"You loved him, S.K.?"

"Yes."

"What was it?"

"His modesty."

"His small-town Christian modesty?"

"Yes, exactly, that's it. It wasn't his decency."

"No."

"The modesty."

"I miss that, too," I confessed. I love such about small towns. But sometimes wonder, where has such modesty gone? (All the big houses now being built in El Camino an especial affront to Dick's sensibility, as I'm sure I've mentioned previously).

I kissed S.K. on the cheek before leaving. She'd nailed me in a way. I'm not sure a Christian would so readily abandon his family as Dick had–but I've never had a family of my own so I don't feel in position to judge such things. I do, simply, miss him. On multiple levels.

I confess, further, I'm incapable now of conjuring up Dick without also thinking of our S.K. And there, below the fetch of wind off the ocean, with the town seemingly gone, and with Dick in fact gone, paradoxically the ghostly moment seemed to bring me closer to both of them.

S.K. had mentioned hadn't she–on some occasion I can't recall when–that her father, K.K., liked to play cards. Asians generally do. I confess to being glad to have such an opening–a pretext, if you will–for possibly contacting her again. Perhaps to further discuss modesty. (Democritus said, "The foolish learn modesty in misfortune." Aristotle claimed that modesty is not a virtue; it is good only as a curb of youthful indiscretion. Further, that it is a feeling more than a state, and only appropriate to youth.)